All 4 Love

NAKIA ROBINSON

Right About It Publications
Baltimore

All 4 Love

Published by Right About It 2014

Print ISBN: 978-0-9890982-6-7
E-Book ISBN: 978-2-9890982-7-4

Please connect with me on FB @ https://www.facebook.com/nakia.robinson.35 Or IG/Nykia8, Twitter @AuthorNakiaR

www.RightAboutItPublication.com

Check out the trailer for You Call That Love:
Production and lyrics by Bmore Ben. Vocal performance by Ashley.
https://www.youtube.com/watch?v=6W9cC8VHooo&feature=youtu.be

"You create your destiny."

Acknowledgments

God, I thank you for bringing me this far. I pray that you continue to bless me with the ability to put words on paper in a way that people can connect and feel the story. I pray that you use me to inspire.

Mommy – You mean so much to me. I love you. Thank you for continued to provide me with that priceless love and support. Never would have made it without you. I'm so grateful that you are in my life. I can't tell the world enough how lucky I am to have you as a mother. Again a precious diamond who deserves nothing but the best.

Antoine – Thank you for having my back and pushing me to do what I had to do. Love you. My kids- I love you. Thanks you for being patient while I wrote this book

Nyki and **Renny** – You two as siblings bring out the best in me and inspire many characters. Thank you!!

My grandmothers – Thank you for the love and support.

Lyndon – My mentor, thank you for the many valuable lessons I absorbed it all and my future is brighter thanks to you. 4 books in a year only made possible by you. Standing ovation to you, I appreciate everything you do. Thanks so much for continuing to be the shining light at the end of the tunnel.

Jacci and **Natalie** – Thank you, thank you, thank you, thank you again for helping me complete yet another project. It is an honor to have the BEST working with me and to believe in my work.

Chaundrae – You are a diva and so inspiring. So much comes out of that mouth of yours it's hard to keep up, lol. Your stories keep me laughing, especially the one about the M#####. It was bananas LOL. Thanks for answering many questions and GENIUNE ALL THE TIME support. Love you.

Fam, Keith and **Tyronna** – You two are my fav. Thank you for the love and constant promotion.

Belinda Sue Rae - my sometimes agent, smile. You are the sunshine for many, looking forward to seeing the one to be the sunshine for you. Linda Selby you and Mr. crack me up. Oh gorgeous one, Christine you ARE QUEEN of all trades. Thank you so much for all your help in so many things. A special thanks to Elaine Ragin and Dorothy Smith. Elaine thank you for inspiring the names and being the inspiration behind Yasmin's strength. Although the storyline is completely different, Yasmin's strength was inspired by you. You've gone through a lot and continue to sacrifice for family. Throughout it all you STILL STAND. Thank you. Dorothy you push me to continue through my obstacles and are one of my biggest supporters. You are the reason for this book. Anyone who is reading this thank Dorothy she truly encouraged me. Your words brushed aside my many doubts and are so appreciated. Can't wait to hear your thoughts on your beloved Braxton after this portion. It's All 4U… CF Crew – I appreciate all of you and your continued support. It really means so much to me.

Source of Knowledge – Ms. Patrice and Mr. Dexter thank you so much for supporting me. Thank you for the kind words and encouragement. You both are WONDERFUL! I'm so grateful for the connection.

Mr. Larry, Antoine "Inch" Thomas and **Mr. Chris Evans** – You were the first to carry my book. I thank you all for the connection, support and encouragement.

Junior and **Keith** – Thank you so much for allowing me into the store and your hospitality. Keith every visit into Jay Books I learn something new. Thanks for the knowledge.

Cretia, Cool Press and **Suga Mama** - Thank you for the love and support. Suga Mama you ready to write a scene?

The BBBClub – Thank you for the love. Looking forward to coming out again and being around you wonderful ladies.

XPress Yo'self Bookclub – Thank you for inviting me out and showing true southern hospitality. Look forward to future connections

To my readers - It has truly been a pleasure to connect with you. I pray that you feel the emotions of the characters and can visualize the script. I hope that you able to understand everything is not always black and white and are able to gain something through Yasmin's evolving journey. Thank you again for supporting my dream.

Dedication

John H. Fraling and Robert Lee Robinson - Your words continue to guide me daily. Every accomplishment I will continue to dedicate to you. It is a blessing to have the BEST in my life. I still feel your spirits surrounding me, thank you for the many lessons and love.

Prologue

Rain On Me

"In sure and certain hope of the resurrection to eternal life through our Lord Jesus Christ, we commend to Almighty God, our sister. Now, we commit her body to the ground; earth to earth; ashes to ashes, dust to dust. May the Lord bless her and keep her, make His face to shine upon her, be gracious unto her, and give her peace. Amen."

I stand still, holding my breath, praying for strength. The wind brutally punches my face like a punching bag; it's trying to bring me down. My body sways. I will not fall. I will not fall. I can do this. I *will* do this. Deep breaths, my heart heavy, each beat echoes in my head, drums a beat I do not want to hear.

As the casket is lowered into the ground I want to yell stop. I want someone to wake me and for it all to be a bad dream. But as the casket crept lower and lower into the ground, no one woke me. It is not a dream. She was gone. This was our final goodbye. I would never see her face or hear her voice again. My body aches. This is too hard. I feel weak, my body can't take this hurt. Just as I'm about to fall, I feel strong arms grab me.

"I got you, beautiful, I got you."

I fall into his arms. He supports me, holds me tight. He stands strong, my rock. I turn to face him, bury my head in his chest, tears fall soaking his shirt, but he doesn't care. He strokes my back, kisses me on my forehead, then my cheek, telling me "it's okay to let it out."

I can't believe she's gone. I never imagined she'd be gone. I thought we had time. I thought we would eventually get things right. The finality of today says so much; our relationship, our connection was no more. Things would remain as they were. There would be no goodbyes, only my tears, and questions to God asking why? God, I'm so tired of the pain.

I just need to put this life of mine on pause and make time stop, so I can breathe, catch my breath, have some peace and happiness, even if it is only momentary. So much has happened in the past year; the drama and chaos never seems to stop. I need time to figure out what to do because this life of mine is too overwhelming; so much pressure, I just want to be free. But there's no pause button or another option. I must keep going.....

1

Every Tear Is A Waterfall

Months ago, I came to the hospital anxious, anticipating the birth of my daughters. I was nervous, scared, and confused, but I was happy. My husband, Braxton, held me and reassured me that I would be alright. My room was comfortable with amenities including music, and plenty of fresh cut flowers that scented the room to make the strenuous task of childbirth as calming as possible. Now I sit in the same hospital where there are no smiles and the décor is sterile. The smell of disinfectant trying to cover up the foul odor of infection and impending death makes the air cold. I sit, anticipating the death of my first real friend, my best friend, my sister. Landon was part of me, responsible in a lot of ways for the woman I have become. I sit numb, unable to accept my world without her.

I look over at my father, Lawrence, and it's evident, in the few days that have past, how his appearance has changed. His normal light skin is dull; his hazel-green eyes lost. Kevin, an attorney at my father's law firm, but more of a brother to me and Landon, is just as lost and unsure what to do. Landon and I kept him busy with our theatrics…Landon more so than I. God, how I wish this wasn't happening!

I look at the TV screen plastered on the hospital's wall; Landon is in the headlines again. She's always a star, a diva, nothing ordinary, never in a million years did I think she would make the news this way. This was not supposed to be her fate, but before me on the screen, it said it all.

Former forward for the Washington Wizards Eric Ayres, is being charged with attempted murder and first-degree aggravated assault after allegedly shooting his ex-wife Landon Taylor-Ayres. The couple who divorced July of this year has a 4-year old son. There is no word on a motive or what may have caused the altercation.

Eric Ayres was recently cut from the Washington Wizards after playing with the team for several seasons.

We've learned that Mrs. Ayres is in grave condition.

Reporters had been scouting for answers, asking the same ridiculous questions. What happened? Why did it happen? How do you feel? I wanted to scream. Why? What do *you* think? How would *you* feel? But I ignored the idiotic questions, silently praying for a miracle.

Braxton, Lawrence, Kevin and I were sitting in the lobby when I saw my mother, Michelle approach. Fortunately, Landon's mother, Jackie, had gone on a mission to find the chief of staff.

"Ma?" I said, surprised to see her.

She barely acknowledges my presence, "Yasmin."

"Lawrence, you don't look so well."

"Michelle?" my father responds, just as shocked to see her.

I try to speak to her. "Ma, what's going on? Why are you here? Are you okay?"

"I saw the news. Is it true? Did your chosen golden child meet her maker?" she spews.

"Ma."

"Shut up, Yasmin. This is between your father and me."

"It's not the time or place," I said, trying to rationalize with her.

"Mrs. Sinclair, please calm down. Not now," said Braxton in agreement with me.

"Oh, you're still playing a protective role, isn't that nice. Yasmin, you're making dumb choices I see, putting your trust in men. Watch!

Both of these mutherfuckers are going to hurt and abandon ya ass again."

"Ma!" I scream.

"No, you need to hear this. You swear you had the worst childhood. You complained no one showed you any emotion or love, but I was trying to prepare you."

"Really ma, that's why you catered to Ashley?"

"Ashley was loveable. Her father was respectable, honest, committed. Your father is a liar, a cheater, and a manipulator. I had to be tough on you because I didn't want you to inherit his ways. Too bad you didn't inherit common sense."

"Michelle, I'm not going to argue with you. My daughter is fighting for her life," Lawrence said sternly.

"You hear that, Yasmin? As I said before, Landon and Jacqueline are more important; they take priority. Don't you see you will never be a factor in his world? He acknowledged Landon, I didn't hear him once acknowledge you. That's why I was tough on you. Instead of crying about your childhood, you should be thanking me."

Lawrence looked at me, "Yasmin, don't listen to her. You are important to me. I always loved you. I apologize to you for letting this evil bitch raise you."

"I'm a bitch now? The only bitch here is that wife of yours, and she raised a bigger bitch. That's why you're in the hospital now. Karma finally caught up with all y'all asses." She smiled.

"Enough! It's time for you to go NOW!" Braxton said sternly.

"I'm not leaving until I see Ms. Jacqueline."

"You're leaving now!" Lawrence grabbed her arm.

"Ma, please go."

"Don't come crying to me when he makes you look like a dumbass. Isn't that what you called me? I did fall for this mutherfucker's bullshit. But I got his ass back, financially and other ways." She looked at Lawerence. "Isn't that right?" She focused her attack back on me. "You, however, choose to stay a dumbass, so you get whatever's coming."

Just then, Jackie returned. She sees my mother, and I watch as her weak demeanor transformed to prepare for battle with Michelle. Appearance-wise, Jackie, as always, was dressed for the runway. Her gray slacks fit like they were made only for her, along with her crisp white shirt showing off her size 4 figure, and her signature chic bob was flawless. She could easily pass for a woman in her late thirties.

"Hello, Ms. Jacqueline."

"Michelle, what the hell do you want?" said Jackie getting straight to the point.

"I heard about your most precious privileged daughter. I couldn't believe it."

"Mrs. Sinclair, please can I take you home? Please don't do this," pleaded Kevin.

She ignores Kevin.

"Michelle, you should know I have no tolerance for your ignorance today. You need to leave now or I will have you escorted out just like before."

"What is it that you told me 29 years ago about our daughters and their differences? You said Landon would be a prominent figure. Where is your daughter now?" Michelle taunted. "Married a successful basketball player that she drove crazy. Poor thing sacrificed his career to kill her. You were right, she was destined to be a bitch and it caught up with her."

Jackie tries to lunge at my mother, but Lawrence restrains her. "She isn't dead!" Michelle said sternly.

Michelle raises her eyebrows.

"Twenty-nine years later, you're still the same miserable whore who dropped her panties for a man who didn't want her. You still haven't accepted that you were never an option. You devalued yourself the minute you laid down for a smile. Get over it. He was never going to be with you. My daughter is fighting for her life. I refuse to entertain your ludicrous behavior any further."

"You know, I know, we all know, I was not the first or the last. Me, devaluing myself? No, your highness, you have it all wrong."

"Leave here now!" barked Jackie.

"Michelle, leave!" Lawrence co-signs.

"Lawrence, I see Jackie's still wearing the pants. Perhaps if you put your foot down and made your own decisions things would have turned out different. Told you years ago Lawrence, man up. Like mother like daughter's sole purpose is to make men grovel at their feet. Your daughter followed her mother's plan only to get killed."

"You will not stand here and disgrace my child, you jealous bitch! My daughter is a fighter! She's gorgeous! Everything I said and more. She is NOT DEAD!"

"Yet. Karma is a beautiful thing." She turns and leaves.

Broken, Jackie falls in a chair and Kevin comes to her aid. She leans over the chair crying, "She is not dead, she is not dead!"

Braxton holds me in a tight bear hug. I lay my head back closing my eyes only to see images of Landon's battered face. My head was pounding from the mounting stress. I had to get out of this hospital, find some type of solace. Just as I turned to Braxton to tell him that we should check on the twins, I see the doctor.

The doctor's face is grim. He advised us to start preparing for the worst. The gorgeous carefree butterfly that impacted me, heart had stopped beating, her body had begun to shut down. The doctor had revived her, but told us to say our goodbyes.

We all go in. Landon's disfigured image took a toll on all of us. One by one with the exception of Jackie, tell Landon how much she means to us, but tell her it's okay for her to leave. We assure her that we will take care of little Eric, make sure he knows she loved him most.

Jackie refused to accept this would be her baby's fate. She dictated to the doctors what to do, to do more, call in any and every specialist or they'd be sued.

I hold my sister's hand and pray God's will be done.

2

Take Control

It's been a month since that unfortunate day. Things were not easier, but I was coping. I simply took one day at a time. My daughters and my husband gave me happiness, love, and comfort, that helped me ease the pain.

I close my eyes trying to erase the image of her that haunted my dreams. Even a month later, the image of her battered face caked with blood, and distorted by the abuse her attacker placed upon her refused to fade away. She was not the image conscious, gorgeous Landon anymore. I knew if she could see her image she would never be able to handle it.

I went months barely saying two words to her. She had delivered a detrimental blow that sent me spiraling. I felt guilt, because, at the time, I did wish death upon her. I never wanted my words to become reality though. Despite her flaws and devastating betrayal, she could never, would never, be replaced in my life. Her impact was too important to ignore or forget. Our bond was forever.

The computer screen inside my office in the Legg Mason building stares at me. I tried to concentrate, focus on this account, but too many things were happening. My office phone buzzes with a call from the guard's station. I am pleasantly surprised when they say Chauncey Smith is here to see me.

Minutes later, Chauncey Smith's smooth butter, 6'7 physique stood in my doorway. His curly hair is unruly, yet sexy. He smiles at me showing his perfect teeth and deep dimples. Yes, we dated briefly, well, almost two years during my break from Braxton. We were still very amicable and managed to keep our friendship intact. In fact, I managed his money on the side for some residual income. He even referred four other wealthy friends to manage.

"Hello Mr. Smith, come have a seat."

He takes a seat, "Hello Miss Lady."

I pout, "No song for me today?"

One thing I could always count on Chauncey for was a good time and a song. He couldn't sing, but he always greeted me with a song hook. It was corny cute but funny.

"My bad, any requests?"

"Hmm, no, you pick."

"A'ight I can pick something, but I have a request for you."

"A request for me?"

"Yes, I need you to keep an open mind. Don't be quick to say no."

I raise my eyebrows, "That big?"

"It is" he said seriously, which was rare for Chauncey.

"Ok, what is it?"

"Yasmin, Eric wants to see you."

I pause. My body goes numb while tears fall. I shake my head, no."

"Yas, you know I hate to approach you, but it's important."

The lump in my throat makes it difficult to talk, "I can't."

"He says he need to tell you something about…" his voice fades.

"No, Chauncey. Leave now."

"Yassy, I didn't.-"

I cut him off, "Don't call me that. Only Landon calls me that."

"I'm sorry, Yasmin. I just think you need to talk to him. It's some things you need to know before it goes public."

"What are you talking about Chauncey?"

"That's Eric's story to tell you. Yasmin, trust me, you need to talk to him."

"Chauncey, I'm not going anywhere near Eric, he is crazy. He --- my friend, my sister. I begged him not to hurt her. He almost killed Braxton," I cried.

"What are you talking about, Yas?"

"Nothing, I don't want to hear anything from Eric. He can rot in hell. "

"Yas. What do you mean he almost killed Braxton?"

"Chauncey get out of my office."

"Just think about it."

"I did. Tell Eric, fuck him. I don't want to hear shit he has to say. Because of him I have an innocent little boy who asks me every day why his mommy won't come back to get him."

Chauncey hesitantly stands. He wisely walks out of my office without saying another word.

I try to focus on the computer screen, but Chauncey's visit unnerved me. I hated Eric for what he did. Part of me wanted to hurt him myself. I recall my visit with him the day I went to him and begged him to stop. His callous eyes, his evil, heartless stare, his possessed demeanor. I was six months pregnant with the twins when Braxton was involved in an automobile accident. At the time, we were barely speaking because I found out he and Landon had a sexual encounter while I was grieving over the loss of our son, Bryan. The one-time hook-up created little Eric. At the time, Landon thought Eric was the father. But years later, a paternity test ordered by Eric revealed that he was excluded as a possibility and another revealed Braxton as the father.

The revelation sent me running, however, I returned later after I found out I was pregnant. Eric chose to retaliate by beating Braxton badly and sending him to the hospital with broken ribs, leg, nose and a bad concussion. On that day, I went to see Eric and related to him that I understood his anger. My best friend had slept with my husband and had a baby. However, I begged Eric to let his hate go. He, in turn, swore to get Landon, saying she deserved to die. I rationalized with him by telling him not to ruin his life. Yes, it was horrible what they did, but move on. I begged him not to hurt her for little Eric's sake. I told him she was really sorry, but she really thought he was the father. At the time, I thought I had gotten through to him. Months later, I still can't believe he pulled that trigger.

But then, I *could* understand. This ultimate betrayal caused me to take a very long time to forgive Braxton. It took me even longer to forgive Landon because we were friends first. She knew how I felt about Braxton. She knew he was the first person I'd gone out on a limb for. I know she was jealous of our relationship. She couldn't accept that there was someone else vying for my time. Do I think she or they intentionally set out to have that sexual encounter? No, but it still hurts because it happened. What I realized was Braxton had my heart. He had that missing beat. He showed me my beauty, taught me how to love me. He knows my heart, knows what I need, he loves me right.

Landon, on the other hand, taught me to have a voice. She taught me it was okay to be a little aggressive, to try things. She showed me how to live life. She also shielded and protected me from a lot of pain and hurt from my mother. She never allowed me to mope and was my first supporter.

I rub my face trying to alleviate the tension and stress that the visit ignited Chauncey opened up old wounds, I needed a release. I gather my belongings and head to BET to see my favorite VP, my husband, Braxton.

*

I approach and see Kim, Braxton's secretary. She holds up her index finger to shush me. I walk over to her desk where she scribbles on the notepad, "Lisa is in the office."

Lisa Stevens is a BITCH. She is Braxton's co-worker who I have warned him for years about. She wanted to jump on his dick. From day one she's been giving me shade. On what supposed to be one of the happiest days of my life, my baby shower this chick announces to everyone that Braxton had a son with Landon. She then called me pathetic. I was mortified. Thinking about it now, I should have pulled every last track from her raggedy head. Instead, all I managed was to slap the chick and give her some choice words. It was one of those unfortunate situations when you say, I should have done this, but when the reality hits you you're too discombobulated to do anything. Damn, I wish I would have dragged the chick.

Kim and I stand quietly outside the office, the door had been left cracked, giving us the opportunity to eavesdrop.

"Hello Braxton, how are you today?"

"Hello, did you get my email about the report?"

"Yes, how is your day going?"

"Lisa, you need to be concerned about the report, not my day."

"Braxton, I apologize again for the incident at the shower. Again, I was out of line. We are colleagues, but we were also friends. Can we be cordial?

"Lisa, I need the report on my desk before 3 pm today."

"Braxton you're being unreasonable."

"So are you."

"You're right. I apologize to you again, Braxton. Please, can we make amends?"

"Lisa, I need the report by three. But before you leave, I need you to sign this."

"Braxton, you're writing me up?"

"Yes, your job performance is a reflection of you. As of late, it seems you are having more difficulty performing the required duties. I'm just putting you on notice."

"You're being unfair, I apologized. You're taking this too far. Fine, we won't be friends, but I am warning you, I'll go to HR."

"Go ahead, everything is documented. I have more than enough incidents showing your incompetence. I also have emails and performance reviews where you were encouraged to take career enhancement workshops to improve your job performance. You've done none."

"Braxton, what can I do? Please, can we work this out?"

"Do you think after the stunt you pulled I would entertain the thought of being an ally of yours? You tried to humiliate my wife, you created a disturbance at my daughter's birth celebration, and you just threatened me."

"I…I've been under a lot of pressure. I wasn't thinking. I'm sorry. I need this job. Truthfully, I am in a financial bind."

"Again, you should have thought before you acted. You knew exactly what you were doing. You need to leave my office now and get the report done by three."

Kim and I are all smiles when the bitch walks out. She sees me and jumps.

I couldn't resist. "Silly bitch, tricks are for kids."

She storms off, shutting the door behind her. Kim and I share a laugh.

I shake my head. "That chick is raggedy

"And desperate," adds Kim.

"Kim, I love the hair," I compliment Kim's new red- colored short do. Kim always wore her hair short cut this cut was more tapered. Kim was very attractive but I was not threatened at all. I didn't get that vibe. Most of the time Braxton was getting on her nerves with his mood swings. Kim also was married with three kids.

"Have you ever considered cutting your hair?"

My thick curly wild tresses hung mid-back consisting of a lot of blond and many shades of brown. The blond bringing out my hazel-green eyes while the browns made my golden honey skin luminescence. Today I wore it all in a bun.

"No, I love my hair. It's like a security blanket and there are a lot of advantages to have all this all this hair. One is being hiding my facial expressions."

She laughs. "You have so much though. Ironically I do like doing little girls hair. I'm always changing my daughter's hair. She gets mad but it's fun to me. I just can't deal with all the hair on my head."

I pick up the picture of Kim's daughter, Ayanna. Her hair is in flat twist and pulled into a ponytail. "Aww, she is so cute. She has you're deep dimples. How old is she now?"

"She is eight, Marcus is eleven and Kyle is six."

"Your babies are getting big."

"I know."

"How long did it take you to do Ayanna hair?"

"An hour and a half."

"That's fast. I know where I'm sending the twins because Yasmin can't do hair."

"You can't. Didn't you play in doll hair when you were younger?"

"Not really. But even if I did, that was years ago."

She laughs. "Your babies already have a lot of hair. They're not even six months and can wear a ponytail."

"Well, I can say they inherited something from me. If I didn't experience the labor I wouldn't think they were mine. They are all Braxton."

Kim and I carry on like we're at a happy hour.

"I should have known," said Braxton startling both of us.

"I'm sorry, Kim. I got you in trouble again. I will correct this though."

"Is that so?" said Braxton.

"Yes, sir. I take full responsibility. Kim, as always, is professional and has been nothing but a delight while I waited. I was the cause of the disruption."

"Kim should know she has to be responsible for her actions. She should know not to let others influence her to act outside a professional manner."

I roll my eyes. "Oh, we're in a cranky mood today."

He narrows his piercing grey eyes on me. "You! I in my office now." he demanded, trying to be threatening.

I go in and take a seat in the chair in front of this desk. I make sure to cross my legs, so he can see my upper thighs. I was glad I chose the brown two-piece suit; the skirt stopped just at my knees and was fitted, but flared on the bottom. I unbutton the top two buttons to reveal part of my gold La Perla bra. I can't hear what he's telling Kim. I hope he doesn't give her a lot of crazy demands.

I hear the door closing when he comes in. I do not turn around. The blue tailored suit I bought him looks good on him. He takes a seat and I study him. My heart skips just like the first day I ever laid eyes on him. He's so damn sexy; his wavy hair cut close, and goatee adding to his sexiness. Those grey eyes had me in a trance, his smooth caramel skin, those lips and the things they did. His tall 6'4 body always felt good on top of my 5'11. He was my love, my honey, my baby, my rock. My everything.

"Yasmin, you can't come to my office carrying on like you're home or at happy hour."

"I'm sorry..."

"Let me finish. Saying hi and a few pleasantries is fine, but you have to be professional. I am Vice President and have a standard to uphold."

I widen my eyes, poke my lips out just a little, giving him my puppy dog look.

"Don't do that no more."

I stand. I know he was a little upset, which he should be, especially after dealing with that chick Lisa Stevens. However, the smell of his Issey Miyake cologne had me feeling a certain way. I was moist doing kegel exercises of all things, which wasn't helping the situation.

"Where are you going?"

"To work."

"So you came here to see Kim?"

"No, you jealous? You want some of my time?"

"Always," he winks.

"You want me?"

"You love starting stuff."

"You love when I do."

"I do."

I walk over to his chair. He scoots back. I sit on his lap and begin a little grind.

He moans.

I lean back and he inhales my neck, causing me to shudder. Now it's my turn to moan.

He chuckles. "You smell too good. What are you wearing?"

"Honey."

"You are sweet like honey."

"Really, Honey by Marc Jacobs."

"Well you smell too good not to have some of. I smell it, now I want to taste that other honey." He puts his hands between my legs.

"And you feel too good. That's why I'm going to give it to you," I whisper.

I kiss him deep. He spreads my legs, slips my panties to the side before inserting his finger in me.

"Mrs. Simms you so wet. Damn, all this honey."

I kiss him again before I stand pushing my skirt up in the process. I straddle him placing each leg on the side armrest. With my hands, I hold on to the bottom of the armrest, lean back grinding slow and steady.

Braxton grabs my waist pulls me up.

"I want to fuck you nice and slow."

I'm glad I shaved my jewel this morning. It was nice, smooth, and hairless, decreasing the risk of getting caught on his zipper.

"You don't have to want. Do it."

Using his desk for support, I ease up just enough for him to unbuckle his pants. Sugar Daddy is out within seconds.

Sugar Daddy was the name I gave to Braxton's smooth, thick, caramel 9 ½ inch dick. Just like the candy, it was long, sweet, and caramel. The way you could suck on it all day was the way I felt about my Sugar Daddy. I couldn't get enough; it could stay in me all day long.

I waste no time putting his massive caramel in. The feeling so sweet I get an instant high. I rock slowly, my body relaxing, going in a trance, being hypnotized by his sex.

My low, slow, moans sound as if I'm in Buddha chant.

"Look at me." His voice demanding yet seductive causes me to shudder, bring me to the verge of climax.

I can't open my eyes.

"Look at me." He grinds in me.

I rock him back. I lean all the way back using the arms on the chair for support. My head inches from the floor, I grind him slow going clockwise only to switch up and go counter-clockwise, alternating every few minutes.

"Look at me." He grinds.

I still can't open my eyes. Instead, I bite my lip.

"Look at me. Look at me." He stops, steadying my hips to prevent me from moving.

Instantaneously, I look at him.

He begins winding in me. I rock with him.

"Don't close your eyes, beautiful. Look at me while I fuck you."

He pounds in me. He stops, kissing me deep. He grinds slooooowly... pound…he stops…kissing me again.

Over and over the cycle continues. All of his teasing has me ready to pull my hair out. I want to ride him hard, but he isn't allowing it. I lean back so I can feel more of him.

He smiles. Wrapping his arms around me, he grabs my shoulders and pounds hard.

"Ahhh…"

"Shhhh."

I feel it coming. He covers my mouth with his hand trying to muffle my moans.

Damn, shit, oh my god! I don't want to come yet, I said in my mind. He drills in me deep, "*Yes, yes, yes, give it to me. Put it all in me. Make me come*." And he does.

I collapse on his shoulder, breathless trying to catch my breath.

Braxton hadn't. He grabs my hips, moving them with him, against him. Normally, I would help him out, rock a little, squeeze it, but my body was still tingling. Trying to regain some composure. I lean back again so he could feel more of me. Minutes later, I feel a puddle between my legs.

He chuckles. "So this is what I got to do to control that mouth. You are amazing."

I smile.

"Give me a kiss, beautiful."

I do.

"As much as I want to go another round with you, I can't. I have a meeting in thirty."

I get up, the weight of my size twelve frame has my legs sore, half asleep from being on the armrest.

"Yeah."

"Are you backed up? You came like you ain't had none in months."

"No, I'm good. My wife takes very good care of me."

"And my husband takes care of me."

Fortunately, after many incidents, Braxton learned it's imperative to keep two suits at work. I on the other hand didn't take heed. Braxton gave me a quick peck, jumped up, and ran in his bathroom to take a shower. I got his suit, underwear, and other disrobed garments and placed them in a dry cleaning bag.

Braxton came out minutes later looking refreshed. I was on my way to the bathroom to freshen up when he stopped me.

"Thank you for making my day better."

"Thank you for the relief; I needed it." I smile.

"What are you thinking about? What has you so stressed?"

"Chauncey came by my office to see me today. He wants me to go see Eric."

"Hell no! You're not going to see him. He lost his damn mind," Braxton rants.

"That's what I told him."

"You stay far away from Eric."

"Chauncey is saying it's some things I need to know."

"Yasmin, seriously, what is wrong with you?"

"Nothing. I guess part of me wants to look him in the face."

"For what? You know why he did what he did. You know what he did to me. It's not important though, because you're not going."

"How you gonna tell me what I'm not going to do?"

"Yasmin, I'm not going to sit here and debate with you why you're not going to see Eric. What the hell can he say? He needs to save that shit for the judge and jury. "

"I see you're confused. I'm not one of your kids."

"Yasmin, I'm not playing. Don't go with Chauncey or anyone else to see Eric. Stay the hell away from him. He officially snapped and I don't want you near him. Do you understand?"

"Later, Braxton."

Now I looooooooooooved making love, fucking, and all that with Braxton, but I hated the aftermath. The feel of slimy cum between my legs was icky. Like now I could feel the sticky glob running down my legs. Gross. I wish I just went into the bathroom. I had to take a shower. I didn't make it to the lobby before I turned around. Luckily, Braxton had left for his meeting. I took care of what I had to and 20 minutes later I was walking out the door.

3

Let's Us Move On

"Hello, Lawrence." I said as I walked into his office.

He gives me a slight smile. "Hello Yasmin. How are you doing?"

"I'm well. How are you coping?"

"You know how it goes, better than Jackie. She is really struggling, which was to be expected. I understand. I wish it was something I could do. I don't like feeling so helpless.

"Unfortunately, right now there is nothing you can do. You have to be supportive, but give her space. Let her know you're there and that you love her, and when she's ready or needs to talk to you, she can."

He stands, walks over, hugs me and kisses me on the head.

"I'm so sorry I wasn't there for you growing up. It was my loss. You are beautiful and wise beyond your years. I thank you for allowing me in your life. I'm so proud of you," he said with remorse. "Despite the injustice your mother and I did to you, you are a wonderful amazing wife, mother, woman. You are forgiving and you've made this difficult time tolerable. Your heart is pure and I admire that. Thank you."

I was caught off guard, but I appreciated his words. Not so long ago, I craved for acceptance from my mother, Michelle and John; the man who I was told was my father. Growing up, I always felt like the black sheep. I never had any connection with John or Michelle. They focused their attention on my younger sister, Ashley, who I still didn't have any bond with. My childhood was filled with forgotten birthdays, no acknowledgements and plenty of ridicule from my "parents" and paternal grandmother. Recently, I would learn that Michelle had an affair with Lawrence and I was the result. What was even more disturbing Landon and I had met in high school and immediately formed a bond. No one said anything. It wasn't until years later, when my mother's sister Patti threatened to tell the truth, that it was revealed that Landon and I were sisters. Lawrence appeared remorseful.

I chose to forgive Lawrence and try to build a relationship. I even reconciled with John, he apologized for his actions and admitted he was wrong. I talk to him once a month. My mother, on the other hand, has so much hate and anger and refuses to make any amends and blames me for ruining her marriage to John, who had filed for divorce.

I wipe my eyes. "Thank you, Lawrence. It means a lot."

"No need to thank me. I wish I could say I hold some responsibility or part for making you the woman you are."

"Well neither can Michelle, but you're trying and you're here now and it means so much."

"Have you talked to her?"

"I called, but she hung up on me. Said I chose my sides and I would regret it."

"Yasmin, she is your mother, but maybe you should step away and try to build a relationship later."

"Yes, she is, and the only one I have. I know we will never have the ideal relationship, but I have to keep trying."

"I just don't want you to get hurt."

"Yes, daddy."

He pauses. I see his eyes glisten. "Thank you, daughter." He said choked up.

"I brought you some pictures of your grandbabies." I hand him an envelope.

He gives me another quick kiss before he takes a seat behind his desk.

"Thank you. I needed this. Look at my girls. I know they are keeping you busy."

"They are."

Kevin abruptly comes barging into the office.

"Hey Lawrence you called me in. Oh, hey, Yas. Sorry to interrupt."

"No need. Come have a seat. Check out the pictures of my beautiful granddaughters."

Kevin comes in and takes the pictures from Lawrence before taking a seat next to me. He goes through them.

"The girls are getting big. They look like just like their daddy. I guess it's true."

"What are you talking about, Kevin?"

"My grandmother says whoever aggravates you the most, your baby will look like them."

Lawrence laughs and I punch Kevin in the arm. "Your sense of humor is just that, yours."

"Mr. Taylor, you have a meeting," Lawrence's short, frumpy, acne having assistant announces. Surely, Jacqueline picked this girl.

"Thank you, Barbara."

He looks at Kevin and I, "Thank you, my daughter, for the pictures. I appreciate your visit. Kevin, I will see you when I return. You can leave my pictures on the desk. I know they are so irresistibly cute, but all of the pictures are mine."

"Not one?" Kevin pretends to be hurt.

"No," growls Lawrence.

"You're welcome, daddy." I laughed and Lawrence left.

"Daddy now," said Kevin inquisitively.

"You catch everything."

"Of course, that's what I do. Kevin Powell Esquire." He pulls out a card.

I shake my head. "It feels awkward, but he's been here, proving that he wants to be a part of my life."

"That's good. I'm happy for you. Lawrence is a good guy."

"Of course you would say that. He's the boss and you are a brown noser."

"Ha ha, you and your jokes. You know he is. So what's up with your crazy husband?"

"Lawrence is good and my husband is not crazy. He is attentive and he is doing well. Although, we did have a disagreement."

He sighs. "This isn't one of your disappearing acts is it?" He asks referring to the two-month hiatus I took when I first found out about Braxton and Landon's hook-up. I stayed in Minnesota for a whole month before Braxton tracked me down. I relocated to another location for a month, only to learn later that Braxton had hired a P.I. to track me down.

"Ha ha, no. He's upset because I told him Chauncey came to my office saying Eric wants to talk to me. He started barking orders saying I was not going to see Eric and to stay away from him. He said I lost my mind for even thinking about it."

"And I agree with him 1000 percent."

"What?"

"No what. It will serve no purpose of you going to see Eric. The evidence against him is mounting by the second. He should have thought before he pulled the trigger. Every day he will be reminded of what he had and lost because of his rage. His ass will die alone in his 6x8 cell. And that still won't be enough." Kevin bangs on the desk startling me.

"Yeah," I say glumly.

"Yasmin, really, why would you even entertain the thought of seeing that criminal?"

"I don't know. I wanted to look him in the face. I thought I had gotten through to him."

"What do you mean?"

"That day when Braxton was in the accident, I knew Eric was the cause, so I confronted Eric. He denied it at first, but then admitted it. He told me Landon would pay. I really thought I'd gotten through to him."

"Yasmin! What the hell? Why am I just finding out about this? You should have mentioned this. We could have brought him up on charges a long time ago, issued a restraining order against him for both Braxton and Landon. We could have avoided this!"

"Kevin, I feel guilty enough. But you and I both know a restraining order wouldn't have done shit. He still would have found a way to shoot her."

"Well, in light of this new evidence you presented I will be pushing the prosecution to go for the death penalty. This proves this was a premeditated crime. He carefully thought this out. He deserves it. You and Braxton will have to testify against Eric."

"Kevin please don't do that to me. Please leave this off the record. I don't want to go anywhere near the court, let alone stand trial. I can't do it."

"You can and will. Justice for Landon."

"Kevin."

"Yasmin, you can't withhold this evidence. I won't withhold this evidence. Do you want to tell Braxton or shall I?"

"Damn Kevin, I came to you as a friend. I told you about this lawyer/friend crap. You seem to not be able to distinguish between the two. I need my friend. How am I supposed to go to Braxton and say I ran my mouth to you about Eric beating you up. That incident was too remain between Eric, Braxton and me. I don't want to reopen that mess up."

"Yasmin, this is for Landon. The jury and the judge needs to know what he is capable of. I will talk to Braxton."

"No, I'll do it, but I won't tell you nothin' again."

4

Refill

"Hey beautiful." I was in the sitting room on the chaise nursing Khouri when Braxton entered our plush master suite. He kisses me and then bends down to kiss Khouri.

"Hey, you."

"Where is Reagan?" He looks around.

"In her crib." He leaves out, minutes later returning through the double doors cradling Reagan. I shake my head.

He starts smothering her with kisses waking her up. "Reagan, daddy missed you. Wake up."

"How was your day?"

"Long. I missed y'all. I'm glad to be home," he sighs.

"I'm glad you're home."

"Yeah, it's no place like home."

"Nope."

I loved my home. A five-bedroom stone colonial with seven bathrooms, five fireplaces, sunroom, pool, 20 foot ceilings, sunken living room, library, media room and three-car garage, resting on three acres. I decorated in rich neutral colors; a lot of browns, beige, and rust with some olive and coral colors. It was my tranquility, my therapy.

"You know we never got a chance to celebrate our anniversary."

"I know. You owe me," I pout.

"I do."

I kiss Khouri

"Everything is so chaotic and stressful we need a break." He says.

"Speaking of stress and chaos, I saw Kevin today." I tell Braxton that I opened my mouth. He was okay. He agreed with Kevin, go figure. He was willing to testify to keep Eric behind bars. Personally, something in my gut told me this just wasn't right.

"Beautiful, we need to get away."

"We do," I nod.

"Let's go to the Cayman islands for the holiday. My parent's anniversary is so close to ours we can take them to babysit. Then we can go get into some things."

"They might have something planned or want to be alone."

"You think my parents going to miss out on their first holiday?" he kisses Reagan again.

"You're right. That sounds like a plan. Do I still get another gift?"

"That five carat emerald center cut on your left hand is a lifetime gift. Your ring cost as much as my car," he said referring to his seven series BMW.

I hold up my five carat center cut. In actuality it was more like seven, he had a carat of round diamonds on each side surrounding the emerald diamond.

"I'm worth it and more."

"You certainly are. We'll see," he winks. "Something like this?"

He presents me with a box and opens it. Inside is a beautiful diamond tennis bracelet.

"Aww, thank you baby, it's beautiful."

"Not as beautiful as you."

I stand to give him an appreciative kiss. Khouri finishes nursing and Braxton grabs her up to burp her. "Hey, Khouri. How daddy princess doing?"

She lays her head on Braxton's shoulder and is content. While Reagan was now alert in an upward position looking around. Khouri and Reagan had him wrapped around their fingers. I know they are going to be the ones to calm him, but drive him crazy just the same.

I take Reagan so I can start nursing her.

"You were happy a few minutes ago, what happened?"

"I was about to pick up the phone to call Landon. It's just not right." I wipe the tears from my eyes.

Braxton comes over wraps his free arm around me. He bends down, kissing me gently on the cheek.

Khouri starts whining and I can't help but laugh. "Just like daddy, she wants all the attention."

"I told you about talking about my daughters." He kisses on Khouri.

"I didn't realize they were only yours."

He smiles. "So we're going to the Cayman Islands?"

"Yes, we are."

I hated to leave with everything so erratic, but I was anxious for a change of scenery. I needed this.

The twins came with us to the island, along with Braxton's parents, Ms. Beverly, who I call mommy, and his father, Mr. Jeff. Braxton's comical Uncle Charles also came with his new lady friend, Stella. Lastly, was Braxton's older brother Vincent and his hooker girlfriend, Ty, who had been around too long. We wanted to bring Eric, but Jackie insisted she need him close. We respected her wishes, allowing her time with Eric. It's understandable that this holiday would be extremely difficult for her and Lawrence.

I held Braxton around his waist and lay my head on his chest. The island was just as beautiful as it was when we came two years ago. Braxton had surprised me with an impromptu wedding. He sent me on a day-long scavenger hunt from store to store shopping for a dress, jewelry, and accessories. Every store handed me a flower at the end of my quest. He stood at Rum's Point dressed in all white asking me to marry him. The flowers I collected throughout the day served as my bouquet, and when the sun kissed the water, the ceremony began.

I took in the scent of flowers, coconuts, palm trees and more. The ambiance, as always, was serene and tranquil. This was our utopia. I couldn't wait to get back to the beach to enjoy everything it had to offer. But before I could do that, we had to unpack. Braxton and I recently purchased the villa we honeymooned in. The 7 bedroom 5 bathroom home allowed us privacy and was large enough to accommodate our family. All three floors have spacious king-sized bedrooms facing the ocean. On the ground floor, there's a large kitchen and dining room with a formal sitting area that leads right to Seven Mile Beach.

As Braxton predicted, Mommy and Mr. Jeff happily volunteered to keep the twins the first night. Braxton and I, along with Vince and Ty, went to a poplar bar and lounge. This evening would be more enjoyable if I had better company. I wish Braxton's two other brothers, Jeff Jr. and Horace could have come. Jeff Jr. and Braxton, the first and fourth son, are younger versions of their father; from height and facial structure to the piercing gray eyes. Jeff Jr, the eldest, is a lawyer in the D.C., Maryland, Virginia area, and his wife, Patrice, reminds me of Olive Oyl from Popeye because of her tall, too skinny, 6'2 stature. Patrice always wore her hair in a bun, and dressed in meek attire. She looks like the old stereotypical school teacher that she is. They have a three-year-old son Jonathan, and this year they were going to North Carolina to spend time with Patrice's family.

Horace is the third born son. Like his father, he pursued a career in the medical field. Mr. Jeff was the head anesthesiologist at Holy Cross Hospital, while Horace was a prominent cardiologist. Horace was the most timid and soft spoken. He is a sweet guy. He's currently dating this woman by the name of Monica. Monica reminded me of the actress Rachel True. Monica has a four-year-old son that she's brought around a few times. She seems sweet, but I'll have to do some more investigating.

Vincent is the second son. Vince and Horace look more like mommy, who resembles Diahann Carroll, so both are very handsome. Their eyes are both big, dark, and seductive drawing you into their heart melting smiles. Vince and I always have some type of battle going on. He's annoying, but I love him. He is always good for a laugh. I knew never to take him seriously. This Simms boy was a male gigolo who unfortunately didn't discriminate. He has brought the weirdest and craziest females home. The first time I met the family, the girl he brought home looked like the horse Seabiscuit. She wore a skin tight, cheetah print bodysuit with thigh high black boots and a blonde ponytail that touched her donkey ass. Yes, she was a hot mess. Two day later, he had someone new, but just as bad. It's normal for him to change girlfriends like underwear, which is why I'm puzzled by Ty still being around. It has to be the head game...it's the head game…has to be.

I'm convinced Ty was born with a missing chromosome at birth or had the umbilical cord wrapped around her neck. She acts like something caused her to lose oxygen, which is causing her problems with comprehension and common sense. I really was going to be nice, but she irritates me and usually within the first two minutes of being around her. Like now, this chick comes to the island with five-inch heels, a spandex dress, and too much makeup. It matches, but it's too much. All the foundation, concealer, eyelashes, blush, eyeliner, the Nicki Minaj look. She was a high price hooker, escort, lady of the night or whatever the title is these days.

I tried to sit content, but I could only take hearing her critique of everyone's attire so much. This chick thought she was Anna Wintour. She gave her opinion too much on what should have been matched, how their body type was all wrong and whatnot. Still I sat with a smile, nodded, every now and then saying, "Yeah. Ok. Really?" Yes, so shallow.

Braxton and Vince talked about a variety of thing from work to sports, movies to cars. I would try to join in with them, but Ty kept tapping me to look at someone. I pinched the heck out of Braxton for making me suffer like this. He laughed because he knew this chick was lame. If he didn't add me to the conversation soon, the joke would be on him. He will get no lovin' tonight.

Two minutes later, I couldn't take it anymore, so I excused myself to the bathroom. Braxton is anti-alcohol since I'm breastfeeding, as he says, *his* daughters. While he drank, I was expected to drink fruit punch. I knew this fool was not above tasting my drink just to make sure it was non-alcoholic. So after leaving the bathroom, I made a detour to the bar. I had already pumped enough milk for a day, so I was good. I needed the drink to deal with Vince's dense video hoe. I must say Ty is very pretty. She was tall, petite, a size three at most, and she flaunted her sexy all day. Her hair long, straight, natural Brazilian. Vince—who was just as tall as Braxton—and Ty made a cute couple.

Her messiness and condescending comments is what irked the hell out of me, and left me little tolerance for her. Tonight though, so far so good, as far as the comments, so I would continue to play nice. I guzzled the drink down, returned to the table to see Ty sitting in Vince's lap, rubbing her hands all over his legs. She was obviously drunk and in heat. Vince isn't any better because his hands are cupping her breast.

I look at Braxton, he just shakes his head.

I will be nice and initiate a meaningful conversation with Vince. "How's business, Vince?"

Vince was a videographer. He did a lot of videos for music artists and documentaries for athletes. Ty is a video vixen. Like I said, she's trying to be a revamped Superhead.

"Business is great and Ty's been assisting me now on a lot of projects. Matter of fact, I just did a music video for Geester. That thing is fire!"

"Yeah, you did your thing. It was good." I give him his props.

"How you know? The video hasn't been released. I just sent him the finished product two days ago."

"I was over Chauncey's when you sent it. You know he and Chauncey are my clients. I help them manage their funds." I say matter-of-factly. This was good for them because Vince is expensive. The quality supported his price, so it was all good.

"So you know all the finances. You know my fee too."

"I do, but I'm so good at what I do, that he made it back already," I laugh.

"Really?" he said with surprise.

"Yeah, I'm sure she did. Yasmin knows how to work numbers, among other things." Braxton kissed me on the shoulder.

"You don't have a problem with her working with Chauncey, Braxton?" said Ty, looking appalled.

Before he could respond, I speak. "Why? I am a professional. In my career, I don't take off my clothes and lie down." My tolerance was gone.

"But you laid down with him for what, two years? Once you sleep with a client, you can only be so professional. Two years...I know you did your share of fucking."

Braxton was quiet, which meant he was pissed. I focus my attention on her and Vince.

"Vince, how do you handle having Ty as your assistant, being as though I KNOW and the industry knows, she's fucked half of them if not more?"

"Ladies, let's play nice. We are supposed to be enjoying this beautiful atmosphere," said Vince.

I roll my eyes. I peek at Braxton and he is sipping on his drink, disposition stiff, getting angrier by the second. I was going to have to pull out the tricks tonight.

Ty goes back to fondling Vince. Vince is just as bad sucking on her neck. I excuse myself for another bathroom break. I would need a little extra in this drink.

On my way back, I see my favorite uncle has appeared. "Vince, have some class with yourself. This ain't one of your video shoots," said Uncle Charles, trying to school his nephew.

"Man, Uncle Charles, this is an adult establishment. We good, just being affectionate," said Vince as he continued to fondle Ty's breast.

"Well, I don't wanna see no soft porn starring my nephew. Ty sit in your chair."

"Hey, Uncle Charles." I give him a hug.

"Sweet Thing," he returns the hug. Sweet Thing is the nickname he gave me when I met the family for the first time. Braxton and I had an argument about Kevin, of all people. Anyway, he had an attitude and Uncle Charles picked up on Braxton's little jealousy. Since I was the only girl Braxton ever brought home, he had a good time seeing his vulnerability. He instigated the whole night calling me sweet thing to piss Braxton off.

"Hello, Ms. Stella," I kiss her on the cheek.

Hey, sweetie." She returns the gesture.

"See, that's what you call manners," Uncle Charles said matter-of-factly while looking at Ty, Vincent and Braxton.

Uncle Charles and Ms. Stella take a seat next to us. They are a lovely couple. To be in his sixties, Uncle Charles still has an athletic build and is in shape, jogging three miles four times a week. His salt and pepper hair made his 6'4 frame of dark skin appear rich and distinguished. Uncle Charles is Braxton's father's older brother and didn't have any kids. His only wife had been killed in a car accident two years into their marriage. Since then, he was a lover of many ladies. Although, Stella has been around for a minute. Maybe, he's slowing down in his old age. Stella was a little younger, in her late forties. She was short, about 5'5. She wasn't as fit as Uncle Charles, about a size 16. She kept her hair in a cute bob. Her skin is brown and flawless. I hoped she would stay around because I really like her; she is so sweet and personable.

"So what are you youngins up too?"

"Nothing," Ty responds half-heartedly.

"Well, I am enjoying the music and taking in this breeze," I said while bopping to the music.

"Why you quiet, Braxton? What got you mad now?" inquired Uncle Charles.

"I'm good," he responds.

"Braxton that attitude is going to cause you more harm than good. After a while, a person gets tired of dealing with it," lectured Uncle Charles.

Vince laughs with Ty still sits in his lap.

"Vincent, I don't know why you laughing. Have some respect. I know how you do, what you into, but we all don't need to see it." Uncle Charles again berates.

"Dag Uncle Charles while you got to be lecturing. You killing my vibe. We adults trying to relax."

"Oh Charles let's do some karaoke." Ms. Stella said after they announced they were going to start the karaoke hour, taking the attention off of Vincent and the hooker.

Uncle Charles and Stella ended up singing Luther's *If This World Were Mine.* That got Braxton laughing. Ty and Vincent even went up there, these real porn stars wanted to do Uncle Luke's Me So Horny. They were really I mean really upset when they didn't have the song. They settled for Sir Mix A lot, *Baby Got Back.*

Braxton wasn't feeling the karaoke and I wasn't doing it alone. I did get an admirer, some guy with an S-curl, big lips, long side burns, big head and little body. Seriously he was like 5'3 weighed about 95 pounds, yes he looked like Prince. Well he decided to sing to me of all songs Prince's *I Will Die 4 U.*

"You got some competition bro." Vincent howled.

"Yasmin, I told you about your friendliness." Braxton cracks.

"Shut up, Braxton."

I grab Braxton's hand.

"Don't try to be up on me now." He continues.

"Oh, you got jokes." I hold up my fist.

"You know you are expensive." He teases.

"Uh-oh Yasmin, you ain't ready for this. He coming for you." Vince stands encouraging little man to come over.

This thing performed too. He gyrated, rolled and humped the floor all while pointing to me. He come up to me did a split, jumped back up, begin rubbing his body and shaking his booty.

Everyone was laughing at this fool. Uncle Charles had pulled out his phone to record the mess, Vincent was encouraging him. Ty and Ms. Stella had tears coming from their eyes.

I was laughing at first but when came up and started licking his hands and grabbing himself it was too much for me. Luckily for me the song ended and he stopped. He grabbed a rose from a nearby table and handed it me. I accepted and he kissed my hand. He left politely and I wiped my hand on the table cloth.

"That's cold Yasmin. You should have gave him a little kiss after that performance" instigated Vince.

"Whatever. I don't know where those lips have been. These lips and the privilege is only for Mr. Braxton Simms." I kiss him on the cheek.

Braxton wraps his arm around me.

"Boo, you phony," howled Vince.

"No, you got me confused. But, you're not use to a woman of my caliber and probably will never be. I'm authentic and loyal." I had to get that winch back.

"That's right, sweet thing. Tell him," cosigned Uncle Charles.

Ty rolls her eyes and Stella tries to stifle a laugh.

It was time to go. I lean over to whisper in Braxton's ear, "There's this sweet caramel candy I love to suck on. Can I have some?"

Braxton stands, grabbing me in the process, literally, almost knocking me off my feet. "Later, we'll see you sometime tomorrow."

"We know what y'all about to do," instigated Vince.

"And we have enough class to do it behind closed doors." I shot back.

"That's why there's a tape floating around with you two getting wet in the shower," Vincent teases, referring to the mishap where Braxton and I had sex in the bathroom during a very public party. Unbeknownst to us, a camera was recording. Our sensual sexual relations had been viewed among many, live, and later on DVD.

Ty bursts out laughing.

"Vince, shutup!" Braxton said annoyed.

"You two have a good night," Uncle Charles shoos us along.

"Boy, who the hell child are you? I know your mother would have your butt laid out looking like the fool you are for acting. I won't do that now. You on notice, you got one more time. Your foolishness killin' *my* vibe."

I hear Uncle Charles grill Vince while we leave the bar. Braxton and I share a laugh.

*

Once in our suite we wasted no time, immediately taking off all our clothes. Braxton led me to our private balcony, there lie the perfect panorama of the beach, unobstructed by neighbors or buildings, the stars vibrant, illuminating the view.

I give Braxton a deep kiss that he appreciates. We explore each other's body as if it's the first time. Taking our time kissing one another, touching each other's most sensitive parts. My moist lips kiss his chest, my hands stroke his dick. His moist lips kiss my face, neck, lips. I saunter behind him; tenderly I massage his muscles with my hands. Moments later, my hands are replaced by my lips. He moans as I daintily kiss him up and down his spine. My hands roam his strong legs, his stern chest and finally land on Sugar Daddy. Meticulously I stroke him, his body responds with a shudder. I continue to place kisses on his back while my hands move up and down his shaft. I tease him a little while longer. I smile when his breathing becomes labored. I squeeze Sugar Daddy with one hand and use the other to squeeze his balls. Seconds later I hear him groan as he coats my hands with his sticky cum.

I step in front of him and deliver a passionate kiss. He stops, turns me around, back to his chest and begins pinching my nipples. I spread my legs and he uses one of his hands to tease my clit. I arch my back, bring my arm around and stroke his neck. He in turn bends down kisses my collarbone and I feel honey trickling down my thigh.

Next he bends me over the balcony, I feel Sugar Daddy on my ass. Braxton spreads my cheeks and I anxiously await my candy. He takes his time rubbing his dick up and down, all around my clit, my honey well never entering. I push back desperately wanting his entry. He doesn't allow it. Instead he gets on his knees and begins licking my clit from behind. My legs wobble and I use the banister for support. Braxton lifts my legs, his head in between sucks on my clit. My entire body trembles. Braxton stands, I lose my hold of the banister. Braxton is strong. He holds me steady as he did on our honeymoon. My stomach to his, arms wrapped around him. The upside down motion rushing the blood to my head giving me a feeling of euphoria. Just as before, his tongue slowly circles around my pearl. He makes his way to my honey well where he laps up my honey. He teases me by sucking on my pearl, willing it to burst. Lick, lick, lick. In and out his tongue goes out of my canal. He, knowing my body, releases his tongue before it does. Just when I think I'm about to pass out, he flips me over, lying me on the lounge chair.

Braxton smiles as he strokes Sugar Daddy, pleased he has me senseless. I take a few moments to regain my composure. It was my turn to please him, I stand, get my blindfold. Braxton hesitantly allows me to place it on him. I guide him to the lounge chair. My mouth was ready for his candy. I would be doing the Grapefruit Method I was taught in Angel's Erotic Solution video. I retrieve the grapefruit I set aside earlier, cutting off each end. With the center of the grapefruit, I cut a hole big enough to fit around Braxton's candy. First, I wet Sugar Daddy with my mouth. Going a quarter of the way down I suck my candy. I open wide going down halfway, pushing his candy to the back of my throat. My mouth reacts slavering all over his candy from top to bottom. I remove Sugar Daddy from my mouth, but he's making an up and down movement performing hypnosis, begging me to taste more.

I would, but not yet. I focus my attention on his rock candy balls. I lick his perineum, teasing him by making small circles with my tongue. He grabs my head, begging me to do it again. Yes, he was ready. I walk over to table where there is an assortment of fruits. Grabbing the grapefruit, I begin to roll it in my hand to make it juicy. I take the knife and horizontally cut across the grapefruit on both ends, removing the navels. Next, I cut a hole in the center of the grapefruit wide enough to fit around Braxton's thickness. Gingerly, I walk over to Braxton who is patiently waiting. Taking the grapefruit I glide it down his shaft. I put my mouth on the tip, and suck my candy. I take the grapefruit twisting it up and down as I suck on the tip of my candy. I make rapid movements with the grapefruit, stroking, jerking, and squeezing his dick. My head bobs indulging in the tastes from the grapefruit and his candy.

Braxton normally the more composed was moaning and hissing.

"Damn, sssshit. Uhhhh, Whosh, Uhhh Shit, Shit, Shit. Ohhhh Shhhhhhhhh!"

In less than two minutes, that candy was melting and the cream was spilling out. Braxton lies still for a moment catching his breath. I remove the grapefruit and pat myself on the back. As I was lying back on the lounge chair, Braxton pulls off the blindfold and pulls me into a decadent kiss.

Minutes later, we are in our king-size bed. Our song, Eric Benet's *Making Love,* played serenely in the background, and we did just that.

I ride him slowly rolling my body as if I'm writing an S. He responds to my body giving me all of him. Slowly, I ride the surfboard on his tide, twisting, turning, relishing in his ocean. Soon he is on top of me giving me more. I was on a natural high. In and out he glides, my breast, my neck is his candy. He drills my honey well continuously going in so deep it's hard for me to catch my breath. Damn his expertise in handling my sweet honey was mind-boggling. Yes, yes, yes, oh hell yes! In and out, out and in, he goes zealously, movements smooth and slick. Slithering in me, dick feeling like silk, he trounces in filling all of me, handling my pussy well.

He grabs my waist, sits up grabbing my shoulders, pushing me harder on Sugar Daddy. He looks me in the eye, licks his lips, his way of telling me to kiss him. I do and it's deep. Our tongues dances with each other's, enjoying each other's flavor. He alternates from dancing to sucking, sucking to nibbling on my bottom lip. Hands remain steady on my shoulder, holding me tight. Grind hard, precise, touching all my sensitive spots. I don't want to cum, I'm not ready for this pleasure to end, but he feels so got damn good. I take deep breaths trying to control my body, fight my building orgasm.

He knows what I'm doing, but he is running the show. His command, his order is for me to let go, concede. He loosens his grip on my shoulders, puts he knees up, the movement causes his candy to slip out and I cry. Just as I am about to protest, he flips me, knees to my buttocks, he slides that candy in, moving in me riding me like a wave.

With his hands he begins massaging my ample breast. Seconds later he grabs my waist, pulls me up and Sugar Daddy is teasing my G-spot, the hair surrounding Sugar Daddy tickles my clit and has me screaming. Movement is smooth yet firm. I gasp when he starts sucking my nipples. My eyes roll back. He always knows exactly what to do. He has my mind, body and soul blown. He covers his mouth with mine, sensually run his fingers through my long hair. The simplicity has me feeling new waves of euphoria. His simple touch causes me to let go.

"I love you, Beautiful." He tells me before he begins placing so kisses on my face and my shoulders. Breathe hot on my neck stirs another arousal within. Gingerly I begin to sway my hips, he pulls me up, lying on his back careful not to allow Sugar Daddy from slipping out. I place my feet flat each on the side of him. I lean back, use my arms for support and begin a butterfly rock.

Something about the island puts me in a trance. My moans, groans, pants so frequent it makes me hoarse. I remember my countless climaxes, our multiple positions of Kama Sutra, even allowing Braxton the pleasure of sliding in the back door. I had no recognition of time or when it all came to a finale.

I wake up the next day with a love hangover. Hair all over my head, sleep in my eyes, I vaguely hear Vince.

"Yeah, can you and Ty watch the twins?" I hear Braxton ask.

My ass sprung up on that one, with the covers wrapped around my naked body.

"Damn, you look a mess," shot Vince.

I was too tired to respond. My body ached. I should have bypassed the last drink. My ass was literally sore. I didn't want that chick babysitting my babies. I couldn't get up though. Mommy would let the trick know nothing better not happen to my babies. I collapsed back on the bed. Hugging the pillow, I close my eyes ready to doze.

As soon as I was about to fall for the sandman, Braxton slides in bed behind me, spooning and wrapping his arms around me. I feel his stiff dick, but groan that I didn't have the energy. Besides, I was sore.

Braxton was ready, wanted more. He lifts one of my legs and wraps his arm around it. Gently, he glides in and I grip the covers. My sweetness, a little swollen, but wet, allows that thick candy to glide in and out, round and round. Braxton moans telling me he loves the snugness. I can't lie, it did start to feel good. Soon, I'm lying on my back, legs pushed back, feet touching the headboard. It's a slow drill and I'm grateful. He takes his time, appreciating every area, giving it all the attention needed. Patiently, he goes in over and over like he's giving me a lesson of whose love is best. I acquiesce; my honey well has run over. Once again, I feel light kisses before sleep took over.

Note to self: Get back to the gym. I needed to up my wind, to keep up with him.

I managed to come out the room around four. I couldn't believe I slept for so long. I was hungry and ready to eat. On my way to the kitchen, I see Vince playing with Reagan. Ty was getting too close, playing with her chubby legs. I didn't want that chick touching all on my baby. I definitely didn't want those former or currently diseased lips touching any parts of her. I ever so sweetly walked over to Vince and scooped up my baby.

"Me and Khouri are bonding. You interfering with our quality time. By the way, you look much better. You were tore up earlier," Vince laughs.

I ignore his insult. "You're holding Raegan."

"Damn, I'm goin get it right. Reagan wants to bond with her favorite uncle. How can you tell again?"

Most people couldn't tell the twins apart. Braxton and I along with Mommy and Mr. Jeff were the only ones who could. I ignore his question and continue to tend to Reagan.

"Aww, I'm sorry. I need to feed her. She was about to start looking for something," I lied.

I look over at Braxton who is lying on the nearby sofa with Khouri. He gives me a look and I see him smirk. He knew I was lying.

"You can't feed her. You've been drinking," Ty snitches.

"You've been drinking?" Braxton sits up on alert.

"Calm down, Papa Braxton. That was hours ago."

"So, I told you about that. My daughters don't drink tainted milk."

"Actually Ty and Braxton, having an occasional drink is okay as long as it is limited. Doctors say it is safe to resume breastfeeding two hours later. It's been several hours for me."

"I don't trust it," huffed Braxton.

"I wouldn't either. You have to be careful with babies," co-signed Ty.

See little stunts like this would have me going off every two seconds.

"Ty, when you birth a baby and get a medical degree, talk to me. Braxton, google it, call the doctor."

Mr. Jeff who is an anesthesiologist, Mommy along with Uncle Charles and Ms. Stella come into the family room and I explain what's going on.

"Actually son, it's okay. The girls are safe. You know Yasmin isn't going to hurt the girls," said Mr. Jeff, in agreement with me.

He was going to drive me crazy being so over protective. I take a seat, covering myself with a towel and proceed to feed Reagan. Braxton still not convinced and was irritated.

Mommy busts out laughing followed by Mr. Jeff and Uncle Charles.

"What's so funny?" Braxton asks.

"You, I told you, you were the most hard-headed nonchalant child. Nothing worked for you. Now I get to sit back see my little princesses drive you crazy. It is really the double the pleasure. You acting like this now. Wait till they start walking, getting into things, dating." said Mommy.

"Hey, enough of that."

Vince adds his nonsense. "Braxton will be alright. After last night, they'll be having another one or two in nine months. Lil' bro, can you make another set of twins?"

"Shutup, Vince." everyone chimed, with the exception of Ty.

We ended up having a BBQ. Braxton and Vince had gone to the store leaving me alone with Ty.

"This is my first time over here in the Caymans. I like it. It's beautiful," she admits.

I play nice. "It is, I love it here."

"Have you gone to the Dominican Republic?"

"No, not yet."

"It's beautiful there as well. I went there a year ago with my friend." She hands me a picture.

I look at the picture. I can't deny her friend is as beautiful as she is, even more. Her skin is a rich brown, high cheek bones, and she's tall and petite like Ty. Her long dark hair was swept over her shoulder. She had an exotic look that screamed, 'I'm sexy, and you can't even try to deny it.'

"That's Melania. We took that picture a year ago in the Dominican Republic."

This chick was so messy. A little pang, ok, a big pang of jealousy touched my heart. So this is the chick I was being compared to. I can't deny, in all honesty, between the body and even face-wise she had the edge.

"Very nice picture."

"Thank you."

"She had plenty of admirers. Everyone wanted her."

"And everyone had her," I wanted to say recalling the time when Braxton came home drunk. Braxton drunkenly discussed how he and his former friends Javon and Cory, agreed she was the best lay. Well, Braxton said he thought that until me, I was the best.

Instead I say, "I bet."

"She wasn't conceited though."

"That's good."

"A lot of people loved just being in her company, no ego just pleasant."

"That's a good quality," I said nonchalantly.

"Her and Braxton were close."

"Are you trying to make a point?" I had grown agitated.

"No, I was reflecting, missing my friend. She died a few months ago."

Ok, curiosity got the cat. "I'm sorry to hear that. How did she die?"

"She was killed."

"Did they catch who killed her?"

"No."

"My condolences on the loss of your friend, I know how difficult that is." I really was sorry for her loss. Part of me softened.

"I always thought Braxton and Melania would settle down. They were good together. It was more than sexual. He gave her $10,000 before she died."

See, can't give this chick an inch. I tried to be nice, now I'm about to go in bitch mode.

"Don't be messy. If Braxton wanted to be with your friend, she would have the title and the ring. What they had was a past sexual relationship. Did she meet the family? No. Did she get the house or acknowledgement? No. Don't stir up a ghost. Let your friend rest in peace."

"You walk around like Landon did, thinking the sun set and rises with you. You're trying to downplay my friend's relationship with Braxton. I'm just letting you know, it was more than a sexual relationship. Landon laid down with plenty of guys. I know she was compensated well. She was a hoe in denial. So you can't talk about me or Melania." She smirks.

"Just like your friend isn't here to defend herself, mine isn't either. But really, what are you proving by bringing all this up? Are you still upset about me calling you what you are, a hoe?"

"I am not a hoe. I date men that are established because I have standards. Just because I don't date blue collars and have a preference doesn't make me a hoe."

"Blah, blah, blah, blah, blah. What do you do during the day? Shop? Do you know what a W-2 is? I must say, I'm surprised you're still messing with Vince. Are you waiting for the NBA or NFL draft to begin before you scout out a new sponsor?"

"I am committed to Vince."

"Oh, which means he's giving you a nice monthly stipend. Sweet. True love, you and his money."

"Wrong."

"Oh that's right the sex is good too. Isn't that what you told me when we first met? Don't tell me you caught feelings and you're settling. I don't believe it." I exaggerated.

"You think you are so smart. Ask your husband about that $10,000, and that little incident."

"Since you're mouth all mighty, speak. Tell me yourself."

Just then, Vince and Braxton return.

Ty jumps up to kiss Vince.

"Vince, I missed you. Let's go take a walk," Ty says sweetly.

"Just walk?"

"No," Ty giggles.

"Alright, see you later," said Vince.

"Not so fast, brother-in-law, Ty was about to tell me something.

Right, Ty?"

"What, Yasmin and Ty bonding? Lightning about to strike," laughed Braxton.

I turn to Braxton, "Glad you're in a humorous mood. Ty was telling me about Melania. She told me how close you were."

"We were cool," he said coolly.

I look at him, "She told me to ask you about $10,000, and an incident."

He looks puzzled. I look at Vince who has a blank expression.

Now, I focus on Ty, "Ty, what is it about $10,000?"

She swallows, "Nothing."

"No, it's something. You wouldn't have brought it up."

"Really, Yasmin. It's so easy to get under your skin. You call me names and think I was going to sit back and take it," She laughed.

"I called you what you were on more than one occasion because you continually show me how messy you are. I don't like you. You don't like me, fine. I don't know what point you were trying to make, but finish it."

"Yasmin, calm down. This is supposed to be family bonding during the holiday. Happy time," coaxed Vince.

"You need to talk to Ty."

Vince looks at Ty, "Ty apologize to Yasmin."

Ty smiles, "I apologize, Yasmin. Let's just let bygones be bygones."

"Ty is there something you want to tell me?"

She shakes her head, "No."

"Yasmin, we are making amends remember," scolded Vince."

Braxton comes up, wrapping his arms around me. I didn't trust her ass, something wasn't right. I couldn't do anything about it now, but I would find out if there was something up with her accusations.

"Something isn't right. Don't play me for stupid. I don't do surprises." I look at each of them. "I'll let it go for now, but I'm not forgetting this." I put on a fake smile. "Yes, let us enjoy the island."

I walk away.

This was the holidays, my babies first. Despite my spat with Ty, Braxton and I were able to rekindle the momentum.

The Cayman Islands was always memorable and exhilarating.

5

I Can't Go For That (No Can Do)

We returned from the islands a day ago and were exhausted. The doorbell rings, and I look on the video monitor display in the family room. One of the first things we did when we purchased our home was install top of the line security cameras and monitors throughout the house and grounds. I can't make out the figure. I go open the door figuring it was one of our neighbors.

I was shocked to see Javon at the door. Javon and Braxton's friendship was terminated after I finally told Braxton that Javon had made sexual passes towards me throughout our relationship, including our on and off breaks. Originally, I didn't say anything because he never got physical. However, there was plenty of double entendre.

"Who's at the door, beautiful?"

"Javon."

Seconds later, Braxton was by my side. "Why the hell are you at my door? I told you to stay the hell away from my wife."

"Man, I apologize, but we boys. I was hoping that after all this time we could be cool again."

"We *were* boys, but you disrespected me and I'm not giving you another opportunity. That shit ain't happenin' again."

"I can respect that. I stopped by also to tell y'all I'm sorry for what happened to Landon. Landon was my girl."

He puts his head down, appearing overwhelmed with grief.

I don't respond, Javon still makes me uneasy. I never was comfortable in his presence.

Braxton's tone softens, but he wasn't feeling this friendship. "Yeah, it's rough. I still can't believe it myself. But I mean what I said, stay away from my wife, my family."

"Hey, I will respect that. Can I say something to your wife?"

"No, you can say it to me."

"I wanted to let Yasmin know Landon and I got close. Landon told me how much she admired and appreciated your friendship. She always talked about you and loved you a lot. You know I know how hard it is losing a friend and I wanted to personally give my condolences. You're in my prayers."

"Alright, you said what you had to say, bye. Don't come back," Braxton slams the door in his face.

Javon's visit was an unwelcomed surprise. Braxton was pissed that he had the audacity to show his face at his house. He said something wasn't right and he wasn't buying that bullshit, and neither was I. I had returned back to work after being on hiatus for three weeks. My boss, Bob called me into the office thirty minutes after I arrived.

"Yasmin, I know you have been under extreme pressure lately, and for the past few months, your performance has been shown it. It is far from the stellar performance you demonstrated in the past."

I knew this was coming. In truth, he was correct. I had been slacking. I had not performed the job duties I was hired for. In the past year, I had worked six months and the amount of accounts I handled were minimal.

"As much as I like you, I also have to make a business decision. Yasmin, I am going to have to let you go."

"I understand."

“I do wish you well in all your future endeavors.

“Bob, I do thank you for the opportunity. I am sorry things are ending on this note.”

“I am too. Our normal HR policy is for management to clear your office, but I’ll make an exception if you’re out in ten minutes.”

“I will. Thank you.”

I walk out of his office, return to mine, and gather my personal items.

Damn, I lost my job. Financially, I would be okay. I saved a nice sum. I still have property that I rent out. We made double my salary renting out our property in the Caymans, plus Braxton made three times my salary. I was more upset that I was fired because I slacked off. I had four major athletes whose finances I was managing. This wasn’t a bad thing, I just wish I had made the choice instead of being forced out.

I called Braxton and Kevin, but both of them were in meetings. I chose to call Chauncey. I had to go over his account anyway. He was always good company. We chose to meet at a local cafe. I saw Chauncey approaching.

Chauncey comes in dressed in business attire. I must say he looked good in a suit. It was a very, very, good look for him.

I greet him with a hug.

“Very nice.”

“Thank you. I’m loving your dress too. You know I love them legs of yours. Something about a woman in stockings and heels gets to me.” He licks his lips.

My green fitted pencil dress was cute, enhancing my 36 DDs. It was a little short, but professional.

“Thanks. How are you today?” I asked.

“I’m good. Yourself?”

“So, so.”

"Hey Yasmin, I just want you to know I'm here if you need me. I know how much you miss your sister."

"Thank you, Chauncey. I do."

"Anytime. I know this is hard."

"Aww, you're so sweet."

"I am. How are the twins? I swear I still can't believe you got kids now?"

"They're spoiled. Daddy and Nana girls. How are your three?"

"My kids good."

"Your baby mamas?"

He shakes his head, "Trouble, trouble and more trouble."

"Aww, I'm sorry you got drama. If you decide to have any more kids make sure it's someone you can stand to be around; someone you can have a conversation with or commit to."

"Like you?" he flirted.

"Yes, like I did."

"So, you and hubby doing well?"

"Yes, we are. We just came back from the Cayman Islands. Stayed a little too long, though. I was fired today." I pout.

"What? How they gonna fire you? You're good. My financial portfolio looks even better thanks to you."

"Thank you. Actually, I can't be mad. I haven't been around with everything with Landon, the twins, making you, Geester, Larry, and Tom money. I haven't been as focused.

"You okay? You need some cash?"

"Chauncey, if I need money, you should have fired me. Rule #1, don't hire anyone to manage your money if they can't manage theirs. Make sure their ish is together. I appreciate the gesture, though."

“True, true. So what are you going to do with all this spare time?”

“Undecided.”

“What did Hubby have to say?”

“Nothing yet, I haven’t told him.”

“You told me before the hubby? Does this mean I still have a chance?”

“You were told by default. Hubby is in a meeting. You were third in line and no chance.” I smiled.

Chauncey grabs his chest, “You know how to shatter hearts, hopes, dreams.”

“You are so funny.”

“I just see what I want.”

“So did Braxton. That’s why he put a ring on it.” I hold up my ring.

“Question is, will it stay on. It came off before, it can come off again. I’m ready. Carpe diem.”

“Whatever.”

“Carpe Diem.”

I shake my head and go over Chauncey’s financial analysis. He is, of course, impressed.

Braxton took me out later, once he found out I was fired, to cheer me up. He helped me feel better by pointing out that I had more leisure time to deal with things concerning Landon, my mother, and of course, spend time with the twins. He encouraged me to build our financial portfolio, and acquire more properties. He also told me I didn’t have to work, but if I did, I could always find some ugly clients to manage.

Mommy was sad I lost my job, but I believe more so because she wouldn’t have the twins as much. I assured her she would see them often. As I said after the Caymans, I had to add some gym time in my life to keep up with Braxton's stamina, and I did. I did acquire a few more properties, but I didn't add other clients.

6

Get Together

Monica asked me to go shopping with her to pick out a gift for Horace's birthday. I drove since I had the twins with me. We ended up going to Tyson's Corner Center where she settled on a watch and a few shirts from Lacoste for Horace. All of the shopping had us famished. Monica treated me to lunch at P.F. Chang's. I decided to use the time wisely, see what her intentions were.

"So how are things with Horace?"

"They're good. Horace is a great guy," she smiled.

"He is, but is he a great guy for you?" I raise my eyebrows.

"He is," she hesitates.

Uh, oh. Flag. "How is your son? Is he with his father this weekend?"

Her body tenses, I can see she is annoyed.

"Yeah, he's wit that thing. I swear he irritates the hell out of me. He's using our son to get to me. He has him asking me why I don't like his daddy. Telling me he can't have things because I said no. I'm the bad one. I'd be wrong if I stopped him from going. Be glad you don't have to deal with that foolishness."

"Oh, that's terrible. Why did you break up?"

"His wife."

My eyes open wide in surprise.

"He was married to the streets. The streets didn't love him back though. I was a few weeks pregnant when he got locked up on a gun charge. It could have turned out worse. He was on probation, but only got two years."

"Wow."

"No, wow was when I went to visit him in my ninth month and some other chick was there. Girl, I was so messed up, I went into labor. It was crazy."

"I bet it was."

"I'm glad it happened that way though. As blinded and stupid as I was, I would have still been waiting, putting my life on hold. My son didn't need that."

"I know dating Horace is a different experience."

"It is. A good one. Yasmin, I really do love Horace."

"That's good, Monica."

"Do you think he'd ever marry someone like me?"

"Why would you say someone like me? You weren't into your ex's lifestyle were you?"

"No, but I won't lie. I did enjoy the benefits. He paid my way through school, bought my car, and a lot of other things."

I'm surprised at her openness. "Are you sure you're over him?"

"Hell, yes! No more drama. So do you think me and Horace will work out?"

"I don't know. Have you told him everything?"

"Yes."

"Horace is laid back and sweet. He's not the type to just date because it's something to do. Like his work, he's serious. If he's dating you, it's for a purpose."

She smiles, "I thought the same thing."

"How does your son take to Horace?"

"He's still shy around him. I know that's because of my ex."

I frown my face. "That's a problem. Horace is not going to take the next step until everything is good."

"Yeah, I can respect that."

We were waiting for the waiter to come take our orders when Chauncey approached.

"Hey, Ms. Lady."

"Hey Chaunce," I stand up to hug him. Chauncey hugs me tight and doesn't want to let me go. "You can let go now."

"But you feel too good and smell even better," he flirted.

"You are a mess," I poke his sides so he would let me go.

"You are so… um, um, um."

"Chaunce! Anyway, this is my friend Monica. Monica, Chauncey." Monica was a little star struck, blushing, fidgeting, looking desperate. We don't do that. I shake my head.

"Hello," Chauncey says coolly. He finally notices the twins in their stroller. "So, they are real. I thought you were lying. You don't look like you had babies."

"Yes, the one in the lavender is Khouri, and the one in the yellow is Reagan."

"Hey, pretty little ladies," coos Chauncey. "Can I hold them?"

"Sure, you like babies. Sit down."

I hand him Reagan first, and then Khouri.

"They're cuties, Yasmin. They will be heartbreakers like their mommy."

Chauncey starts bouncing them on his knee trying to get them to laugh. Khouri cracked a smile. Reagan wasn't feeling it and burst out crying.

I grab her and she immediately stops.

"What I tell you. Reagan broke my heart already."

"These are daddy babies. She's funny like that. Reagan only likes Braxton. She'll deal with her uncles, but she's already a true daddy's girl."

I put Reagan in the stroller and hand her a bottle.

"Well, I still got a chance with Khouri," said Chauncey. She was smiling at him, showing her new two bottom teeth."

Chauncey looks over at Monica who was still star struck.

"What are you doing in Virginia?" I ask, bringing his attention back to me since Monica got all gaga like a groupie. She's looking all desperate because of a star status. At the end of the day, he ain't different.

"Car shopping."

Khouri began fidgeting so I take her, put her in the stroller, and hand her a bottle.

"Don't you have enough?" I say referring to his Bentley, Range Rover and Benz.

"You know I like my toys and since I got the sexiest, smartest financial planner looking over my accounts, this will be like spending pocket change. Matter of fact, lunch is on me." He pulls out a wad of money and counts out ten $100 bills.

"Aren't you sweet?"

"But you taste even sweeter," he licks his lips.

"Chaunce enough, and for the record **my husband** agrees."

"You so wrong. You know I like to pick with you. No disrespect. I know about your husband."

"You need to. Mr. Simms don't play."

"Can I take a picture with you?" Monica blurts out.

We both look at her like she's crazy.

"Ah, sure."

Monica jumps up, hands me her phone, and tells me to take a picture. I took the picture, but would have to have a talk with her. The way she was acting, Horace may have to cut ties. Especially since she admitted she loved reaping the benefits of her ex's street hustle. Seeing her with Chauncey confirmed she was attracted to lots of money.

"Well, Miss Yasmin. I'm going to grab something to eat." He gives me a kiss on the cheek.

Normally, I had no problem with Chauncey joining us, but with Monica acting like a groupie, I was hesitant. Being polite I ask, "You can join us if you want?"

Monica looks like she about to pass out.

"I'm waiting on Geester, so I'm good."

On cue, Geester comes in heading straight towards us.

"Hey Yas," he hugs me. Unlike Chauncey, he lets go within seconds.

"Hey Gee."

Geester notices Monica, "My bad, how you?"

She blushes again.

He doesn't pay her any mind because he was going gaga over the twins.

"Your daughters are gorgeous."

I thank him for the compliment. Before Monica could hand me her phone and tell me to take a picture, I rush them off.

"Well you two enjoy. I'll see you next week."

"OMG Chauncey is tall and foine! No he so got damn sexy and Geester, give me some water."

"Monica you need to calm down. You acting like a crazed groupie. You can't be doing that. They are my clients, which means you need to be professional. They also are my friends and you are dating my brother. You're not going to be acting all possessed on my watch."

"I'm sorry Yasmin. I just never seen any famous people. They were so nice.

I still was very annoyed, but I let it slide. "They're people just like you and I."

"You really use to date Chauncey."

"Yes, that was a while ago."

"Why did you break up?"

It really was none of her business, but I chose to let her know, "Because I love Braxton Simms."

"I hear that."

"You sound like Ty, and we both know I don't like that chick."

"No, not Ty. I need to get myself together. I'm so sorry." Monica giggles.

Monica and I did a little more shopping before going home. I still had some reservations. I hope she was with him for love, not money. Time would tell if I would welcome Monica into the family, one Ty was enough.

*

"What the hell is this?" Braxton stomps into the sunroom slinging the newspaper in front of me.

I look at him like the crazy he is.

"Why the hell is this punk holding my baby girls?"

It had been a few days since I went to Virginia with Monica. I forgot about the encounter. That's the media for you, always lurking stirring drama, an aspect that I hated dealing with when I dated Chauncey.

I grab the paper, scan the contents. It was a picture from a few weeks ago when Monica and I ran into Chauncey. Chauncey is holding the girls and I am standing over him. Monica is cut out and we look very close.

Chauncey Smith: Life is Good!

New contract, wife and twins?

It's two pictures side-by-side. The one on the left is Chauncey holding me, placing a kiss on my cheek. The picture on the right is Chauncey sitting down holding the twins. The caption reads: Looks like Chauncey Smith is celebrating a new contract and two new additions.

Chauncey hasn't been on the scene in a minute, now we know why. Observers said the happy couple were very affectionate and in love. No word if the wedding has taken place, but we see that rock. Nice, Chauncey. Congratulations on your new additions, they are adorable.

"That was the day Monica and I went shopping for Horace. I ran into Chauncey. As you see the media was obviously there and are loud and wrong."

"Y'all were too close and he shouldn't have been holding my babies. I don't want him around my daughters."

"Baby, I understand you're upset, but it wasn't serious. He saw the twins and asked if he could hold them."

"My babies don't need strangers touching them. I'm their daddy and I don't like that. Matter of fact, I don't like your relationship with Chauncey."

“Braxton, I wouldn’t let just anyone around our daughters. Furthermore, Chauncey isn’t just anyone he is a client, but more than that, a friend.”

“Yeah, yeah, a friend that you fucked.”

See Ty done got in his head.

“In the past. That was a long time ago.

“His ass looked too comfortable with my daughters and you. He trying to resurrect the past. He still got feelings. Find him someone else to handle his affairs.”

“I can’t just get rid of him like that, off something the media speculated.”

“I don’t like the relationship. I don’t trust him. He too close.”

“Chauncey has never crossed the line. He knows I’m happily married.”

“Yasmin, I don’t trust him.”

I walk up and kiss him, “He can want me all he wants. I want you. Besides you stay up in me. You have the only candy I want.”

“You ain’t slick. I know what I’m talking about. I will tell you this. I will stomp the mutherfucker. I ain’t feeling none of this.”

“I know.”

“No, you don’t know. Ignore me if you want. I’m not playing with you. I don’t want him around my daughters or we’re going to have a problem. Make that the first and last time he looks, sees, or breathes on my babies. First thing, you contact the paper and get them to issue a retraction.”

“I will.”

7

Stormy Weather

"Jackie, don't make this difficult. Go get my son." Said Braxton trying to hold on to the little calm he has left.

"He is staying here with me."

Braxton and I had went to Lawrence and Jackie's house to get little Eric. Since the ordeal with Landon, Jackie has had little Eric. Braxton has seen him twice in the last few months. He has talked to him, and each time, little Eric has said he wanted to see his sisters. Each time we tried to arrange something, Jackie makes an excuse. We have been patient. I know this has been extremely hard on her, but enough is enough.

"Landon would want me and Braxton involved in raising him," I reason.

"Jackie you've had him long enough. You haven't allowed me any contact. Even now, I had to just come over and hope you were here," said Braxton.

"You've talked to him several times," said Jackie

"Jackie, he is my son and I need to spend some time with him. I know it's been rough and you are adjusting, but he still has a parent that loves him and is able to care for him."

"Are you forgetting your name was never added to the birth

certificate? According to the state of Maryland, I am his guardian and have reign to care for him as I see best. As I said, he will remain with me."

"Jackie don't force my hand. I have resources as well," said Braxton in a strained voice.

"Braxton, your resources are just that. While you get them together, I'll be out of the country with my grandson."

"Jackie, please."

"You're not going to take my son."

"Oh, yes I am."

I squeeze Braxton hand signaling for him to let me try.

"Jackie, please, all of this isn't necessary. I…we understand you want little Eric with you, but Braxton is his father. He loves him too. He wants the same thing you want, to love him. We both want what's best for him."

"Well, being with me is what's best for him. Understood?"

"No, not understood. He is my son. I'm not going to step back while you run things."

"Jackie, little Eric has gone through so much. He lost big Eric, now Landon is…"

"Don't you ever say anything about that bastard in my presence. The things he did to my baby. I will make sure them thugs in there rip him a new asshole and then make sure he gets buried under the jail. That is why I'm changing his name. He won't be named after that criminal. You are to refer him as Lathan now.

"Hell no! How the hell you gonna make that call? That's it! Go get my son now."

She doesn't.

"Jackie little Eric has bonded with Braxton, me, his sisters, the family. Despite everything, he is transitioning well and he has a strong support system. Taking him away will hurt him," I try again to reason with her.

"If I need a psychiatrist's opinion, I will call a licensed legit one. And his name is Lathan."

"Enough of this bullshit, go get my son."

"According to the state of Maryland, I am his parent."

Braxton pulls out his cellphone and makes a call.

I attempt again to reason with her.

"Jackie can we try to compromise. How long do you want to have him out of the country?"

"As long as necessary."

"Yes, I want to report a kidnapping," Braxton announced on the phone.

"Kidnapping?" she retorts.

"Yes, I'm at 6703 Silverlake Drive. I came to pick up my son, but his grandmother is refusing to give him to me or tell me his whereabouts."

I call Lawrence but the phone goes straight to voicemail.

"Yes, yes, yes." I hear Braxton say.

"Jackie all of this isn't necessary. Just please, get Eric."

"The police are on their way."

"Good because I'm ready for you to leave. I have a plane to catch."

Braxton is pacing back and forth in the foyer using all his restraint. I know his temper and he's seconds from blowing up. I have to do something before he kicks a wall, punch a hole, or do any damage.

Jackie leaves and goes to the study, she returns as there is a knock on the door.

Braxton doesn't hesitate to open the door, "Officer she has my son and refuses to give him to me."

In walks two officers, the first officer is a tall, white male appearing to be in his mid-thirties. The second one is a brown-skin black male, I would guess in his late twenties. From his tightly fitted uniform I could tell he stayed in the gym. The grimace on his face told me he was cocky and no nonsense.

Jackie ever so sweetly and calmly said, "Hello officers. I'm sorry you had to come over here and your time was wasted."

"Ma'am, that is for me to determine," said the short muscular officer.

"Yes, of course officer."

"Before any of you say anything else, I will do the questioning. Speak only when you are spoken to," he said.

We all nod.

"Who are you?" the short officer directs at me.

"I'm Yasmin Simms, and this is my husband, Braxton Simms," I grab Braxton's arm.

"Braxton Simms, you are the one who called."

"Yes, officer."

"What is your connection?" He points to Jackie.

"Officer, I am Mrs. Jacqueline Taylor, mother of Landon Taylor. I-"

"That's enough for now, ma'am. Your relationship to Mrs. Taylor?"

"She is my son's grandmother."

"How old is your son?"

"Four."

"Do you have a custody agreement and where is his mother?"

"The monster, Eric Ayres shot my daughter. As stated in the legal documents, if by any unforeseen accident or trauma should occur to Landon Taylor, sole custody should be granted to Jacqueline Taylor.

Also, here is a copy of my grandson's birth certificate. It lists Eric Ayres as his father."

The officers look at each other, both smirk. I cringe. I know forgiving Braxton meant accepting all associated with Eric's paternity. However, it wasn't easy. The judgment, the looks, were still a challenge.

"Officer, a paternity test was done and it was determined that I was the biological father."

"Sir, was the original birth certificate modified and do you have legal documents to support this?" the tall one asks.

"No," Braxton says regret tingly.

"So you had an affair with Ms. Taylor. Another man, Eric Ayres signed the birth certificate. You did a paternity test later, and you were determined to be the biological father."

Irritated, Braxton responds. "Yes."

"When was the test done, sir?"

"A year ago."

"Exactly a year ago?" asked the short officer, being smart.

"A little over a year ago."

"In over a years' time, you have not gone to court to establish paternity and correct the birth certificate?"

He looks at me doing a toe to head evaluation.

"No," Braxton says irritated.

"The reason, sir?"

Braxton sighs, temper flaring, "None."

"Officer, as I stated earlier, a waste of time. Now, will you escort Mr. Simms off of my property?"

"Well, she is correct. Legally, you have no rights and you have to vacate her property."

"Jackie, so you just gonna take my son?"

"I told you earlier, and you heard the officer, you did not do your due diligence. You have no rights. I am his guardian."

"Your daughter got it honestly."

"Braxton!"

"Are you threatening me?"

"Braxton, let's go." I tug his hand hard. "Don't say it, don't say anything, let's go."

"Officer, please have him leave. I'm beginning to fear for my safety and I definitely fear for my grandson.

That was it. Braxton turned around and kicked a hole in the wall.

"Officer, I'm pressing charges. You see this man is violent. Destruction of property…"

"Jackie, enough. Don't do this. Please drop this. This has gone too far."

Jackie plays scared, "Officer, remove him now, please."

"Braxton Simms you are under arrest. Anything you say can and will be used against you," the tall officer began to read Braxton his Miranda rights.

"Jackie, really. Where's Lawrence?"

"Yasmin, you're going to have to leave."

"Jackie, you are not pressing charges. Get them to release him now. Don't do it, Jackie."

"Officer, I'll be down to press charges."

"You bitch!" I yelled, shaking in anger. This was ridiculous.

The short one stayed in to talk to Jackie. I followed the tall one out while he put Braxton in the squad car.

The image of Braxton being escorted in handcuffs had me sick. My stomach couldn't take it and I threw up right on Jackie's white rug.

I get in the car and call Jeff Jr. to get him on this. The cops took too long to pull off. I was able to fill Jeff in on what transpired. It was late Friday evening, so unfortunately papers wouldn't be processed until Monday. Jeff then informed me that Braxton would not go before the judge until Monday, which meant jail for the weekend. I couldn't hold any composure after that. I just hung up. What the hell was going to happen to him? We just came to get Eric. Braxton can't go to jail. He don't belong in jail. They're going to hurt him in jail. Crocodile tears, snot, hyper-ventilating. I was shaking so bad, I needed a drink, a pill, something. After about 20 minutes, the officer finally started the engine, immediately pulling off the property. I couldn't get my nerves together. My hands were shaking so bad, I couldn't steer the vehicle. Thank God for BMW's Servotronic control technology, in particular, which adjusts the amount of steering assistance to suit the speed of the vehicle. I needed that and more.

The officer pulled over after two blocks. The tall officer gets out the vehicle and I know he's going to tell me not to follow him. I get a tissue to try and get my face together.

"Ma'am, I need you to calm down."

I couldn't even talk. Tears were just running from my eyes.

"Breathe. It's okay. We're releasing him."

I pause. I still couldn't talk.

"Mrs. Taylor decided not to press charges. However, you are not to return to her property under any circumstances. I told your husband we're cutting him a break. We're going to pretend we didn't see him damage the property."

I nod.

"Do you understand? DO NOT return to the premises. You and your husband need to get your business handled. First thing, get that birth certificate rectified."

"Yes, thank you officer," I say in a shaky voice.

"Okay, I'm going to release your husband."

I get out of the car, anxiously awaiting Braxton's release. The officer assists him out of the car before uncuffing him. He says something, Braxton nods. The short one adds something that I can't hear before Braxton walks toward the car.

I know he is enraged, which he has every right to be. It's taking everything in him to keep a calm composure.

I couldn't hug him fast enough. "Baby, you okay. They didn't hurt you did they?"

"Hell no! That bitch! When I get this shit straightened out, her ass will not see Eric at all. The bitch gonna try and change his name. Hell no! I need to call JR to get on this."

"I already called him, baby. It's been handled," I said, still holding him tight.

He gives me a kiss on the cheek. "Come on, I need to get away from here."

I hated to let him go, but I agreed we had to get far away from there.

Braxton took over the driving. While in the car, I called Jeff Jr. to let them know Braxton wasn't arrested. We all met up at Mommy's to get everything prepped for Monday.

*

Braxton couldn't get out the car fast enough. He rushed into the house, grabbing the twins from Mommy.

"Yasmin, don't you ever try to pull no shit like that."

I know he was emotional, but I wasn't the one. "Braxton watch your tone and don't insult me. You should know me better than that. Why would I?"

"You get mad and you do this running thing."

"With cause. Don't do shit to piss me off."

“Yasmin, I’m not fucking playing with you. Don’t ever try to take my kids,” he said, tightening his grip on the twins.”

“Again fool, I never did. When I found out I was pregnant you were included in the process.”

“You didn’t tell me until five months later. Another thing, remember what I told you. I DON’T want any mutherfuckers around my daughters. *I’m* their father.” He kisses them both.

I roll my eyes. This fool was tripping. Khouri was getting agitated and Braxton was trying to settle her down.

“I caught that. I mean what I said.”

“Can I hold one of my daughters? You know, to feed her.”

“Have a seat. Feed her right here,” He nodded to the spot beside him.

I take Khouri and gave her a kiss before feeding her. Then, I take Reagan, all under Braxton’s watchful eye. He takes both of them when I’m done, and for the remainder of the day he barely allowed anyone to have them longer than five minutes.

8

Talk to Me

Braxton had filed papers with the court and was in attack mode. True to form, Jackie had disappeared making it impossible to serve her or have any contact with Eric. He was obsessed with his cause, cranky, and barely tolerable, a horror to deal with. The twins, or I should say his daughters, kept him sane and calmed him, however he was still overly possessive.

Chauncey wanted me to go with him to hear a business proposition. I really didn't want to go, but a break from the chaos was good. Chauncey drove, while my mind was preoccupied with life. I appreciated that he didn't talk. I needed the silence to regroup. When he stopped in front of a house, I look confused.

"Where are we?"

"A friend of mine's."

"I'll wait in the car."

"Come on in with me."

"Chauncey, I'm not in the mood to be social. Let me just wait in the car."

"Yas, I want you to check out something."

I sigh, "I don't need any more clients right now."

"I know. I just need you to give him some advice. Please, for me."

I get out the car and allow Chauncey to lead me into the condominium complex. Our ride to the top floor is silent. The door is open and we go right in. The condo is sparse, only a couch and two chairs. There wasn't a TV, or carpet on the floor. No pictures were hung, just white walls and dark curtains that were closed. Chauncey directs me to the couch while he closes the door. Soon he takes a seat next to me. He grabs my hands.

I try to pull back, but his grip is strong.

"Chauncey, what the hell are you doing?"

"Yasmin, I need you to hear me out. I brought you here because there's some things you need to know about Landon and Eric."

I try to remove my hands again. "Chauncey, I don't want to talk about this here. Why am I here? I'm leaving."

"Yas, I didn't do it. I didn't shoot her."

Eric walks out of the bedroom looking like a shell of himself. He had lost a substantial amount of weight, at least 50 pounds. His 6'8" frame was bent over, face ashen, hair on his face wild and unkempt just like the hair on top of his head.

"I gotta get out of here. Chauncey, let me go!"

"Yas, please here him out."

"Yasmin, I'm not lying I didn't do it. I swear to you, it wasn't me."

"Eric, you told me she deserved to die. You told me she was going to get what was due."

"I know I was mad, but I…"

"Just like you were when you almost killed Braxton."

Eric takes a seat in the chair.

"Your ass denied it then. You called me here for what, to lie again? I don't want to hear shit else you have to say. Chauncey, get off me now."

"Yassy…" said Eric.

"Don't call me that. Only Landon can... You did the same thing you did to Braxton. You fucked up her face, stomped her like she was trash. The same fucking thing you did to Braxton! Then you shot her like you told me you would. I begged you to leave her alone. I begged you for little Eric's sake. He asks for his mommy every time I talk to him. I told you to leave her alone and you didn't. Do you really expect compassion from me?"

"I know you did. I went to see Landon that day, but I left. I wanted to strangle her, kill her but I didn't do it. I couldn't do it. I'm not going to say I didn't touch her at all. I did, but I didn't shoot her. I swear to you, I left. I saw that picture of little Eric and I froze." He pauses. "Yasmin, I really love that little boy. He was my son. Everything I did was for him. He made things better, then I found out it was a lie. I was mad, but I didn't do it. I know how it is to lose a mother. I couldn't do that to him. I couldn't. I just want my son back."

I knew Eric loved little Eric. I knew finding out destroyed him, but what he did to my sister I couldn't accept or give him a pass.

"You're lying," I cried. "You told me she deserved to die and told me you would get her. You're the only one who would do it."

"Yasmin, I'm not. There a lot of things about Landon you don't know. Look at me Yasmin," pleaded Eric.

I looked at him and his eyes screamed fear and spoke truth.

"I didn't shoot her."

"He's telling the truth, Yas. Landon was involved in some shit," confirmed Chauncey.

"What? Y'all lyin'."

"Yasmin, she was in business with Javon. They had parties." Chauncey speaks again.

I shake my head no, "That doesn't make sense. Landon sold real estate. What kind of business would they be in together?"

"Yasmin, I wanted to warn you that some things are about to come out." Eric warns.

"I don't know all the details, but it was heavy," said Chauncey.

"Landon didn't have time or patience to do multiple ventures unless it involved shopping."

"You don't know what Landon had been up to. You and her stopped talking, right?" Eric asks.

"Yes. So Eric, she was in business with Javon. I know what you told me. I also know someone saw you leaving Landon's house."

"I told you I was there, but I left. I didn't shoot her."

"Who did?"

"Javon is a pimp." Chauncey blurts.

"Why are you telling me this? What am I supposed to do? What's your point?"

"I want to warn you, Yasmin. I'm fighting for my freedom. There are some things that are about to come out. I'm about to tell you shit you don't want to hear but need to," warned Eric.

"Eric this is too much. Your lawyer should be handling this."

"I've been prosecuted and judged. I knew you were the only one who could help me."

I grab my head.

"Braxton used to mess with this girl, Melania." Eric pauses.

My heart pangs with familiarity of the name, Melania again. I recall the picture Ty had shown me weeks ago of the flawless beauty.

"I know Melania."

"She's dead. She was found a few months before Landon in an abandoned building brutalized." Eric words sent a sharp pain through my chest.

Chauncey continues, "Javon owns an escort service. She was one of his escorts. They had an exclusive clientele. She wanted out of the business, but it's never easy getting out. Melania and Braxton dated on and off for five years and Braxton helped her out financially."

"How do you know this?" I asked in a tone to let them know I was pissed.

"I know her cousin Rico. He used to work as Melania's assistant. He said Braxton gave them money for the funeral and looked out for her son."

"Don't tell me her son is Braxton's." My chest tightens. "I can't deal with this shit."

"I don't know." Eric hesitates.

Ain't this some shit? That mutherfucker! Giving me grief about my relationship with Chauncey and he giving out money. Hell no, I thought as I felt my legs twitching.

"So you telling me Braxton was still messing with her?"

"I don't think so. She told me they were close at one time, but since he was married now, their relationship was over." Eric says.

Chauncey rubs my back.

Eric picks up, "After Landon and I divorced, I hooked up with Melania a few times. She told me some things. She told me Javon was the front man, and Landon used her real estate connection to rent houses, among other things. Melania groomed the girls; she was the Madame. But Rocco was the one who controlled them all. She was tired of that life, and scared.

"So you think Melania was killed by Javon?"

"Yes, it was set up. Melania was not a drug addict. She was so pretty, but cool, not arrogant, real laid back. She loved her son. I know she didn't go out on drugs. They killed her."

I swallow hard.

"Yasmin, I'm fighting for my life. I can't afford to hold anything back. With that being said, I'm not holding back. The sex parties, the men, including Braxton and Landon's relationship is all on the table. There's a press conference scheduled two days from now" explained Eric.

I fall back in the couch shaking my head no. Damn, I was not prepared for my life to be displayed in the paper or gossip blog. I take deep breaths trying to control my anxiety of what was about to happen. The incident a few weeks ago was enough. This story is scandal.

"Yas, you always been cool with me. That's why I wanted to talk to you. Give you a heads up."

I nod.

"I also need a huge favor, Yas."

My head was pounding from the impending chaos. All this newfound information, I take deep breaths in and blow out of my mouth. This was surreal.

"I need you to help me."

"Help you? What am I supposed to do? I can't help you? That's what you got lawyers for."

Eric looks at Chauncey. "I need you to get into Landon's bank account and get her statements."

"I can't get that. Jackie is in charge. She's handling her paperwork, and you know Jackie is a BEAST."

"Can you go to the house and look for anything?"

"Eric, I can't go to that house."

"Please Yasmin. You're the only one who can help me."

"Eric you have my mind all messed up right now. Really, I can't go to Landon's. I can't."

"I'll go with you Yasmin," volunteers Chauncey. "You gotta help him out."

I was still trying to process everything, and was unconsciously shaking my head.

"Yas, I know you not just gonna let this man go down for some shit he ain't do?" Chauncey asked incredulously.

"No! It's not that simple. Like you said, Landon and I wasn't talking. The day she was shot, I went and made amends with her. That was my first time at her place. I don't have any idea where she kept anything, including a spare key."

"What about your father? Can you get one from him?"

"No. He and Jackie are M.I.A. I've been trying to get in contact with them for two weeks now."

"Kevin?"

"No, he wouldn't have a key. Kevin mentioned going over there several times trying to get her to open up with him, but said Landon was evasive with him. If Kevin had a key, he would have gone in, especially now, to build a case against you."

"Damn, I need something concrete."

"Can you get into her office?" asked Chauncey.

"Landon changed her passcode every 60-90 days. We weren't talking. I don't know what it is."

"Yas, I appreciate anything. I'm glad you listened to me. I hate to drag you in this mess, but this is my life. My press conference is at 2 pm Friday.

"I understand."

Chauncey didn't speak on the ride back to his place. Other than him singing along on the radio every now and then, he was quiet and I was appreciative.

"You gonna be okay?"

"Yeah."

"You sure? You can chill here if you want."

"I'm good. I gotta get home to my girls."

"Alright. You know I'm here if you need me. I got your back."

"Thanks, Chaunce."

He gives me a hug and a kiss on the check before I get out of his truck.

*

I wanted so bad to ask Braxton about his generosity, but he wouldn't be back from business until tomorrow. I needed to see his face. Look him in the eyes when he talked to me. I picked up the phone to dial his ass so many times, but we had to discuss this face-to-face. I had to see his eyes when I confronted him.

Since I was a ticking time bomb, I ignored all of his calls. This fool made sure he got through though. The phone rings again, and I see Mommy's number. I take a deep breath before answering.

"Hello," I said groggily, already knowing it's a set up.

"Yasmin, why haven't you answered the phone?" Braxton asked in a concerned voice.

"Because I was sleep," I roll my eyes as if he can see me.

Mommy jumps in. "Yasmin, you looked tired earlier. I told you to leave my babies. Jeff and I love ourselves some Reagan and Khouri,"

"Thanks mommy. You do so much. I am so grateful for both of you. I miss them too though. We are having a girl's night."

"Aww, they are so precious. I love to see them interact with one another. The way they babble and now they have started kissing each other. Oh, I miss my babies. They are so cute. Khouri has this thing she does..."

"Alright, Ma," Braxton cuts her off. "We already established my girls are beautiful. You will see the twins tomorrow. You want to watch them overnight, so I can take my beautiful wife out?"

"You don't want to spend the evening with your sweet daughters? Didn't you miss them?" I said quickly.

"You know I did. I get in tomorrow afternoon around noon. I was going to spoil my princesses until six and then spoil you," he said.

I roll my eyes. That's what he thinks. Hell about to break loose in less than 48 hours.

"You know I will keep the girls. You two go have fun," encouraged Mommy.

"Yasmin, I'm going to call you right back."

"Braxton, I'm tired. I'm going to lie down. I'll see you tomorrow evening."

"You don't want to talk to me?"

"Braxton, she's tired."

"Alright, see you tomorrow, Yasmin. Love you, love you too, Ma."

He called me Yasmin. His ass knew something was up. He called me by my name only when he was mad or something was wrong. He'd be calling me back.

"Love y'all both. See you in the morning, Yasmin."

"Okay mommy, love you."

I hung up. Sure enough, immediately the phone was ringing again.

"Whats up?" he asked as soon as I pick up.

"Nothing."

"Something ain't right. What's the problem?"

"Nothing."

"Oh, so you playing that game?"

"Braxton, I'm not playing any game. I was sleeping," I lied.

"You haven't figured out yet that I know you? I know something's up."

Just then, one of the babies started crying.

"Braxton, the baby's crying. I gotta go."

"No, you don't. Put the phone up to her ear. Which one crying?"

"Checking now. It's Reagan." I say entering the nursery. She sees me and lifts her arms up. I rush to get her. I didn't want her waking up Khouri. I was really being sarcastic earlier when I called them sweet. Yes, they were mine. I love them dearly, but I was not in denial. At seven months, their personalities were forming. They are stubborn, moody, have to have their way, just like daddy. My daughters were spoiled. At seven months, they still weren't really crawling, thanks to daddy and Nana, who believed they should be held and didn't belong on the floor. Mr. Jeff was my ally at first, but he's gotten just as bad.

"Little girl what you fussing for?" I pick her up and give her a kiss on the cheek. She still fusses and no surprise Khouri wakes. Phone in the crook of my neck, I scoop up Khouri and carry them both to my room.

"Why are they so fussy?"

"Because they're spoiled."

"Hey mommy babies. What's the matter?" I give Khouri a kiss.

"Put the phone on speaker."

I oblige and Braxton starts talking. Both of his babies got quiet looking around smiling. He goes on for a few minutes, both now settled and content.

"Take the phone off speaker, Yasmin."

"Yeah," I said irritated.

"Why are you ignoring my calls?"

"I'm not."

"Why are you lying to me?" he said even more irritated.

"I've had a very long day. I am not going to sit and listen to you argue. Have a good night. I will see you tomorrow. Later." I hung up the phone.

Of course he kept calling, but I turned off the ringer. He lost his damn mind.

9

Trouble

After our phone conversation, Braxton switched flights. He startled me this morning when he slipped in bed, attempting to get some morning loving, which I quickly put to a halt. Of course, he didn't like that. I told him later we'd have our time and there would be plenty of screaming. Mr. Cocky liked that, leaving me alone while he tended to his daughters. All day, I've been quiet, waiting for the right time to grill his ass. My in-laws just picked up the twins. Now we are in the family room, Braxton was getting all the screaming I promised.

"You gave her money?"

"She was in a bind."

"What the hell. Was that payment for a blowjob, sex, what?"

"No, it was a loan. I don't pay for sex."

"Loan for what?"

"I don't know, she was in a bind."

"Am I supposed to believe that she came to you, asked you for money, and you gave it up without questioning what it was for?!"

Braxton doesn't respond.

"Is that the only time you gave money to Melania or her family?"

"Yeah."

"You sure?" I narrow my eyes.

"Yeah!"

"Her son?"

"What about him?"

"Did you give him money?"

"Why would I give him money?"

"Oh, you really want to play stupid and think I'm some fool."

"No, Yasmin."

"You know what, stop playing with me. I know you gave Melania's mother money for her son, so tell me everything."

"I just gave her mother a little money in case her son needed anything."

"Out of obligation?"

"What?" he scratches his head.

"Are you the daddy? Do you have another kid?"

"What?! No! I'm not. Not at all."

"Then why were you so generous?"

"I knew Melania loved her son. It wasn't much, I knew Ms. Rosa could use some help."

"Oh, so you're close with the family. On a first name basis."

Braxton shakes his head.

"You're not the father of that kid, but was there a possibility?"

Braxton got that, "damn" look on his face confirming what Eric told me.

"Damn, you a sloppy mess. Almost getting a hooker pregnant? Really? I thought you always wore protection? Lying ass," I throw the pillow from the sofa at him.

"I did. There was an accident with the condom."

"How did that happen?"

"Yasmin, really? It happens. The same shit happened with you and me when were first got together. Pool table, your strip tease, yeah, you remember."

I give him a disgusted look.

"We weren't even together when this happened. It was years ago and doesn't matter because I am not the father."

"It does matter! Obviously, you were close for you to make huge monetary contributions. Notice I said contributions, as in plural, meaning this was a regular occurrence with you."

"Melania was a good person. She just got hooked up in some shady mess. I know she loved her son. Our relationship, on a sexual level, ended when you and I got back together."

"So when I went to Minnesota, you didn't call her to relieve your sexual tension?"

"Yasmin, when you and I got back together all that ended. No, I didn't have sex with Melania or anyone else. When you had your disappearing act, when you came back, or when you took months after the twins were born to make up your mind. I haven't been with anybody."

I roll my eyes.

"Where is all this coming from?"

"Why did Melania need the money?"

"I told you, she got in a bind."

"What kind of bind?"

"I don't know."

"Braxton stop lying to me. You don't just give out $10,000 to anyone without a reason and explanation."

He looks puzzled. His ass shook on how I knew the amount. I help him out.

"I guess Ty messy ass was telling the truth. Her messy ass told me how you always looked out for her girl. You were very generous giving her $10,000. I told you then, I wasn't for anymore damn surprises. You didn't say anything, so I dismissed it, thought she was starting ish just because. Especially after you and Vince looked at me like I'm exaggerating. Once again, Yasmin is the clueless one." I throw the other pillow.

"She got caught up in some bad business."

"Oh, you know. Really?" I act surprised.

"Yasmin."

"Braxton."

"She owed some money to some people."

"Javon and Rocco," I said recalling Eric's accusations.

"How do you know Rocco?" asked Braxton, substantiating Eric's claim. My head is spinning and my heart has dropped. This was too much to process.

"I don't. I see you do though. He wasn't lying."

"Who is *he*?"

I ignore his ass. "So you recently gave her money, like around the time she died?"

He looks at me in disbelief. "Who is he?"

"She was killed?" I shudder.

"Who are you talking to? Where are you getting this information from? How do you know about Rocco?"

"How do you know about Rocco?"

"Yasmin enough of this ring around the rosey shit. You need to stay the hell away from Rocco. What do you know about him?"

"Not much, other than him and Javon are into business together. It's obvious, he is ruthless. Eric, Chauncey and now you, are saying the same thing," I said, still in disbelief that Eric's words were truth.

"You saw Eric? I told you to stay away from him."

"You also told me you were done lying," I snap.

"I ain't lying."

"You got so much shit with you. You gave money to your ex-girlfriend, paid for her funeral, and taking care of her kid? You don't think it's something wrong?"

He rubs his head.

"You were fucking a hooker. You were fucking her while you were with me and it's obvious you caught feelings."

He takes a deep breath.

"Aww, how insensitive of me. You are still mourning. Maybe you should go be with Ms. Rosa and your almost son."

He looks me in the eye. "I'm where I want to be. Melania was a friend. I did have a sexual relationship with her, but we were friends for a while. Our sexual relationship ended when I committed to you. I talked to her every now and then, but that was it."

"Did she console you while I was gone? Did you confide in her while I was gone?"

He lowers his eyes.

"Oh, hell no! You got a lot of damn shit with you. You give me grief about Chauncey, Kevin, and your ass was doing some sneaky, conniving shit. Let me get a $10,000 loan from either one of them, your ass would be having a fit. You gave her money, paid for her funeral, and didn't tell me. I had to find out from that bitch Ty, and Eric."

"I apologize. I was just helping a friend. When she died we were barely talking. You and I were separated. I didn't know what I was supposed to say or how to say it. I didn't want to complicate things."

"Is that supposed to make it okay? You were fucking me while you were with her."

"I wasn't. I told you I stop messing with her when we got serious."

"Whatever. You had feelings for her, confided in her, told her about our relationship, and supported her."

"What was I supposed to do? I helped her family out because I knew they couldn't afford to bury her. She didn't deserve to go out like that."

"I can't deal with this."

"What are you saying?"

"I'm tired of your surprises and your shit slapping me in the face."

"I'm sorry."

"Again, is that supposed to make it better? Make it alright? I'm always compromising; making sacrifices and your ass always got some shit you haven't told me because I can't handle it. I'm tired of this shit."

He grabs me in his arms. "Yasmin, all that was in the past. I haven't cheated on you. I was wrong for not telling you, but it wasn't like that. It's in the past. We need to focus on moving on."

I push myself away from him. "That's just it. The past has a way of coming back to life. Eric is fighting to save his life. Meaning, he is going to do all he can do to prove his innocence and be acquitted."

"Okay, what's that got to do with us?"

"Everything! He is telling all. From Landon dealings with Javon and Rocco to you fucking her and having a son. So be prepared for your life, my life to be in chaos. Yes, I gotta deal with your shit again. Relive it in the news, on TV. Lisa, a thousand times worse."

He puts his head down. "Shit," he grunted.

"Just like that bitch, Lisa. I kept saying 'Braxton, you can't trust her. She wants you. She is conniving.' You swore it wasn't like that. What the fuck happen? Yeah, you're quiet now. That bitch embarrassed me at my damn baby shower. It was me looking stupid. Everyone staring at me like, poor Yasmin. Like I said I'm always the one getting slapped," I wipe the tears from my eyes. "Cheated on me with your hooker ex, break up with me because you got my sister knocked up, had a coworker embarrass me, paying for funerals, supporting a kid that was almost yours. All these goddamn lies!"

"Yasmin."

"Braxton, get the hell away from me!"

"Yasmin, we not doing this separation shit again," he said sternly.

"You don't have any right to tell me what the hell to do."

He grabs me, "Yasmin, look at me. Look at me. I am committed to you. I did not cheat on you. I love you. Melania was just a friend and never a threat. She knew I was committed to you. I never loved her. You are the only one. That's why you're my wife." He takes a breath. "In the past I made a lot of stupid, stupid mistakes. I'm not the same person. You and our daughters are my life. I'm sorry for the position I put you in yet again, but don't doubt my love."

I sniff.

"Yasmin, really I was just helping out her family."

"You don't give up that type of money for just any friend. Your relationship with her was more than you're willing to admit."

"Yasmin."

"Braxton, I have to wonder if she wasn't a call girl, if she'd be wearing this ring."

"Yasmin, the right person is wearing the ring. My relationship with Melania was never that serious."

"Stop the damn lying. I told you when Ty brought it up not to lie to me. I'm tired of people knowing all this shit and me being in the dark. Got me looking stupid again."

"Yasmin you're not looking stupid. I should have told you about the money, but we barely talking. I just knew she was in a bind. I did it as a favor, really."

"Braxton, I'm tired of you and your 50 million reasons of justifying shit. I stand by what I said. You don't give any friend $10,000. Then, you constantly putting me in situations where hoes like Ty got the upper hand."

"Yasmin."

"How much of me did you discuss with your not so serious friend that you fucked while we were dating and on and off."

He takes a deep breath.

"Answer the damn question!"

"Yasmin, what's that going to prove?"

"Are you being defensive because you said things you shouldn't have? When was the last time you fucked her Braxton, honestly."

"Yasmin she knew about our situation. But I told you, I didn't mess with her."

"Really?"

"I'm serious."

"I need a break from you. Leave me alone, don't bother me."

"Yasmin, we're not doing another separation."

I shove him before attempting to go upstairs. He grabs me.

I remove myself from Braxton and walk upstairs and shut the door. I took a long bath in the huge Jacuzzi tub, adding coconut oil and lavender hoping the aroma would calm me. My life was about to get crazy. Stand by your lying ass husband or run. I'm so glad the girls are with mommy.

When I came out the bathroom, the room was still empty. When I walked into the massive hallway I could hear Braxton on the phone with someone, probably Vince. I could have eavesdropped but why even bother. I walked away I was reaching my limit with Braxton Simms. I slid on my plain cotton night gown, and slid into my bed. My head was foggy. I wish I could sleep the stress away, but it would take more than sleep.

*

"Unh, unh, uuunh" I gasped as Braxton slid in and out of me, waking me.

His slick ass had slid that caramel candy of his, Sugar Daddy, in me and it was so sweet, hitting every spot. Sleek, sweet, sticky, my walls soaked him all up, salivating, begging for more. Damn!

"Mmmmm," I moaned.

"You feel so good." He sucks on my neck, my nipples. My eyes roll in the back of my head and I squeeze his sugar tight.

He slides in, out, in, out, in, out, in, in, pushing in."

I whimper.

He slides all the way out and I admit I cried, "Put it in me, Put it in me."

"Not yet. I'm not ready for you to cum."

He bends down and kisses me deep. I wasn't feeling that. I needed to cum.

"Let me ride you. I need to ride you"

"Nope," he slides in sloooow.

"Get me the dick." I beg.

"You want your dick."

"Yes, give me that dick." I cry.

"You love this dick don't you?"

"Yeeeessssss," I groan.

He gives me three hard grinds, "How this dick feel."

'"Ahhhhhh, oh, oouuuuu," I scratch his back.

He grinds again, "How this dick feel."

"So damn good."

"This your dick." He stops.

"Yes!"

"You want your dick?"

"Yes, yes, yes. Give me some of my big dick. I need me dick. Give me my big dick. Put it in me. Put it all in me. Fuck me hard." I begged.

He kisses me.

I begin to gyrate my hips begging him to fuck me hard. My pussy is pulsating.

"Damn, my pussy always feels so good." He groans. "Squeeze the dick back, beautiful." He slides in. Use them muscles push the dick out."

I do.

He slides in again and my pussy squeezes his 9 ½ inches.

"That's it just like that. That's my girl. This dick feels good don't it." He hammers.

I wimper.

In, out, in, out, in, out, in, out, 1/4in, out, 1/4 in, ½ in, out, ½ in, out, ¼ in, hold it, hold in, I'm shaking. He goes all the way in hard, pound, pound, pound, pound, pound, pound, pound, and pound.

I'm about to let go.

He stops. "Tell me you love me."

"Asshole."

He glides in slow. "Tell me you love me."

"No."

In and out he goes slow. He alternates sucking my nipples, nibbling.

"Tell me you love me."

He slides out of me.

I moan.

"Tell me you love me."

"I love you. I love you. I love you."

"I love you, beautiful."

He pounds, pounds, pounds, pounds, pounds, pounds.

"Oh, oh Ahhhhh."

"Let it out. Don't hold it in. Let it out. "

And I do.

*

"Good Afternoon, I'd like to thank you all for taking the time out to come out and just hear me out today, I will be brief. First, no words can adequately capture my feelings about the devastating accident that has caused such heartache for everyone involved. The pain and sadness, especially for Landon's parents, family and friends, consumes me with sorrow."

He pauses.

We're here today so I can give you a statement. I, Eric Ayres stand before you today, declaring my innocence. Over the last few months there has been a lot of speculation in regards to my marriage. I want to clear up the discrepancies, while my ex-wife and I ended our marriage recently, it was a mutual decision. Furthermore, I have not caused any physical harm towards her. I did not shoot her. I, in no way was involved in her attack, meaning I did not orchestrate or enlist others to harm Landon Taylor. I am not here to place blame or speculate on who did shoot Landon Taylor. I am here to clear my name. It also is not my intent to defame my ex-wife, but, facts are facts. As the trial unfolds you will find my ex-wife carried on several affairs and lied regarding the paternity of our son. You will also find she was involved in illegal activity such as money laundering, among other things. With that being said, I am confident in our legal system and believe that the evidence and due diligence will find me not guilty on all charges. I do pray her family finds the justice they seek. I however, am not the man they seek. I am not guilty. I repeat, I did not shoot Landon Taylor.

All the hurt, pain, so much turmoil, present on his face. My heart ached for him.

At this time since this is an ongoing trial I will only take a few questions.

The questions begin.

"Who do you think shot her?"

"I don't know who did it. I know I didn't."

"Do you have a theory on who shot her and why?

"No."

"Did your wife have any affairs with your teammates?"

"Yes."

The questions shot off. "Who? How did you find out? What was her response? Were there any reasons for the divorce? Who is the father of Ms. Taylor's son? How did you find out he wasn't your son? Who do you think did it? What did Ms. Taylor say to you? How did you feel?"

As far as the father…" He gets choked up, and pauses for several moments.

I hold my breath.

"All I will say is, it was someone I thought was a friend."

I look over at Braxton who looks relieved.

"There will be no more questions," were Eric's last words before walking off stage.

I was grateful he didn't say Braxton's name, but I wasn't naïve. I know by him not naming Braxton it was out of respect for me. It was also his way of saying I did you a favor, do me one. But even though he didn't name him today, someone would.

I shake my head. I grab Khouri who puts up a fuss because she wanted Braxton.

"Khouri wants her daddy. Hey, Khouri. You want daddy don't you?"

She instantly starts smiling trying to jump to him.

"I was going to feed her." I look at Reagan who is content laying on Braxton.

"Sit next to me."

I oblige. I feed Khouri while Braxton plays with Raegan.

The next morning we were awaken by the phone ringing off the hook.

Braxton answers with a growl, "What?!"

I hear Vince's voice, but can't make out what he is saying.

Braxton sits up and turns on the TV.

"This is Adam Groggin ESPN and we have learned, based on court documents filed in the District court of Montgomery County, that Braxton Simms has filed for full custody of the minor known as Eric Ayres Jr. Now another question is, who is Braxton Simms?"

Gotdamn Jackie! If her ass would have let us get Eric, there'd been no need to file papers. Eric's father would still be listed as Eric Ayres, and the truth behind his paternity would still be a mystery. Damn Jackie, damn!

A picture of the four of us at the BET awards appears on the screen.

If I wasn't already lying down I would have fell back. I knew it was coming, but with some things you can never be prepared enough for it.

"Beautiful, you okay? He reaches for my hand, but I pull away."

"I need some space," I hold my hand up.

"Yasmin, I know it's hard, but remember we're in this together."

"Of course it's easy for you to say. I get the 'dumb chick' comments. All I said was give me space. I still have to get my head right. This is a lot to deal with."

"That's fair. I know it's hard. Give me a hug," he holds his arms out.

"Did I not just say give me some space?"

He ignores me, pulling me into a bear hug.

"Braxton, stop!" I break away from his embrace and lock myself in the bathroom.

I take a seat at my vanity, staring at my reflection. Eyes puffy, tears threaten to fall. I was tired of crying. Crying solved nothing. I grip the sides of the vanity.

You will not cry. You will not cry. You will not cry! Get it together! You are strong. You can and will handle this. Breathe. Breathe. No tears. No tears. "Aargh" I growl. Breathe. Breathe. No tears.

10

Find A Way

I called Kevin. I had to find out if there was any word on Jackie and Lawrence. I also wanted to discuss this Eric issue.

"Hello, hello, hello Kev, are you there?" I said hearing heavy breathing in the phone.

Now moaning.

"Kevin Powell, really?"

I was surprised to hear Nicole's voice on the phone.

"Kevin can't come to the phone right now. He is handling me, I mean his business," she giggled, before slamming the phone hard in my ear.

Obviously, he wasn't handling it right because if he was you wouldn't have been thinking of a phone. I thought. I swear, more and more that chick was showing me something wasn't bright with her. I feel bad because I told him she was wife material. She got a ring and the chick lost her mind. Twenty minutes later Kevin was calling.

"That was real fast," I couldn't resist.

"More like real good."

"I doubt that since you're calling. If it was *real good* you'd be catching your breath, about to pass out 'cause you did the damn thing. But anyway, I called because I need to see you."

"I'm real busy with Lawrence and Jackie on hiatus."

"Keeeviiiiiiin," I hear Nicole call out.

Oh, this chick had worked my nerves. This is juvenile crap. It wasn't my place, but this chick needs to stop. I don't want your man, so just stop. Seriously, we did need to have a talk, clear the air. Her feelings, however, were on the bottom of my list of things to do. I had bigger problems, so she was just going have to deal.

"I'll be right there. Give me ten minutes." Kevin tells Nicole.

I get straight to the point. "Where are Jackie and Lawrence?"

"I don't know."

"I know you know. I'm not going to go back and forth with you. You won't disclose that information, fine. So pass this message to Lawrence, if he wants to have any kind of relationship with me or his granddaughters he needs to call me in the next 72 hours.

"Yasmin, really, I don't know where they are. I can't get in contact with them either. When I come in the office, there's usually a memo and a voice message."

"So if there's an emergency, you are to handle it? He leaves his multi-million dollar company for you to run as you please? I don't believe it."

"I am more than capable of handling business, I've done so for a few years. I take my job very seriously. Unlike you, who runs away when you feel the pressure. Furthermore, my life is drama free. By the way, before I laid it down in the bedroom, I caught the morning news. Instead of insulting me and giving me orders on what I need to tell my *partner* you need to focus on your mess."

"You arrogant mutherfucker, the only thing you can lay right is the tongue and it wasn't all that. I called to inform you about information I came across in Landon's case."

"I got this. I do my job well. I hold the degree and the credentials. Your information I'm sure I'm aware of and Eric will pay for his crime."

"You ass. You so damn arrogant and WRONG!"

"I gathered evidence and witnesses for the prosecution. The only thing left is the trial and the guilty verdict. Like I told you, worry about your mess."

"Kevin, fuck your arrogant ass and your ignorant fiancé. Consider our friendship over."

"There you go acting like a little kid."

"There you go acting like an asshole."

"Kevin, honey," Desperate calls out.

"I'm going to give you a few days to cool off. I'm about to hang up."

"You don't have to give me nothing. I stand by what I said." I slammed the phone in his ear.

The blogs had dug and they dug deep. It doesn't take much for people to talk. Landon had acquired a few enemies and they were spilling the tea. One in particular was a scorned woman by the name of Tonya Duke. Tonya was the wife of Thomas Duke. He, like Eric, had played for the Washington Wizards. Tonya did an interview with a popular blog after she was arrested. Yes, she was arrested for stabbing her husband, Thomas.

She claimed that her husband cheated on her with Landon and as a result she caught syphilis. She even had pictures of Landon with her husband and some other man. She said the humiliation and disease caused her to go temporarily insane. I admit it does. I could relate since I stabbed Braxton when I found out about him and Landon's hook-up.

That was mild though. There were more pictures and more people trying to cash in on fifteen minutes of fame. First, the pictures. There were pictures of Landon and me at the Espy awards. I was with Chauncey and then with Braxton at the BET awards. I was labeled a groupie, and Landon and I shared men.

Now, to my husband. Pictures of him with some scorned hooker he fucked giving fabricated stories on their love affair. His dumbass took pictures with her sitting in his lap at one of Javon's charity events. The blog dug and found out the hooker had been arrested four times for prostitution. Then there were pictures of him with Melania, and people had theories on how she really died.

Eric had numerous people coming forth vouching for his character, but there still was a tremendous amount of evidence against him. This was a high profile messy case. It was Basketball Wives: Reloaded, better than reality TV. People couldn't get enough. I was surprised, yet grateful, that the news didn't get out that Landon and I were sisters.

I still had my clients which kept me sane through the chaos and I used my work to get away, but it was useless. Due to the severity of the case and the extreme media attention, Braxton was on leave. You know ethic and morality clause, this was negative press. Therefore, Braxton and BET agreed it was best for him to take a leave of absence pending the outcome of this case. He still got paid, which was good, but not an issue because, thanks to me, we were financially well. It's just having him here was too much.

Never before did I have a reason to have my number listed as private. I wish I took that precaution because every day all day the phone rang requesting interviews. Reporters had even found out my address.

Mommy and Mr. Jeff had come over to get the twins. I was pissed about it. Since it was so much going on with this case, they decided to take the twins away for a week in hopes that the media attention would die down some. They, along with Jeff Jr. and Patrice, were going on a little vacation down in Virginia to some retreat. I was going to go and leave Braxton, but I had been subpoenaed to appear in court. Jury selection was scheduled to begin in three days. Although, it more than likely would be postponed, Braxton and I had to be available.

I held on to my babies rocking back and forth. Both of them laughing and giggling made me cry. I missed my babies already.

"Don't cry, sweetheart. You know I'm going to take care of these princesses."

I nod.

"We'll be right back. Get some rest." Mommy rubs my shoulders.

"I know it's not easy." Mr. Jeff walks beside me.

"Khouri, kiss kiss. Reagan, kiss kiss." I kiss them both.

Braxton hesitantly walks over giving me a pitiful look. I cut my eyes at him. He takes Reagan and starts tickling and kissing her.

"Braxton, put the stuff in the car now," Mommy ordered.

"I did, Ma," he said.

"You don't make no kind of sense. I don't know what the hell you were thinking. Acting like you were brought up without sense. A hooker… hookers. Jeff, that's *your* son. "

"I know," he said exasperated.

"Beverly, calm down," said Mr. Jeff. "Braxton knows he was stupid."

"He was more than stupid. What is wrong with you? Just embarrassing." She continues.

She takes Reagan from him.

"Ma, let me give my daughter a kiss."

"Do you hear me talking to you?" Mommy grills.

"Yes, I'm stupid. I get it," he grabs Khouri from his father.

"You better. Just don't make no kind of sense," Mommy continued.

Braxton bends down to kiss Reagan. She reaches for him.

Ms. Beverly hands her over. Her disposition changes at the sight of Braxton with the girls.

"You did something right. Look at my babies. Yasmin, honey, come take a picture with your family."

I do and they're gone twenty minutes later. The large house is too empty. Braxton comes behind me wrapping his arms around me, startling me.

"Now is not the time."

I attempt to break away. "I want my babies."

"I know. I do too. This is just temporary."

"Let me go."

"I know you mad at me but all this shit was before you and I was together."

"And I'm paying for your shit. I'm paying for staying with you. All your shit is out on the table and I'm suffering."

"I apologize."

"Fuck an apology. It's always something with you. You always got something that you think isn't relevant so there's no need to tell me and then it comes slapping me in the face."

"Yasmin, I didn't you about all my *past* relationships like you didn't tell me about yours. They weren't relevant and had no importance in this relationship."

"You dated known escorts who spread their legs for a buck."

"So all the people in your past were *good?* No, they weren't, particularly Chauncey. Didn't he get somebody pregnant when you were together? Didn't our business get out when that happened?"

"No you didn't go there." I say through clenched teeth.

"All I want you to do is realize that sometimes shit gets out. It ain't right, but the media will always add a spin to it and make it worse by twisting the facts."

"My miscarriage with our son was put out there, true. The media did falsify documents to make it appear as if I miscarried Chauncey's kid. I broke up with Chauncey for that reason along with other things. Everything they said about you, however, was true, so own it."

"I am owning it."

"No you're not throwing that in my face. And for the record Chauncey, and I never got as serious as you and I."

"Oh, so he had a pass to cheat?"

"No, but he didn't impregnate my sister."

"There you go throwing shit back in my face again. I thought we were moving past that. Every time something gets you mad, you want to hit below the belt. You told me you were done throwing shit up in my face. Here you go again. I did you wrong. I know. You think I don't feel bad for hurting you? For doing that shit. You think I meant to? You think I don't get upset and depressed about all the shit I put you through and still do?"

"What am I getting? What are the benefits? Yes, I accepted Eric, now you expect me to accept all your other shit because we're married with kids? Which aren't here because of your bullshit! Yeah, this is easy for you because there's a double standard. You're just a man that was getting it in with beautiful women. I am a reformed groupie who you turned into a housewife."

"Yasmin, I don't want to hurt you. If I thought this would be a factor I would have told you. As for benefits, you have me, a man that loves you and is completely committed to only you."

"By process of elimination. You've been with the roster of escorts sampling."

He takes a breath.

"I am tired of looking like a desperate dumbass. I need to go to the store." I walk away.

"Yasmin, we are not done talking."

"I am." I grab my keys.

"Yasmin, where are you going?"

"For a ride. I'll be back."

"There you go. Always trying to run away when you get mad."

"I'm going for a ride."

"You need to calm down and stay in the house. It's raining and slippery."

"I know how to drive and I need to go get some feminine products," I lied.

"Unh, hunh."

"I'll be back."

11

I Gotcha

Trying to sort through all of the mess and chaos in my world, I drove around trying to clear my head. Braxton kept calling my phone, but I turned it on silent. My truck felt like it was pulling to the right and it was a strange sound when I tried to accelerate.

Lost in my thoughts, I didn't realize I'd driven into familiar territory. I picked up my phone to make a call.

"Hey, Chaunce."

"Hey, Ms. Lady."

"I need a favor. My car is acting up. Can I stop by in a few minutes? It's raining and …."

"Yas," He cuts me off.

"I'm sorry. Do you have company?"

"No, just come. No reason needed. Can you make it?"

"Yes, I'm about ten minutes away."

I slid my way to Chauncey's. Just as I pulled into his development, my car jumped a curb sliding into a fence. I heard a loud pop that frazzled my nerves. Scared out of my mind, I held on the steering wheel so tight my nails made piercing indentions into the leather steering wheel. My car wobbled at five mph until I saw Chauncey's massive mansion. I was so relived to finally make it.

Chauncey waiting by the door, came out with an umbrella. I couldn't open the door fast enough. As soon as I got out of my truck Chauncey pulled me into an embrace.

"You ok, Yas?"

I pull back, "Yeah, just got a little shook. I'm good. I think I blew my tire out."

"You did. Come on in, it's cold."

I walk over to the passenger side, not caring that I was getting drenched from the rain and ice.

"Shit," I said taking in the damage to the bumper and blown out tire. "I hope I didn't mess up my rim."

"You can't do nothin' about it now. Let's get in the house. It's cold."

I follow Chauncey into the massive foyer. I take off my wet coat and shoes appreciative of the heat. I notice Chauncey watching me.

"I'm sorry. I just came in your house taking off shoes invading your space," I smile.

"You good. Continue undressing, I'm ready for the show."

"Haha. There will be none of that."

"So what happened with your car?"

"It's been acting crazy for a minute. With so much going on, I kept putting off taking it to the shop. But it's pulling and not accelerating right, if that makes sense."

"Sounds like it might be the transmission."

"Oh, so you know a little something about cars? I thought you just liked to buy them."

"I do, Miss."

"Hopefully, it isn't. I don't feel like being bothered with car problems now. I have enough to deal with."

"Yeah," Chauncey gives me a sympathetic look.

I could see the clock in Chauncey's hall and saw it was a little after eight. "Let me call AAA first and Braxton."

AAA, to no surprise, was backed up and couldn't give me an idea when they would be able to send a dispatch. I could call Braxton to come get me, but him coming to Chauncey's would be a headache I wasn't ready for. His bipolar ass would go off. One, for me ending up at Chauncey's house; Two, for driving thirty minutes away from home in this weather; Three for not answering my phone; Four, for just calling him; Five, for being so damn difficult. And when he sees that I didn't go to the store at all. Yeah, I would tell him, but not tonight. I'll take that battle in the a.m. Besides, his ass has put me through enough, he'll be okay. I need the break.

I called Braxton's cell, let it ring once, hung up and called right back to get his voice mail. *"Braxton, it's me. First, I am ok. It's slippery, so I'm just going to chill where I am. I'm with a friend. I will be home later. Waiting on AAA. My phone is about to die, but I am ok and will see you later."*

You know the phone rang right back. I sent it straight to voice mail and powered the sucker off. Yeah, I deal with Mr. later.

"You get everything straight?"

"No, AAA can't come out till later."

"So that means you gotta chill with me. Looks like it's gonna be a good night."

"Not too good."

"Ha ha, you never know."

I give him a serious look, "I know."

"You want something to drink?"

"Yes, please."

"You're wet. You can put on one of my T-shirts. You remember where they are?"

"I do."

In Chauncey's room, I take off my wet clothes and bra and put on one of his t-shirts. I took my wet clothes and threw them in the dryer. When I came back, Chauncey had drinks and food. I took a sip, immediately scrunching my nose.

"You don't like your drink?"

"It's too damn strong. Here you go." I hand it back to him. "I'll make my own."

Chauncey shakes his head while I mix a concoction of Peach Ciroc, Sprite and Malibu Rum.

We go into his game room. He has Jason's Lyric playing.

I take a seat on Chauncey's plush sectional.

"You and your subliminal messages. You can put on porn, strip, or whatever, I ain't fuckin' ya ass. Those days are over and never returning."

"Never say never."

"I'm 99.9999999 percent sure I am not fuckin' ya ass again."

Chauncey falls out, "You know how to bring a man down. You so mean. He got ya ass trained. You scared to make a move. He put dat Anna Mae on dat ass."

I laugh. "It's called being committed and honoring my vows. Besides, my husband takes care of all my needs. So, you can say he definitely does put it on me in a lovely way."

"He also lies."

"And you didn't?"

"Your legs are so umm, umm."

"Nice way of changing the subject."

I sit up Indian style covering my legs.

"I was immature. Still new to the game chasing, I don't know what. Guess I thought I was missing something. I finally realized I wasn't."

"And when did you come to that conclusion?"

He looks at me, "Eric situation. It's fucked up, but it makes you realize in our world you come across women who want the fame and fortune not us. When shit go down like an injury or finances, 98% of them will be gone with it. At the end of the day, it's good coming home to someone who cares and who you can have a *real* conversation with."

"True," I say softly.

He gives me the most sincere look, "I had that with you."

"Chaunce, our season is over. Even though Braxton and I are having problems, I'm committed."

He laughs. "So tell me about Mr. What is it about him that has your ass so trained? Other than what he does in the bed."

"Braxton and I have a connection. It's more than sex. He is the first person that made me feel beautiful. I feel his love without him telling me. He has his faults, but I know he's genuine with his feelings."

"Faults?"

"Yes."

"That's what you call having a kid by your sister?"

Just like that even though I accepted reality, the sharp pain still came. Like a low blow rendering me speechless.

"My bad."

"I took him back. Part of that is dealing with opinions. With all the media coverage, I should be used to it."

"I'm sorry. I know it still doesn't make it easier," he said sincerely.

"I'm fine. Back to his *faults*, the main one is his temper."

"We never had that problem."

"When we were together it was fun, but I knew it wouldn't work."

"So you never really gave us a chance?"

"Like you did. Didn't you have a baby?" I raise my eyebrows.

"So how is having a kid while y'all were together different than when we were together?"

"It's not that simple. He was wrong. I was dealing with a miscarriage and…"

He cuts me off, "He should have been there. How many more surprises are you going to take?"

"You had unresolved feelings for an ex as well. What's up with Toya?"

"Once again, a good girl gone bad, and she's gone forever." He sang in Jay Z voice. "This life wasn't meant for Toya. She wanted things to be like they were before the fame. She couldn't understand you grow up and some people can't go for the ride. You got to eliminate the toxic things, people. Surround yourself with the right people."

Wow, how Chauncey had matured. My mind drifts to memories of Landon.

"What you thinking about, pretty woman? And for the record, I always thought you were...are beautiful. I wish I was the one who made you feel that way. Guess the timing wasn't right."

"Thank you, Chauncey. Just thinking about Landon. She did a lot of things that I didn't agree with. She definitely didn't take any ish and had her ways, but she did have a heart. No doubt what she did to Eric and me was really fucked up. Not making excuses, it's just Landon always acted without thinking. She always had Jackie to cover her and she told Lawrence what to do," I pause. "She had plenty of faults but if it wasn't for her, I'd still be in shell."

"You think so?"

"I know so. When I met Landon, I had no friends. She didn't either." I laugh. "I stayed to myself. I didn't get along with my parents. I was the black sheep. I went home stayed in my room, read a book, went to school. I did nothing. She was the first person who took an interest in me. We started doing things and formed a bond. I was her project at first, but she got me doing things and wouldn't let me accept being anyone's doormat."

"So you don't think you're one now?"

I breathe in deeply, "I do think I'm getting more ish than I deserve. Is it worth it?" I shrug. "I do believe Braxton's actions weren't intentional. I believe Landon's weren't either. Does Braxton love me? Yes, he does. Is he taking advantage? I would say no to that as well. So, no, I don't think I'm a doormat."

"So you're going to stay committed?"

"I'm trying."

"Sometimes you just can't force things. You have to let some people go."

Chauncey and I had a few more drinks, deep conversation and fun. He showed me current pics and videos of his kids and so did I. We ended up upstairs having a pillow fight, singing karaoke and playing hide and go seek. I know, juvenile, but I needed the release. It felt good to talk to someone who wasn't directly involved in the madness. I vaguely remembered Chauncey climbing in bed with me before I drifted to sleep.

12

Can You Stand The Rain

Chauncey and I were in his kitchen having breakfast I prepared that consisted of scrambled eggs, blueberry pancakes, and turkey bacon.

"Thank you for breakfast," Chauncey said, giving me a smile showing off his deep dimples

"Thank you for letting me use your spare room."

"Any time."

"No, this is the last time. I need to go home to my husband." Which I did. I left a message on his cell earlier telling him where I was and would be home by 12. I was grateful he didn't blow up my phone. I wasn't ready to battle with him.

"Are you ready for that?"

"No, but staying here is not appropriate and it's the last place I need to be."

"You're good. I like your company," he said while giving me his most seductive look, eyes exploring every aspect of my body.

I laugh.

"What's so funny?"

"You. You just like having a cook."

"It's a nice perk, but it's you." He then starts singing Raheem Devaughn's song, *You*.

"You are so entertaining."

Just then the doorbell rang, "I'll get that."

As I was drinking my orange juice, I hear Chauncey call me.

"Yasmin, you have company!"

As I approach, I hear a deep baritone voice respond, "Company? This ain't her goddamn house."

"Braxton, chill," coaxed Vince.

Braxton gives Vince a menacing stare and then focuses on me, giving me the stare of death. He scans my attire of Chauncey's t-shirt, messy ponytail, and bare legs, while Chauncey stood in jogging pants, shirtless, toned six-pack present. He is far past livid.

Yes, he had every right to be mad, but so did I. "Hello, Vince, Braxton."

"Get your keys, your stuff, let's go."

"My car isn't drivable. One of my tires is blown out."

"I'll get it later. Let's go now," ordered Braxton.

"Chauncey called AAA, I'm waiting on them."

His stare somehow intensifies causing me to flinch.

"Yasmin, you ok." Chauncey asks.

"Yeah, she's ok," answered Braxton.

"I was talkin' to Yas. She can answer for herself."

"I'm fine, Chauncey."

"Everything's a'ight, Chauncey. I'll wait for Yasmin's car," volunteered Vince.

I know I needed to run put on my clothes and leave with Braxton, but at the same time I needed to stay close before things escalated.

Chauncey walks up to me, his eyes asking me if I was really okay. I nod.

Through my peripheral vision, I see Braxton give Vince a look that screams, *What the fuck?*

"You don't have to go," Chauncey said softly.

"Yasmin is my wife. I got this."

"Yeah, technically she is, but Yasmin's getting tired of your surprises. With me, I don't sugarcoat. I'm honest and she respects that. She knows what she's getting. She doesn't want to go through life waiting for the other shoe to drop, dealing with all the bullshit."

"Chauncey, what the fu..." I said surprised at his outburst.

"Who the fuck you think you talkin to?!" yelled Braxton, stepping to Chauncey, who is three inches taller.

"You, muth-"

Before Chauncey could get another word out, Braxton had his hand around his throat in a death grip.

Vince steps in and manages to break Braxton's grip while I restrain Chauncey.

I look at Chauncey, who is now coughing and hacking, my eyes pleading. "Chauncey, stop. Please shutup, we're leaving."

"Mutherfucker, your business with **MY** wife is done. Don't contact her under any circumstances."

"That's not your call to make," said Chauncey in a strained voice.

I stand tall, hand on Chauncey's chest trying to push him as far away as possible. "Chauncey enough! Shut the hell up! Please go upstairs, downstairs, anywhere."

"Like I said, it's done! Stay the hell away from my family," growled Braxton.

"Your little girls are cute too," Chauncey smirked.

Braxton abruptly pushes me aside, knocking me down and lunges at Chauncey, fist going straight for his jaw. Chauncey is prepared, blocks Braxton's punch and hits Braxton is the shoulder. Braxton throws a combination of punches landing on Chauncey's chin, eye and neck. Chauncey, not a lightweight, attacks Braxton's sides.

By now, I'm scared to step in-between. I choose to yell at Vince, "Vince, break them up!"

"Yasmin, I love you, sis, but hell naw. Chauncey's ass was wrong. Braxton, get his ass or I'm going to beat yours," ordered Vince, like his father.

Braxton dives in sending Chauncey crashing hard to the floor. Chauncey bringing Braxton down with him, the two scuffle. Braxton landing powerful blows, I know breaking Chauncey's nose because blood is going everywhere. Chauncey hits Braxton on the side of his ribs. They go back and forth punch for punch, Braxton succeeding, weakening Chauncey.

"Vince!" I pleaded.

He finally grabs Chauncey, restraining him and allowing Braxton to get a few more punches. I grab Braxton's arm, but he just shakes me off. Going back at Chauncey, who is desperately trying to free himself from Vince, I step in front of Chauncey.

"Braxton, stop!"

"Move the fuck out the way!"

"No! Stop! Enough! You've proved your point. It's done. I'm leaving with you. Please go to the car. Let me get my stuff," I pleaded.

"Yasmin, move," he huffed.

"Braxton, please."

He doesn't respond and I know he isn't done with Chauncey.

"Braxton, let's go home please. Braxton, please stop, please."

"Yasmin, get your shit and let's go."

I grab Braxton's arm, leading him to the guest room where my stuff is. I quickly take off Chauncey's shirt and dress. Braxton stares inspecting my body of any passion marks or any other questionable marks. When we return, Vince is talking to the tow man. Chauncey is holding a rag to his face. I want to check his wounds, but I knew to stay the hell away. My eyes plead sorry as I walk out the door. Vince catches it and gives me an *Are you crazy* look. The tow man looks intrigued.

"It's the black Armada on the side. Tow it to the dealer."

Vince opened the door, handing him some cash, and sending him on his way. The tow man hesitantly leaves.

"Braxton, Yasmin, let's go," ordered Vince.

I don't know what transpired between Vince and Chauncey while we were away, but Chauncey was mute and kept a far distance. Too afraid to speak or look at Chauncey, I grab on Braxton's arm, but he snatches it away. Fortunately, he follows me out the door. Vince is the last to leave, closing the door behind him.

Of course I go straight for the back seat of the BMW. I'm seat belted up before Braxton could object. They get into the car, and within seconds, Chauncey's house is fading away. Vince turns on the radio.

Braxton walks in, heading straight upstairs. Vince grills me.

"What the hell was you thinking?"

"Who the hell are you talking to?" I responded.

"Yasmin, you know your ass was wrong. This running off thing you do when you get pissed gotta stop. It was like déjà vu," chastised Vince.

"Vince, that's not what I was trying to do. I really got stuck. I admit I was pissed, but I didn't realize the weather was going to get crazy like that."

"So out of a million of places you could've went, you went to an ex's house. Tell me that doesn't sound crazy. Shit, fucking around with y'all, I'm missing out on my winter storm loving."

"Chauncey is a client."

"*Was* a client."

"Vincent."

"Vincent nothing. Braxton is pissed with your ass and he should be. To add insult, you come out half-dressed like that was your house."

"Braxton is not so innocent either. Why didn't you tell me about Melania?"

"That don't have nothing to do with today. You need to get yourself together."

"Excuse you."

"No, listen to me Yasmin. You mad, I get that. But you out there looking like a Chauncey groupie. Please tell me you didn't really fuck him."

"Hell no! What the hell? No. Hell no. I didn't fuck Chauncey."

"Good. You need to go make amends. Yeah, Braxton did some fucked up shit, was wrong, but you did and still doing fucked up shit. You need to get a grip. Use some common sense."

"I am. I needed a break. My life is being broadcasted all over the damn place. My kids…"

"Yasmin!" Braxton voice booms startling the crap out of me. "Before your smart ass says anything else, tell me what this is about."

Braxton has a tablet on the counter. He shows an Instagram video of me sprawled out on the bed, Chauncey in bed with me, while John Legend sings, Best You Ever Had in the background. Chauncey is smiling he says this is all natural. Then he adds hashtags #NoMakeup #NoWeave #BeautyandBrains #RealSleepingBeauty #ImInLove. The video only six hours old has over 100,000 likes.

My mouth stuck on the letter "O". I'm unable to finish the phrase with "shit." My hands cover my mouth. My head goes back, then forth, covering my face from shame. It is hot, too hot. I'm sweating, discombobulated, speechless.

"Dammmnnn!" exclaimed Vince. "I'm going to leave on that. You good, bro?"

"No! I need to go back to that punk house and stomp his ass."

"Don't worry about that. Handle home." Vince walked out the back door.

"What you have to say smart ass?"

"I'm sorry."

"Sorry for what?"

"Going to Chauncey's."

"Why cause he got you out there looking like a groupie, a fuck quest?"

I open my mouth to respond, but I'm pissed. This issue with Braxton and I takes precedence, but Chauncey betrayed my trust. I wish I would have let Braxton continue to beat his ass.

"That's your problem, you think you know everything. I told you to stay away from Chauncey. Told you he couldn't be trusted. But you had to prove me wrong. Look at this shit!" He throws the tablet, screen shattering.

"I warned you about Lisa. I told you don't trust her. I trusted Chauncey like you did with Lisa. It was a mistake. We both trusted the wrong people. Please, I'm sorry." I pleaded

"Hell no. I was never laid up in a bed with that bitch. And your ass ain't have on no damn clothes."

Tears run from my eyes. Chauncey's ass set me up. I confided in his ass. Trusted he was a friend and he did this. Now, however, I have to get things right with Braxton. He is fuming. He has every right to be, I have to figure out how to get him to accept my apology.

"I know mutherfuckers like Chauncey. I'm around them all the time. I tried to tell you, but I didn't know what I was talking about. You thought I was jealous overrating so you do shit behind my back. You the first one hollering I can't trust you. Yasmin, I don't trust you."

"Baby, I swear I didn't do anything with Chauncey. Nothing happened, honestly. I'm sorry."

I grab his hand, he snatches it back.

"Get off me," he growled.

"Braxton, nothing happened," I cried.

"Oh, something happened. You went over there talking to him about our business. He got you drunk, pumped you up, you kept talking, got sleepy. You don't know what the fuck you did while you was sleep or what he did to you," he kicked the wall.

"Braxton, I know I did not fuck him. There was nothing sexual at all."

"I don't believe you."

I was not use to being on this end. "Braxton, I was upset with you, but I would never just go fuck anyone else drunk or sober."

"I don't know."

"Seriously, that's not me and you know it."

"I also told you I didn't want any mutherfuckers around my kids. Why the hell you have my daughters around that clown?!"

"That was just coincidence. I ran into him at the store."

"Yeah, whatever."

"It was. I never intentionally took them to see Chauncey," I pleaded.

"Just like yesterday, right? You told me you were going to the store. Somehow you end up there."

"My truck was acting up."

"I thought I knew you. I thought you wouldn't lie about going to see someone."

"I didn't lie. I didn't intend on going there. I saw Chauncey for business and he took me with him to see Eric," I confessed.

Braxton shakes his head.

"I'm sorry. You were right."

"I ain't trying to hear that shit."

I cautiously walk up to Braxton and attempt to wrap my arms around him.

He stops me, "Get off me."

"Braxton, I'm sorry. What do you want to do? I don't want Chauncey, never have. I only was with him because-."

"Don't even say it. Don't say it."

Braxton, what you want me to do?"

"Leave me alone, Yasmin."

"I didn't fuck him."

He grunts.

"I didn't. You want to do a pelvic exam," I said frustrated.

He gives me a piercing stare.

"Braxton, baby," I grab his hand.

Braxton pulls away and walks out of the room.

I take a sit at the bar stool and sulk. Punk ass Chauncey! I wanted so bad to call him and cuss him out for that juvenile shit but I dare not do that with Braxton lurking around. I confided in that punk and he betrays me like this. I thought we had a bond. Oh, I was going to get his ass. Dumbass should know not to fuck with me, especially since I have access to his money.

I walk into the media room to see House of Cards playing. Braxton, however, isn't focused on the screen. He's focused on the glass filled with a dark cognac. I ease back out of the room and am on my way upstairs. I would have to pull some tricks out tonight.

*

Glad he slid in bed with me. I knew not to touch him yet. His breathing soon became shallow. Fortunately, Braxton has only boxers on. I put my hand on the opening pull out Sugar Daddy. I knew my window of opportunity was narrow, I ease my mouth down and go to work sucking, taking my hand massaging it up and down his shaft. Braxton moans. I open my mouth more to take in more of him, sucking him more.

He cums in my mouth, I don't hesitate drinking him in. His hardness still present, but not as firm. I quickly sit up and straddle him. I ease my body up, and just as I was about to ease on to my sugar, he flips me. I spread my legs wider, so he can enter me. Braxton chooses to insert two fingers in me. He's rough, catching me off guard. His fingers explore me, but they're not turning me on. In fact, they're doing the opposite.

"Baby, put in Sugar Daddy."

He gives me a crazy look, "That's what you want?"

"Yes, baby, put it in me."

Abruptly, he pulls his fingers out and stands, "Nope, I'll pass."

"What?"

"I don't trust your ass."

Hold up! Did his ass really just do a pelvic exam on me? "Braxton, I didn't do anything." I cried, hot tears burning my face.

He grabs some clothes and walks toward the door.

"Where are you going?" I panic following behind him.

"Don't worry about it."

"Braxton."

"Last night, I didn't know where the fuck you was. I couldn't get in contact with you. Didn't know if you was alright."

"I'm sorry. Stay with me, please."

"Your ass was laid up with that mutherfucker looking content. You ain't lose no sleep, but I did."

I grab his arm, "It won't happen again. I apologize."

He yanks his arm. "Every time you get mad you run away. You have kids. What the fuck you thinkin', acting like a little kid. You need to stop this shit."

"You're right. I didn't go there to run. My car started acting up and he was close."

"You were supposed to call me. That's my job. Now you got this mutherfucker posting shit. You know what the fuck you did! What kind of position you put me in!"

"You're right. I apologize."

"I ain't trying to hear all that. I'm fucking tired of you disrespecting me. I did a fucked up thing to you, I get that. Your ass keep doing shit to take it on another level. Tired of this shit," he stormed out of the room.

I watch as he goes into the spare bedroom and slams the door.

13

Nobody Said It Was Easy

Three days later, Braxton was still not talking to me, still sleeping in the spare room. Well he talked to me once yesterday, but that was by force. The transmission in my Armada was kaput. He went with me to pick out a new truck. He ended up purchasing me a Toyota Land Cruiser. He didn't like putting the kids in cars, only sturdy big vehicles. My in-laws were the same way. When Johnathan was born, they bought a Honda Pilot. Recently, they had upgraded to a Lexus LX 570.

I missed my kids. Couldn't wait to hold them and was even more stressed than before. Chauncey had sent me several text messages and filled my voicemail with just as many. Each text saying I deserve to be treated right. Telling me to come stay with him. The voicemails always playing T.I.'s *Why You Wanna*.

The doorbell rings. I look on the monitor in the kitchen to see Vince. I get up to let him in.

"Hey, Vince."

"Yasmin," He said sternly.

"So you still mad too?" I roll my eyes.

"Question, you still my sister?"

"That's messed up, Vince."

"So was what you did."

I hit him in the arm. He starts laughing.

"Vince, tell me what to do. He's pissed."

"You know what you gotta do. Have another bathroom scene. That was some funny ish right there. Damn, I wish I had my camera. That would have been some good quick cash." He says referring again to the erogenous bathroom scene where Braxton and I were recorded fucking the shit out of each other. Let's just say the shower didn't cool us off. Later, I would find out Chauncey, Geester, and quite a few others viewed the footage.

"He won't let me," I whispered.

"Damn, lil' bro is mad. You got him all messed up."

"Alright, Vince, later for all that, what can I do?"

"I don't know, sex always works for me."

I shake my head, "I don't know why I expected you to be useful."

He laughs and Braxton walks in the foyer. It's evident he's going somewhere upscale. Braxton's dressed in dark jeans, Polo sweater and Louis Vuitton sneakers. The scent of his Versace cologne filling the air.

"I'm ready," Braxton tells Vince.

"Where are you going?" I asked.

"I'll be back."

I was tired of Braxton's tantrum, tired of biting my tongue. "That's not what I asked you."

Braxton ignored me and walked toward the door.

"You really acting like a baby. I get your point. Your tantrum is old. Talk to me."

He walks out the door. I pick up the vase to throw at him, but Vince stops me.

"I'll talk to him."

"Where are you going?"

"Out," he laughed.

"I can't stand you or your brother right now."

He shuts the door.

Braxton reached his limit. I admitted my mistakes but this was too much. Angry and sad tears ran down my face. I was pissed at Braxton for being an ass, but I was sad because I really needed my sister right now.

If Landon was here, there'd be no tears. Instead, I'd be putting on my freakum dress and be forced to a club to be admired by men, receive free drinks, and Landon's carefree attitude. I'd protest, give her evil stares all the while enjoying my time with my sister. I really hated all the male attention, but I loved my sister more. I wouldn't be moping I'd be relieving tension dancing, partying, having a girl's night out. I'd return with confidence, determined to make things right. My heart heavy, eyes blind from tears I still couldn't fathom her not being here. I can't fathom not hearing her voice, seeing her pretty face, her fashion sense. The year away from her was hard, but then I used my anger to mask my feelings. Masking away that, in truth, I did miss her and needed her presence. Now there was no anger, just overwhelming loneliness. I could never replace our bond just like I never could replace the loss of a child with another.

*

Since I could not repair my relationship with Braxton right now, I chose to attempt to repair another. The drive to my mother's house was long. The neighborhood the same as I remembered. It's been over two years since my last visit. I pull into the cul- de-sac, the split foyer still one of the best landscaped on the block. The snow on the archway supported by the massive columns, trees, and floral decorated bay window, ironically gave the home a welcoming appearance. I hoped my visit would warrant just that.

I sit for a while, playing with the gadgets in my new truck trying to work up the nerve. Twenty minutes later, I ring the bell.

Ashley opened the door, her smile disappearing when she sees me.

"Hello, Ashley."

"Hey."

She steps aside so I can walk in.

"So what's going on with you?"

"Nothing much, planning my wedding."

"Oh, okay that's exciting. What are your colors?"

"Burgundy and gold. Daniel loves the Redskins."

"Ash, honey, who's at the door?" My mother called out.

"Yasmin."

There's silence.

I follow Ashley into the kitchen which has magazines spread across the table along with notepads and photo albums.

I look at my mother. She looked like she'd aged ten years. When I saw her months ago at the hospital, I didn't really look at her. She looked stressed, broken, perhaps today she'd be willing to try to mend our non-existent relationship.

Ashley's cell phone rang, "That's Daniel. I'll be right back." She ran off to the other room.

"Hello, how are you?"

"Where's the father of the year?" my mother asked.

"Away."

"You weren't invited? He tired of you already like before?" She antagonized.

"Ma, please. I don't want to talk about Lawrence."

"Why not? When I came to the hospital you laid me out. You defended him like he was there for you. I raised you for years, provided clothes and food. I sacrificed for you. What he do? He turned his back on you and raised his precious Landon, while you standing around begging for scraps."

I ignore her. "What you said was inappropriate. It wasn't right. All I was saying was have some compassion."

"Like you did for me?"

"That was different."

"No it wasn't. You choose to remain dumb. You father abandons you twice and your husband knocked up your sister and yet you stay loyal. Didn't you call me stupid before? You're the dumb one."

I took her comment. She was my mother. I close my eyes. *No tears! No tears! No tears!* "I apologize for calling you dumb. I'm sorry. I want to move forward and build a relationship with you. You have granddaughters you've never met and that isn't right. We need to stop this."

She looks at me.

"I brought you over some pictures of them. They're names are Khouri and Reagan."

"Daniel says hello," Ashley came back into the room, breaking the momentum.

"Oh, you have a good man Ashley. He will be a wonderful committed husband. I can't wait to see you say, I do."

"Neither can I," My mother and Ashley share a hug.

The two fall into a natural conversation. Both agreeing on wedding details easily. I made several suggestions to be ignored.

"Do you need any help with anything?" I asked.

"No, we're good," gloated Ashley.

My mother never acknowledges my comment.

It was obvious I didn't belong. My chest burned from the constant stabs. It was evident that she and Ashley had a bond that she and I never would. Maybe we'd get to a point where she wouldn't cringe at the sight of me. Hopefully there'd be a time where we could have a conversation. But today, she didn't want me here and my heart couldn't take anymore.

"Alright. Well I'm going to go. I'll see you later."

"See you, Yasmin," responded Ashley.

My mother again never utters a word.

14

Where's The Love

The ride home I refused to cry. Not only had she rejected me, but now my daughters. I wouldn't allow them to feel the hurt I did. If that's how she wants to keep it, fine. I don't need her. I was done with being weak. *No tears! No tears! No tears!*

Braxton still wasn't home. The aloneness, silence threatening to shatter me. I head straight to my master bathroom suite. I shake my head when I enter, Braxton, as always, has his discarded clothes all over the floor. His sink a mess, containing opening containers of cologne, toothpaste, and lotion. His laziness was irritating. I ignore his sloppiness, and instead draw a hot bath and add coconut oil and lavender trying to regroup.

Yasmin be strong. You are strong. Forget what the media says. Forget what your mother says. You are not stupid. You will get through this. You have Reagan and Khouri. They love you and will always love you. So no tears.

I really miss my babies. Two more days, 48 hours, I can do this.

I needed, wanted to be touched. I needed some to tell me it would be ok, even it was a lie.

My cell phone rings. I pray its Braxton, but it's Chauncey. I answer, but don't speak. Staying consistent, he got that damn T.I. *Why You Wanna* playing in the background.

"Yasmin. I know you're mad. I'm sorry. Well I'm not. I just want you to know you can come here. No games. I can be the man you need. No surprises. No lies. I'll give you space. You don't have to accept bullshit. You deserve better. Stop fighting and let go. I got you. I want you."

I hold on for a few minutes before hanging up. This is a problem. I was getting weak.

Dazed, confused, and in a fog after Chauncey's call, I walk into my master suite absentmindedly nude. I jump at the sight of Braxton in boxers. I never heard him come in or noticed him on the security monitor. He was in the room getting a t-shirt from his drawer. I was mentally drained. I prayed he didn't have any snide remarks or comments. I couldn't take it. I walk pass him to get to my drawer. Braxton watches my every move. I turn my back to him, grabbing the first thing I see, a green silk nighty.

I lift my arms to put the nightie over me. Before I can slip my arms through the straps, Braxton picks me up, body slamming me to the bed. There's no warning, my legs are spread, and he goes in.

He drills me into the bed, my legs naturally wrapping around his waist, opening, pulling him further into me. No talking, just fucking.

"Ahh, hmm, oh, ahh, ouu." I moaned.

"Uh, Uh, Uh," he grunted.

He rolls out of me, flips me around, forcing me on my stomach. He spreads my legs apart before placing his heavy frame on top of me. He roughly enters me, his torso smacking hard against my ass. He yanks my hair, forcing my chin up. I teeth grazes my chin before bites down on my neck. He's shows no mercy, fucking me so hard I can't talk or moan just grunt. I grab hold of the covers and hold tight as he hammers on. His breath hot, breathing heavy, teeth still embedded in my neck. I'm finally shown mercy when he slides out. In a blink of an eye, I'm on my back, legs are in the air and his dick is far up in me.

Grinding in me deep, he takes my breath. Moving in and out of me as if he's riding an elliptical machine. Round and round, in and out, up and down. He's getting his cardio in going steady, pace consistent going for the long haul.

We roll, I'm on top. Back arched, each hand grasping his ankles. Taking his thumb, he begins flickering my clit, he rubs it round and round up and down, it's swelling, ready to bust. I ride him hard, fast, vigorously, round and round, up and down I go. The bed shaking, covers unraveling. He grabs my waist, pulling me close. I slow it down some. Our faces inches apart, he grabs mine kissing me hard. Sucking my tongue, lips. I slowly begin to roll my hips, soon I pick up the pace. Braxton takes both hands, grabs my ass, and bounces it hard up and down his shaft. I take his hands intertwine his fingers with mine. Then I begin my own booty bounce. I bounce each cheek, bounce both, making it clap. His breathing labored, he's ready to cum. I move vigorously, my booty claps louder, the impact stimulating.

He flips me. He's on top. He pushes my legs back, my feet touching the padded headboard. Pound, pound, pound, pound, pa-pound, pa-pound, pa-pound, pa-pound, pound, pound, pound, pa, pa, pa, pa, pa, pa, poooooooound. I swear he's trying to pound me through this bed. I'm squirting, I can feel my sugared waters flowing from my honey well, soaking the sheets beneath me. He switches up, one leg up in the back, the other flat on the bed. His movements precise, deep, long and hard.

"Ah, ah, ah, ah, ah, ah, ah, ah, ah, ah, ah, Ouuuuuuuuuu," I whimpered.

He lets go, collapsing his heavy frame on me. He's heavy. I don't complain. I hold on tight, scared to let go. I need this contact. Even though rough, and not our usual sensual contact, I didn't want it to end. Slowly, I began relaxing. I'm feeling vulnerable, insecure. I want to talk to him, tell him I do love him. I'm sorry. Don't leave, stay. I open my mouth to speak. Before I can utter a word, he rolls off of me, with his back to me. He's silent, his breathing becoming shallow, a sign he would be going to sleep. A tear rolls down my cheek. I pinch myself. *"No tears, no tears. No tears! Toughen up."*

I stand grabbing the green nighty that had been discarded. Hurriedly, I put it on. I turn off the lights and climb in bed. My back to Braxton, I grab covers which had been separated in our fucking. He grabs his own. One bed with separate covers. The union we shared moments earlier is over. The only thing remaining, reminding me that it did happen is the throbbing pain between my thighs matching the throbbing pain in my heart.

15

Hear My Call

It's been a few weeks since Braxton and I had our fuck quest. The good news, my babies were home. Having twins was a good thing, each of us got a baby. We'd interact at a minimal for their sake, but I swear they'd give us crazy looks. Braxton and I was still was in the same bed, covers were being shared. We had more encounters, not as rough, but still no words. No, it wasn't right, but some contact was better than none.

I'd be lying ifI didn't say I didn't think about Chauncey's proposition. He was right, I didn't deserve this. However, going with him wouldn't work, like before, my heart or desire wasn't in it. Chauncey's calls were frequent, but I haven't answered.

Kevin also called twice, but I refused his call. Braxton did ask me about that. I told him I didn't want to talk about it. After that, he had nothing else to say.

Fortunately, the spotlight had temporarily been taken off of Eric. As with news, there was another big story. The Oscar Pitorus scandal. The South African sprint runner had killed his girlfriend, Reeva Steenkamp after allegedly mistaking her for an intruder. The media finally getting bored with me, phone calls had subsided. Another unfortunate headline, police confirm the body found weeks ago is the body of missing 16-year-old Janay Watkins. She had been missing for months. Her body was found in a landfill a week ago. The preliminary autopsy indicated that she died of blunt force trauma and suffered sexual assault. Both stories were disheartening. My prayers are with both families. It was disturbing that their deaths took the spotlight off my scandal. Once Eric's trial began, I knew it would be back on and poppin'. In the meantime, I would try to get back to some normalcy.

Braxton had gone somewhere. I didn't ask, didn't care at this point. He was still being petty trying to prove a point by doing his disappearing acts. And guess what, I never called his cell to ask.

I was holding Khouri when the phone rang. I answer only because it was my aunt. Aunt Patti was my mother's only sibling, who unlike her sister, accepted me. She and my maternal grandmother are actually very loving. Sadly, my grandmother passed when I was younger, and my aunt moved to North Carolina, so I rarely saw her.

"Hey Aunt Patti."

"Hello, sweetie." Her voice sounded strained like she was holding back.

"Auntie, is everything okay."

"No, honey it isn't. Who's home with you?"

"The twins, why?"

"When will Braxton be home?"

"What's going on?"

She takes a deep breath. My heart thumps as I feel my chest tighten and a lump form. Khouri, sensing the change in me, begins to cry. I try to soothe her, kiss her, but my anxiety only elevated her cries, waking up Reagan. I put them both in the crib, and gave them toys. I walk out of the room and return my attention back to my aunt.

"Aunt Patti, what's wrong?"

"Yasmin, I need you to be strong."

"Aunt Patti?"

"Yasmin, please, I wish I could be there with you right now. I hate to tell you this..."

"Tell me what's going on?"

"Yasmin, I really hate to tell you this. Have a seat."

"Aunt Patti, you're scaring me. Please, just tell me what's going on."

"Yasmin," she sniffs, "your mother died, sweetie."

"What? No. What do you mean died? I just talked to her," I said as I feel my body slide to the floor.

"I know, it's unbelievable. I'm at the hospital now."

"How?" I wailed.

"She was sick."

"Why didn't anyone tell me? Why didn't you call me, so I could have seen her? Not again. I can't do this again." My entire body was stinging, burning.

"Yasmin, I'm sorry honey. She was already gone when I got here. I didn't even say goodbye."

"No! I'm sorry. I didn't want her to die. I didn't want her to die. I didn't hate her. I'm sorry. She hated me, but I didn't hate her. I just wanted her to like me."

Aunt Patti is saying something, but I don't hear her. The phone is now lying beside me on the floor and I shake my head no. The twins are crying, but I don't have the strength to get them or to call and ask for help.

I don't know how long I'm on the floor before Braxton comes in.

He hears the babies and I hear him run up the stairs. He sees me and pauses; he looks confused.

"Yasmin, what's wrong?"

I can't speak, he does a quick assessment to makes sure he doesn't see me bleeding or near death. He scoops me up and sits me on the chaise in the hallway.

"I'll be right back. Let me check on the twins." He isn't gone long. "What's wrong, Yasmin?"

I take a deep breath, "My mother is dead."

"Hunh, what? How?"

I solemnly respond, "I don't know."

Braxton pulls out his cell phone. A few moments later, I hear his voice, but I can't comprehend what he's saying. I'm unresponsive as he pulls me into an embrace I've wanted for weeks, but I'm numb. His embrace, too little, too late. His embrace forced out of pity and I don't want it.

I break away and go into the bedroom. He follows behind.

"Aunt Patti said she had a complication with anesthesia. She had, what was supposed to be, a minor surgery. She didn't tell anyone and passed away on the table."

I look at him.

"Do you want to go to the hospital to say your goodbyes?"

I shake my head no.

"Yasmin, talk to me. Tell me what you want me to do?"

"Nothing."

"I know it's hard. You know I'm here for you?"

"Really?"

"Yes, I know the last couple of weeks we haven't been getting along. It's been crazy, but I got your back. I'm here for you. Let me know what you need."

"I needed you. This relationship has been one punch after another. I tried to stand strong and take the punches, but I got tired. I make one bad decision after you made several and I'm penalized."

"I'm sorry."

"You expect me to be strong. Deal with everything. I told you I was tired. Punch after punch, I keep losing. Landon's gone. My mother's..." I ball my hand into a fist, stopping the tears. "I never lied. Never compromised your health. I didn't cross the line with Chauncey. I told him I was committed to you. I needed you to be that strong one I needed. Let me know I could count on you. What you do, push me aside, isolate me, and hurt me."

"You're right. I did it again. I'm sorry. Let me make it right."

"I'm tired of being right, done with the apologies and hearing the same crap."

He nods.

"I saw my mother a few weeks ago. Her last words to me were, I was a dumbass for being with you after you got me looking like a fool. I took her insult. That was the night you came home and fucked me like one of the prostitutes you're used to. You rolled off of me, turned your back on me, had no words for me. Just like them, my only use for you was sex and I had served my purpose. What you can do is keep your back turned. Let me deal with this alone like I always have."

He stopped me and held his arms open.

"My mother died hating me. You're showing concern now, but it's from pity. If she was still alive, your ass would still be acting like the selfish bastard you are. I don't want your pity. Leave me alone!"

I walked into the bathroom, locking the door behind me. I slid to the floor, slowly rocking myself. I was so tempted to call Chauncey, but I knew he would only be a temporary solution. This was another pain I couldn't deal with. No words can describe the pain I feel thinking about Bryan. My baby boy, my first the baby I never got to hold, he left me before I had a chance to hold and say I love you. Now I have to deal with the pain of losing a mother whose touch I never got to feel.

I don't know how long I stayed in the bathroom. When I came out, Braxton was feeding the twins. Braxton follows me with his eyes while I play with our daughters.

The week was a blur. I was overwhelmed. I loved my mother-in-law dearly. She, from day one, welcomed me into her heart. She gave me the mother's love I sought. When I had the miscarriage with Bryan, she was there hugging me, telling me it would be okay. Even when Braxton and I broke up for a year, she was there, still persisting that I call her Ma, treating me no differently. She'd done all she could, but she wasn't my mother. All I wanted was to be left alone. I needed to get myself together, alone, by myself, like always.

*

Kevin and Nicole stop before me in the line. "Yasmin, I'm so sorry for your loss." Nicole clings on to Kevin. I just nod and I focus on whoever's next in line. Face after face pass by with condolences. Many I never knew. Braxton sat beside me unsure whether to touch me. I look up when I hear him grumble. There stood Chauncey. I'd spoken with him briefly, telling him of my mother's passing. I never expected that he'd show. I stand, he grabs me into an embrace. "I told you. I got you. Anything you need I got you. All you have to do is let him go." He gives me a kiss on the cheek, holding me longer than needed. I appreciated his gesture, he didn't have to be here. It meant a lot. He hands me an envelope before walking away.

I stare at Chauncey's note afraid to open it. I decide to open it later. Braxton is ready to blow. He tries to grab my envelope, but I hold it tight. We're in a stare down. My aunt nudges me, giving me a quizzical look. Braxton relinquishes envelope and we sit amicably.

The reverend allows family to see my mother's body one last time. I walk to my mother's casket. For the first time, I look. She looks at peace. It was surreal, I couldn't believe she was gone. This would be the last time I saw her face. This was my final encounter, she was gone. No more chances to get it right, reconcile. I stood there willing myself to give her a kiss or touch, but I didn't know how. This was so unnatural for me. We never had a bond or that type of relationship. It wasn't right for my only touch or contact to be cold. Slowly, I bend down, kissing my mother on the cheek. I lift, unaware I'm trembling until I feel Braxton steady me.

I sit through the service feeling more disconnected. I would not cry. The service was short and to the point. I manage to stay strong, no tears. Even when attendees, mourners told me, I didn't realize Michelle had another daughter. I refused to cry. Ashley, however, was having a hard time. I look over to see her being consoled by John and Daniel. Braxton was about to put his arm around me. My look screams no. He puts his hands down, face screaming frustration.

At the burial, I'm shocked at the number of mourners. So many people I've never met or seen. I overhear conversations of how she would be missed, how she was a pleasure. Strangers knew a person I had never met. Confirmation that I never was a factor in her world, her life.

The final walk to the gravesite was exhausting. It took so much out of me. Despite it all, knowing she never accepted me, never acknowledged me, I still wanted my mother's love.

The undertaker recites the dreaded prayer, "*Earth to earth, ashes to ashes, dust to dust. The Lord bless her and keep her, the Lord make His face to shine upon her, and be gracious unto her, and give her peace. Amen.*"

I stand still, holding my breath, praying for strength. The wind brutally punches my face like a punching bag; it's trying to bring me down. My body sways. I will not fall. I will not fall. I can do this. I *will* do this. Deep breaths, my heart heavy, each beat echoes in my head, drums a beat I do not want to hear.

As the casket is lowered into the ground, I want to yell stop. I want someone to wake me and for it all to be a bad dream. But as the casket crept lower and lower into the ground, no one woke me. It is not a dream. She was gone. This was our final goodbye. I would never see her face or hear her voice again. My body aches. This is too hard. I feel weak; my body can't take this hurt. Just as I'm about to fall, I feel strong arms grab me.

"I got you, beautiful, I got you."

I fall into his arms. He supports me, holds me tight. He stands strong, my rock. I turn to face him, bury my head in his chest, tears fall soaking his shirt, but he doesn't care. He strokes my back, kisses me on my forehead, then my cheek, telling me, "It's okay to let it out."

"I got you, beautiful, I got you. It's ok. You're going to be okay. Let it out," he soothingly assured me.

I did, briefly, but I couldn't be weak. He's here now, but as soon as I do something to piss him off, he'd push me away. *No tears, no tears, no tears!*

I wiped the few tears that were shed and compose myself. I found my aunt Patti to tell her I was not going to the repast, opting to go get my babies. Going to the repast meant engaging in conversations with strangers, being scrutinized, and analyzed. Being with my babies was best.

*

Braxton and I make the thirty-minute ride in silence. The only noise is the sound of our breathing. I rub my hands over my face, immediately smelling the scent of Chauncey's Burberry cologne. Reminding me of his letter, my curiosity piqued. Since I was sitting next to Braxton, the letter would have to wait. My cellphone vibrates. I'm not surprised to see a text message from Chauncey. Slyly, I look at the message. It's an electronic card saying, "My thoughts and prayers are with you." Internally, I smile, he was definitely making his presence known, causing me a lot of emotional conflict.

Mommy and Jeff were entertainers, they love company. Walking in, it's no surprise that it's packed with the Simms clan.

"Hey, sweetie," Mommy gives me a kiss.

"Hello."

"Does my sweet thing need anything?" asked Uncle Charles.

"I'm fine, Uncle Charles," I give a weak smile. "Where are my babies?

Mr. Jeff carries them in. They both get happy when they see me, bringing an instant smile to my face. I grab them one-by-one showering them with kisses. Braxton comes over wrapping his arms around us. His touch, repulsing me. I, unconsciously cringe, rolling my eyes.

Mr. Jeff, Mommy, and Uncle Charles caught my annoyance, all looking at each other and giving a knowing glance that there was big trouble. We stay for a few hours, Mommy persisted that she keep the twins so I could get some rest. Braxton kept grabbing my hand kissing it. He was so annoying. I played sleep on the ride home.

Once home, I retreated to my bathroom. I stayed in the tub until the steamy water was chilled. Stepping out, I prayed Braxton was asleep. Relief washed over me when I saw him snoring, wrapped in my 1000 thread count Egyptian cotton sheets. I ease into the bed, close my eyes, and pray for strength.

16

Tsunami

Lawrence called eight days later. Word had gotten to him about Michelle's death. Two months, no call, no show. Well I know I inherited this act from him. I see it's nerve wrecking being on the other end. I didn't like it and he would know he royally fucked up our relationship.

"Hello, my daughter."

"Lawrence." I said, not in the mood for his shenanigans.

"Yasmin, I thought you were going to call me daddy. We're regressing."

"I was, but your actions for the last two months show me I foolishly acted prematurely."

"No, you didn't. Please call me daddy."

"No. So you heard Michelle is dead. It must be a relief."

"No, not at all. I'm sorry that she passed. But more so for you."

"Lawrence, you can cut the façade. I know you're glad your biggest regret is gone. Didn't you tell me I should distant myself from her? Well can't get any more distant than this."

"Yasmin, that's not true. Your mother and I had plenty of animosity, but I did care for her at one time. More importantly, I never regretted you. I love you. I'm sorry I wasn't there for you. I'm sorry I failed you again."

I take a deep breath.

"Yasmin, I'm so sorry. I know it hurts. I'm here for you. I will take care of you."

"Lawrence, you have showed me, yet again, how much of a poor excuse of a father you are. All that crap sounds good but the reality of it is, it's just words. But what do I expect, you *are* a lawyer; a master of word manipulation."

"Yasmin, why would you say that? I know I could have handled things much better and haven't been there emotionally. Everything that happened with Landon has me at a loss."

"What happened to Landon affected me too. She and I were each other's support system. I understand you're emotional. But that's a poor excuse for cutting all contact with me. You showed me I held no significance. So what, I needed you. So what, you have granddaughters. The icing on the cake though, was that bitch wife of yours. She cut off all contact with Eric like I would harm him, and she almost had Braxton arrested. The cherry on top of all this conniving shit, which should have been settled privately, had to become public because I had to file emergency papers."

"You're right."

"I'm not done! This became public which irreversibly did more damage to a volatile situation. My character, Braxton's, and your sweet Landon's character, all tarnished because the bitch wanted to be selfish."

"How can we correct this?"

"You can't. What you will do is bring little Eric home."

"His name has been changed to Lathan."

"His name is Eric. How are you going to tell a little boy who's been taught for four years his name is Eric that his name is now Lathan? He's already confused. You and your wife are ridiculous. Bring him home now."

"We're still out of state in Pennsylvania."

"Lawrence, I'm not playing these games with you anymore. Have him here tomorrow by three pm or any relationship you have with me or my daughters **will** be non-existent."

"Yasmin…" he begins, but I slam the phone down. Enough of this foolishness.

I look at the note Chauncey left and open it. Inside, there are two pictures of us at a charity event I attended with him. With Chauncey there was never stress. He had his faults, but his mood, demeanor never changed. In a room full of people, I had all of his attention. I never frowned. I never cried.

In the first picture, Chauncey had cracked a joke and I'm looking at him laughing. His arms wrapped tightly around me, he's looking at me with a cheesy grin on his face. In the second picture, we're kissing, but he's lifting me up off the ground, and my knees are bent at 90 degrees.

The note says,

You deserve to be happy.

You shouldn't have anymore tears.

You don't have to accept anymore bullshit.

You need someone who respects you.

I made you happy and will make you happy.

Let me be the man you need.

Let me love you the RIGHT way.

I am the one.

Chauncey

I hear Braxton coming up the stairs. I quickly hide the letter in the bottom of my drawer.

"Hey." he said hesitantly, looking at me not sure of my mood.

"I talked to Lawrence. Eric will be here tomorrow by three."

"Why didn't you let me talk to him?"

I give him an amused look. "You can talk to him tomorrow when he brings Eric home."

"You should have let me talk to him. He needs to know that…"

"Whoa. First off, you're welcome. I handled it. Do you not remember what happened at Jackie's when you went off? Get your son first, because legally, as of right now, you have no rights. Again, you're welcome."

"This don't make no damn sense."

"You're welcome," I said, frustrated.

"Thank you. What did you say to him?"

"I told him if he didn't bring Eric home any relationship between me and my daughters and him would be non-existent."

"Good. I'm going to make sure J.R. is here. His ass is getting served. He about to lose his damn rights."

"I have to warn you, he said Eric's name has been legally changed to Lathan."

"What the fuck? Their asses have taken shit too far. What the fuck, they think I'm just gonna sit back and let them run things? I'm ready for their asses."

I sigh. I did not feel like listening to him go on and on. Yes, I agree, Jackie and Lawrence are irrational, absurd, senseless, foolish, yes, all that and more. But, I didn't feel like harping on it anymore. My head was beginning to hurt.

"You hear me talking to you, Yasmin?!"

I scrunch my face up, "Why are you yelling?"

"You act like you can't hear. I was asking you a question. You hear what I just asked you?"

"No. What did you ask me?"

"That irritating. Why you ignoring me?"

"I have a lot on my mind."

"I do too. You bein' rude."

"Really? That isn't polite, is it? Pardon my rudeness. I dare not impose it on you any longer. Therefore, I'm going to go."

"Now you're being sarcastic."

"Later, Braxton."

"We're not done talking."

"I am."

"Where you goin'?"

"Out."

"There you go with that running."

"There you go with that ridicule. Being selfish, yet again. Expecting me to jump through hoops to appease you."

"What are you talking about?"

"You're stressed, I get that. But hell, so am I. I got a lot of stuff I'm dealing with. You ranting and raving expecting me to have all the answers, criticizing me because I didn't let you talk to Lawrence. Forgetting that I have him bringing him home. You're still going to find fault. I don't deserve this."

"I'm sorry, come here." He opened his arms.

"No. Even now, you're in the wrong but I got to come to you. Yeah, ok." I turn to walk out the door.

Braxton grabs me from behind, "I love you, beautiful. I'm sorry." He kisses me on the cheek.

"Get off. I'll be back. You want something from the store. "

"I'll go to the store."

"No, I need a break from you."

"Why you always gotta run?"

"I'm not running. I wouldn't leave my kids."

"Oh, just me?"

I sigh.

"I'll tell you one thing, you can go. My daughters aren't going anywhere. They stay with me."

"There you go. I'm going to get some air," I said through gritted teeth.

*

No surprise, I ended up at Chauncey's. We were in his game room playing a game of Uno, of all things.

"When was the last time you went out?" He asked.

"I haven't been out like you. I saw your picture in the NY Post," I said referring to the picture of him shopping with an attractive woman."

"Are you jealous?" He smiled. Them damn dimples.

"No, y'all look cute," I lied. They did look cute, but I was a little jealous and this was not a good thing at all.

"You lyin'."

"I'm not. You deserve to be happy and be with someone who can make you happy."

"The politically correct, corny answer. You talkin' to me, cut the bullshit."

I bust out laughing.

"So are you admitting you're jealous?" He gives me a look that makes me moist.

"Nope."

"What are you then?"

"Nosy. So tell me about your *friend*."

"Good one. Nothing to tell, she's my cousin."

I roll my eyes.

"You don't believe me?" He pulls out his phone, makes a call, and puts it on speaker.

A woman answers. "What do you want, Ugly?"

"That's how you talk to your favorite cousin?"

"Yeah."

"So what you got going on this weekend?" asked Chauncey.

"Going to Cali with my friend."

"Male or female?"

"None of your business. Although, thanks to you, I'm all messed up."

"You still got people hittin' you up 'bout that pic?"

"Yes, got my picture out there with you. People need to fact check. People looking at me all crazy. Hello people, I am his cousin. Ewww, just nasty. Females giving me shade."

"Oh, aiight I'll talk to you later."

"That's all you called me about, a picture?"

He shakes his head, "Yeah! Sike, no, I got a call coming in from my agent, I need to hit you back."

"Bye, ugly. And ya mama said she better see your narrow, high yellow ass this weekend or else."

"Bye, Quianna."

He disconnected.

"Chauncey, all that was unnecessary. You don't have to prove anything to me. We're not in a relationship."

"If I have my way we will be. I did that because I wanted to prove to you what I say is 100. I don't need to lie. You don't need any surprises in a relationship. It is, what it is. See how we having a good time? It can be like this all the time. Me and you never argued because we didn't need to. We work. Ball in your court. You ready to make a move?"

"It's not that easy. You're the cause of my grief. I never got to slap you for that mess."

"Give me your best shot." He laughs.

"Don't tempt me, I punch hard."

"I doubt that."

"You don't know what I'm capable of." I narrow my eyes on him.

"You just talk. You on't have any fight." He opens his arms. "What you going do?"

I walk forward and punch Chauncey hard in the chest. "That's for that Instagram stunt."

He grabs his chest and bends over. "Damn."

My turn to laugh.

"Damn Laila Ali."

"You deserve that and more. I came to you as a friend, confided in you and you posted that crap. You were wrong and that hurt me."

"I'm sorry for real. I was wrong. I just see what I want. He don't treat you right."

"Chauncey that was wrong. It was disrespectful. At the end of the day I am his wife. You wouldn't appreciate your wife picture being put out there like that."

"My wife wouldn't doubt my love or loyalty. He don't appreciate you like I do or treat you right."

"He does. He does loves me. He just got a bad temper."

"That ain't no excuse or reason to talk to you any kind of way. He wouldn't get upset if he was handling his business, right. Yeah I posted the picture but you were here for a reason, right. He did some foul shit, right. He should be mad at himself, not taking it out on you. "

I bite my lip.

"Why you still there? What's holding you back? Your girls? You know just like I will take care of you, I will take care of your girls."

"I know you would."

"I see you're still conflicted. I don't like you stressed. Let's have some fun. So when was the last time you went out?"

"I don't know."

"You need to go out somewhere. I would love to take you on a plane to Anguilla. See you in a black and red lil' something."

I laugh. "You are a mess."

"I like how those jeans are hugging those hips and thighs."

"Thank you."

"Want to go to the club? You can dance with me."

"Nah, I could dance, but you're too much of a public figure," I said.

"Well, dance with me here."

"Ha."

"You scared."

"You know I can dance, whatever."

He gives me a look, them dimples, damn.

"Turn on the radio."

"Being as though I'm lovin' your outfit." He puts on The Dream's *Rockin That Shit*.

We started dancing, having fun. He'd gotten better, but not better than me. But he started grinding on me, singing he's hooked on my body.

"Ain't just tryna get in your clothes
Okay, I'm lying
Damn, you fine and umm
You rockin' that shit like"

Chauncey pushes me against the wall and kisses me. His kissing has improved drastically. Gone were the sloppy kisses, now they were sensual, sweet. I run my fingers through his unruly curls. He lifts me, I wrap my legs around him, and we make our way to the couch, him on top. His hands go up my blouse. He begins to explore my breasts. His caress is what I've been yearning for, what I needed. He goes for the button of my pants. In seconds, they are around my ankles. My legs are spread. He rubs his hand over my pussy I and shudder. Just as his hands are about to make their way in my panties, I push him, breaking away from him. The common sense switch in my brain finally clicked on. His touch wasn't right. It didn't feel right down there and his body wasn't right against mine. I gotta go. I can't be here. This will not solve anything.

I scoot away.

"Don't stop," he said tenderly.

"This is wrong. I won't do this. I am married. This is not going to work. I'm leaving."

Too ashamed to look at him, I keep my head down only to see his erection. Damn.

"Yasmin, stay. Don't fight it. No secrets. No surprises. You deserve someone who respects you. Someone who will make you happy. I am that person. I love you."

"I'm sorry, Chauncey. No."

I pull my pants up, and then rush out the door to my car. I had to get it together. First thing I needed was a drink. There would be no breast feeding tonight. I stopped at some lounge and ordered a shot of tequila.

17

Runaway

Oh my god, what did I do? I almost fucked Chauncey. Braxton, damn. I have kids. I got to be smart. I don't believe I just did that. How am I going to face Braxton with a straight face? I know I smell like Chauncey. His scent was on my lips. My ass ordered one more shot. I'd go home with tequila on my lips and clothes before smelling like Chauncey. Hell to the no. Chauncey kept calling, but I ignored each call. I sat there for 30 minutes. Multiple guys approached me, trying to get my number. Despite showing my ring, they still pursued me. I got tired and left. I did change my mind about going home with tequila on my breath. I stopped at the convenience store and bought a watermelon blow pop. Mints would have been too obvious. I also couldn't take a shower right away. That would be the tricky part.

It was fairly early a little after seven. I prayed that the twins had Braxton occupied. It was quiet. I go upstairs into my bedroom. I take a seat on the bed. Braxton bipolar ass is on fire. I can see it in his eyes. I really wasn't in the mood. I didn't have the tolerance. I'm just going to let him rant. I will be quiet. Act as if I agree with the bullshit he is about to say.

"Hello." I said evenly, tequila doing its job.

"Hey." He is staring me down like he knows something. Stay calm, stay calm.

"Where are the girls?"

"My mother said she was missing her babies. She came to get them."

"Oh."

"Where were you?"

"Out."

"You dropped something."

"Hunh?"

He holds up a picture. It's a picture of me dressed up as a sexy Miami Cheerleader. I have on my provocative thigh high boots, a red and black bustier with too much cleavage spilling out. I have on black spandex shorts that make my thighs look like they were ready to wrap them around someone's back, yup Chauncey's. I have pom-poms on each side, face sexy, giving that, *it's on, tonight* look. I'd be envious. I remember Chauncey's ass reveling that night because eyes were, most definitely, on me. Knowing Chauncey I can only imagine what he scribbled on the back.

"*Ish. It must have fell out of the envelope Chauncey gave me.*"

"You left your envelope on the table."

"You read my letter?"

"What letter?"

Shit. I put the letter in the bottom of the drawer. I must have left the envelope on the desk. How did I slip up like that? Dumb, dumb, dumb, dumb, dumb. The picture was in the envelope. "Never mind."

"Where is the letter, Yasmin?" he said in his dictator voice.

"In the room."

"Where?"

"It's my letter. It's private. It doesn't matter." I go into our walk-in closet.

Braxton is right on my heels, "I want to see the letter."

"No, seeing that letter would not do anyone any good. I can't deal with anymore drama."

"Yasmin, give me the damn letter."

"Braxton give me a copy of the check you wrote Melania. Just like that ain't gonna settle anything, seeing my letter won't either."

"Yasmin."

"Braxton."

"Give me the letter."

"Really, what will showing you the letter accomplish? What are you to do, but get pissed?"

"I want to see what that mutherfucker said."

"For what?" I throw my hands up in the air. "He said the same stuff he said at his house. That he wouldn't take me for granted."

"Let me see it."

I don't put up a fight I get the letter and give it to him. "Before you storm off to Chauncey's house, he's not home. He's on his way to California."

"You got the whole itinerary too?" he growled.

"Actually no, but I could get it."

"Why the hell you entertaining this shit. Saving letters. Is that where you want to be?"

"No," I said half-heartedly, unconvincingly, sounding weak to myself.

"Oh, so you tryin' to be with Chauncey? You want that mutherfucker?"

"I don't want Chauncey. I am where I want to be with you and the girls," I said unsure.

He looks at me. I will not break. I will not cry.

"You're lying!"

"I'm not lying," I fight to hold my composure.

"You are."

"Like you were about wanting Melania?"

"You take everything to the extreme. I'm tired of you acting like a damn kid having a tantrum because you mad. Yeah, I gave Melania money so what. You took on a mutherfucker that you fucked as a client. The mutherfucker constantly disrespecting me, this marriage, and you still entertaining his bullshit."

"So what are you saying?"

"You know what. You right. Too much damage has been done. Go be with that mutherfucker."

"You leave."

"Chauncey got everything you want. You get out. My daughters aren't going anywhere. You want to see them, you come here alone." He flicks the picture at me. I want to pick it up and read the back, but I knew better.

"You really are crazy and need psychiatric help."

"You need psychiatric help. You the one who keeps running. I'm good."

"I'm not running away. I took a break. I don't want Chauncey. I am where I want to be."

He gets so close in my face I can see the steak stuck in-between his teeth, and smell the steak, onions, and garlic mashed potatoes I cooked for dinner.

"You are running. So you done with that mutherfucker?" he asked.

"Yes."

"If you see him in the store and you have MY daughters, you better go the other way and leave. I better never catch him touching or even looking at them or their way. Do you understand?"

This is the mess I can't stand. Argh! He got on every damn nerve I had. He irked me like no other. "You need to learn how to talk to me."

He ignores me. "Do you understand what the hell I said?"

"Talk to me like you got some sense."

"You been drinkin'? I told you about the drinking. What is your problem? Do you think?" he said with disgust.

I feel the tears coming. I can't deal with this shit. Don't cry. Don't cry. Don't cry. Don't cry. It's too late, I am.

"Now you want to cry. I ain't trying to hear all that." He leaves out of the room.

I go right after him. "I can't stand you. Yelling at me like I'm your kid. I am your wife. I do think. My only problem is you and your damn moods."

"I ain't trying to hear all of that. Go be with punk ass Chauncey. Bye."

My heart palpitates, my chest too heavy. I will the tears to stop, and let out a frustrated groan. I stayed there for minutes crying all the while Braxton ignored me.

18

Say What

Lawrence took my threat seriously. Little Eric, I mean Lathan, was at our house by one o'clock that next day. Braxton made sure the girls weren't there. He was going to give Lawrence a taste of his own medicine. Also, as he said, he had J.R and a processor there to serve Lawrence. He was planning to strip all visitation from Lawrence and Jackie. J.R. tried to get him to compromise, do some mediation, so we could quickly resolve this matter. But his stubborn ass wasn't hearing it. We would battle.

Lawrence tried to talk to me, but I couldn't. I was feeling defeated, depressed. I didn't want to be bothered. I had little words for him and everyone else, including Mommy. She knew something wasn't right. I'm sure she was tired of Braxton and my drama.

Braxton was just as stubborn as me. It's been five days since we'd spoken. It was ridiculous.

"Mimi," yelled Little Eric as he came in the kitchen, breaking me from my trance.

I smile. Little Eric could never say Yasmin, Mimi was his adaption of my name. It had been a few months since I saw him, he'd grown three inches and his hair had been cut into a low fade.

"Eric, how are you?"

"Mimi, I got a new name 'memba."

I swallow. This is some mess. I do need to talk to Braxton to see how he's going to handle this.

"I do, I'm sorry. How are you *Lathan*?"

"Good. I miss my sisters, you, my daddy, Unc Vince, Unc Horse. Nana, papa, ev body."

I laughed, "We missed you too."

"Mimi, is mommy coming to get me."

"No honey."

"Why mommy didn't take me."

"Mommy couldn't, but mommy loves you. She told me you are her bestest friend. The bestest son and she love you more than everyone in this whole wide world. Mommy always will be right here," I touch his heart.

He looks at me confused. "She can't fit there. She too big."

"I know. Remember how Mommy used to tickle you and make you laugh?"

"Yes," he said with his eyes big and confused.

"Remember how she used to give you kisses like this." I kiss all over him.

He giggles.

"You feel happy? You like how that makes you feel?"

"Yes."

"That's from Mommy. When you get kisses and tickles and happy, that's Mommy letting you know she loves you."

"I want my Mommy to come get me."

"I know, but she can't. I miss your Mommy too." I wipe tears away.

"Don't cry, Mimi," he said as he wiped away some of my tears.

"Where my daddy?"

"He's upstairs."

"Not that daddy. My other daddy."

Oh ok, this. How do I explain this?

Fortunately, Braxton comes in. I recap him and he looks just as lost as I for an explanation. It was time for me to get some air. Braxton was able to distract Eric by putting on the movie *Frozen*. I was happy he was back, but truthfully, this conversation had opened too many wounds. I do love him, but it's still difficult. My mind was cloudy, mood horrible. I couldn't right now.

His mother and father were out of his life. I didn't want him to have abandonment issues like me. Eric, I mean Lathan, needed to be reassured that he is loved. I would do what I could, but I was broken with my own issues right now... I still needed reassurance.

As much as I didn't want to do it, I had to see Chauncey.

Braxton is in the media room with Eric when I call him into the other room.

"I need to get some air. I'm going for a ride."

"How long will you be gone? Where are you going?"

This would be a test. No reason to lie. "To see Chauncey.'"

In a blink of an eye, his cool calm became hot anger. "No the hell you're not! I told you, that relationship and business is over. I thought you didn't want Chauncey."

"I don't."

"You don't act like it. You're not going over there!"

"I need to tie up some business. I won't be long," I sigh deeply.

"You're right. You're not going to be long because you're not going."

"You are not my father."

"You're not going over Chauncey's."

"You know me well enough to know I'm not going to listen."

He takes several deep breaths. "I know you going through something. I'm sorry for that. But I'm here, Yasmin. Talk to me. I'm here. Let me in. You can trust me. I'm not going anywhere. If you are committed like you say are, you need to cut all ties with Chauncey."

I agreed. He was right. I had to end all ties with Chauncey. Fantasy is the attraction he has for me, the growing attraction I had. Combined with the incident from days prior, I had to sever ties. I had really grown attached to Chauncey. I valued his friendship. He definitely has helped me a lot during these trying months, which was why I was going to see Chauncey. I just wasn't telling Braxton yet. But while I have love for Chauncey, I am in love with my crazy, moody, difficult husband. The lines had been crossed, and the two relationships could not coexist.

I test him. I had to know if he meant what he said. "That's what you say. I'm always jumping through hoops dealing with your mood swings and tantrums. I need a break. I'm not fucking Chauncey. I am talking to him. I'm going through a lot Braxton."

"Yeah, you puttin' me through a lot."

"Think about everything you put me through and the stuff I'm going through."

"Yasmin, you getting' on my nerves. First, I had to deal with Kevin, I'm not dealing with Chauncey. You going too far now."

"Braxton, don't tell me what I'm going to do. Let me handle things my way."

"Yasmin."

"I told you where I was going out of respect. I didn't lie. Do you think I'm just going to go fuck Chauncey? I'm not. I just need a loan." I smirked.

"You just don't know how to let shit go."

"At least I'm letting you know. I'm just trying to get a male perspective on things like you did!"

"Who you think you yellin' at? You need to lower your voice."

"You, obviously."

"Yasmin, I'm not going to sit here and play this game with you. You're acting like a kid."

"And if I go, what are you going to do? You leavin' me? You're gonna file for divorce because I didn't listen to your ass and obey?" I didn't want him to leave, but he was irking me.

"I'm not going to let you keep disrespecting me, Yasmin. If you go there you're telling me that's where you want to be. Like I said, play that game and see what happens."

"No, it's not where I want to be. I'm just going over for a few. I told you as a courtesy. As I said before, if I had something to hide or planned something I wouldn't have told you."

"Yasmin, go ahead and do that. I'm going to do what I need to do."

"What's that supposed to mean?" I asked, my heart dropped. Pride prevented me from being weak and telling him I was scared; that I needed him to prove that he wasn't going anywhere; that there would be no more hurt; and that he wouldn't push me away yet again.

"Exactly what I said?"

"So it's your way? I'm supposed to jump at your command?"

"Now you puttin' words in my mouth. You gettin' on my nerves. "

"Every time I turn around your ass is dictating some damn order or yelling, just being a damn ass. Enough! Why can't you be nice, calm, and supportive?"

"I've been here for you. I've been trying. You don't want to be bothered. You tell me to leave you alone. I touch you, you get jumpy. But let that clown Chauncey come or call and your ass go running. Hugging on that clown, letting him kiss on you right in my damn face. How the hell you think that feels?"

He gets in my face.

"My mother died hating me. How the hell do you think that feels?"

His face softens. “I know it’s fucked up. I’m trying. You won’t let me help you. You’re pushing me away.”

“Pushing you away! Really? You haven’t been trying.”

He lets out a frustrated sigh.

“You expect me to accept that half ass attempt? Your actions say otherwise. You don’t know how to talk to me. I have to check your mood to see if you have tolerance and if you can make accommodations for me. All on your time, your schedule.”

“I’m done talking about it.” He walked away.

He dismissed me, so I leave out the house making sure I slam the door. Once I’m in my truck, I sit there for ten minutes, praying he’d come after me, but he didn’t. I open the garage door and back out. I’m only down the block when my phone rings. It’s Braxton. I smile, but don’t answer. He calls again, this time I answer.

“Yes.”

“Come home,” he said in a low voice.

“I will… Later.”

“Now.” He sighed.

I hang up and turn the truck back around. When I pull in he is waiting for me. I open the back door to get my bag, Braxton comes behind me and bends me over. He unties his jogging pants and pushes my leggings down around my ankles. With my legs spread, he teases me placing one finger at a time in me, stirring up all my honey. He hovers close, the smell of his Issey Miyake intoxicating me, putting me in a trance. He rubs my derriere before sliding in me.

He fucks me hard. Grabbing my shoulders he thumps in and out of me. My 7,000 pound truck rocks with each thrust forcing me to bounce back harder on his tool. I take it all, reaching back and holding on, so he could give me more. Back and forth he pounces in me hitting my cervix, awakening nerves I never knew existed.

I can’t take much more of this. That’s it. Pound, pound, pound, pound, pound, pound, pound. My honey well responding oozing, squirting, my body in a spasm.

"Uh," I hear Braxton moan.

He gives me a minute to recover. He turns me around, takes off my shirt. I kick off my shoes, managing to get one leg out before he slides in me again. This round, he does a pace of nice sand slow. I wrap my legs around his waist, my arms around his neck, burying my head in his neck, inhaling more of the intoxicating scent.

"Look at me, beautiful."

I do.

"I love you," he pounds.

I close my eyes.

"Un, unh, look at me." He grabs my face. In a soothing voice he said, "I love you. I love you. I love you. I love you. I love you."

I wrap my arms around his neck and kiss him. I break away from our kiss, "I love you, Braxton."

He buries his head in my neck, sucks on neck. I hold him tight pull more of him on me, in me. Sucking my neck hard, he pounds. He takes turns sucking on parts of my neck, my chest. I know I'm bruised.

"Mmm, Uh, uuh. O, Hmm, Mmm Uh, Uh, Uh, Uh, Uh," we both moan. Nice and slow, deep and long. Soon, we both let go.

He's still in me when my phone rings. The phone, which is sitting in the arm rest, displays Chauncey. I look at Braxton just as he tenses. I reach for the phone and it fallsfrom the chair onto the hard carpeted floor. Braxton beats me to the phone.

I hear Chauncey voice echo through the phone. "Hey, Miss Lady. You got me waiting."

"Mutherfucker, didn't I tell your ass don't contact my wife. I'mma run across your ass. This time, my brother won't be there to save your ass."

"Fuck you! You ain't gonna do shit," Chauncey growled into the phone.

"Braxton!" I regain posture and reach for my phone.

He looks at me like I lost my mind. "Yasmin, tell this mutherfucker don't contact you anymore."

I take a deep breath. "Chauncey, I will call you back."

"Aiiight, Yas," he chuckled before hanging up.

"What the hell is your problem?" scolded Braxton.

"What the hell is your problem doing that juvenile shit?"

"I told you. I told him, y'all communication is over. His ass got one coming. That kiss on the cheek, mutherfucker knew when to pull that shit."

"Mr. Simms, calm ya ass down."

"I am calm. I'm tired of that mutherfucker and I'm tired of you pumping him up, encouraging his ass. Is that what you want? You want that mutherfucker?"

"No!"

"You ain't actin' like it. You have no business going to his house."

"Braxton, please. Chauncey is not a threat. The only threat is your bipolar ass with your demands."

"You bitchin' about Melania, who is dead. Even when she was alive, she knew our relationship was over and never crossed the line. That mutherfucker posting videos and shit doing bitch ass shit and you don't have respect for me to put that mutherfucker in his place. Your ass is out of order."

"Braxton, I will handle Chauncey."

"How?"

I shake my head. I can't believe we're both in the garage with our pants down, truck door open. "I'm about to go talk to him like I was planning to earlier. I'm ending all communication."

"I'm going with you."

"Oh, hell no. This isn't going to be a heavyweight Tyson knock out. I'll be back."

"I'm going."

"No, you're not. What, you don't trust me?"

"I don't trust him."

"You said the same thing about Kevin? And you fucked him." He says referring to the one and only sexual encounter I had with Kevin. The unfortunate incident happened right before Braxton and I reconciled. Like he said we had an argument, Kevin was there. A huge regret, but again technically we weren't together.

"That was your fault. And that was a low blow."

"You punch too. You keep bringing up shit that happened in the past. It's aight as long as you do it but when I say something, you got a problem. And Kevin's my fault, that's some bullshit."

"You shouldn't have pissed me off."

"Like you are now? My point exactly. Which is why I'm going with you."

I punched him in the arm, "Braxton Joseph Simms, you know damn well the circumstances were different. Don't stand there and insult me. For you to even come out of your mouth with that bullshit, *your* ass is out of order. So you think I would fuck him?" I asked through gritted teeth.

"Nah, I took care of that." He took his hand and spread my legs.

If only he knew how close I come to doing just that.

"Get off, cocky ass." I slapped his hand away.

"I am and you love it." I attempt to close my legs. He forbids it. With his other hand and that candy I affectionately love. He grabs my leg and place it over the second row seat, I fall back and he climbs on top of me.

I'm mad at myself, I don't believe I'm fucking this bipolar fool. Then again why the hell not, he feels so good. I use my free leg to wrap around his waist, pulling him close I grind and he fucks me hard. "Oh, yes."

"That's it. That's my girl."

My pussy is contracting, pushing all the goodness out.

"Put it all in me, baby, fuck me. Yes. Yes. Yes. You feel so damn good," I panted.

He bends down and bites my lower lip. My leather seats are squeaking. He's grinding me back. He nibbles on my neck, he knows that's my spot.

As soon as Braxton releases, we hear the door rattle.

"Daddy?" Eric, Lathan, calls out.

Braxton pulls up his pants and I struggle to untwist my leggings.

"Hold up, buddy."

Eric ignores him and walks through the door and I close my partially nude body in the truck.

"Mimi" he looks at me like why you sitting in the back of the car.

"Hey Er, Lathan."

"Can I go wit'choo?"

"Not this time. Nana bringing your sisters home."

"Yay."

I give Braxton a look, telling him to take him in the house so I can get my clothes on.

"Come on, buddy. You want some ice cream?"

"Yes."

When they leave, I scramble to put my clothes on. My shirt wrinkled, leggings sticky. I walk in through the garage into the kitchen. Lathan is sitting at the table eating an ice cream cone. He lays it on the table, creating a mess before announcing he has to go pee.

I give Lathan a kiss before he runs off to the bathroom, telling him to make sure he washes his hands.

"Braxton I'm about to go over Chauncey's for a minute." I smirked. His ass wasn't getting his way that easy.

"Why you goin' upstairs?"

"I need to take a shower, change my clothes."

"For what? What you tryin' to impress him for?"

"I'm not. Thanks to you though, I'm sticky."

He smiled, "Come here."

"Braxton, I don't feel like going another round with you. I got your point."

"Come here."

I walk over and he pulls me down and tackles me. He bites my neck. "I love you, Yasmin. I do. I do trust you. Besides, I just handled mine," he smacked my ass.

"You are so arrogant."

He whispers in my ear, "You got one hour, or as you say, I will bring my bipolar ass over there to get you. And I'm still going to beat his ass when I see him. Do you understand?"

"I am not your child. You got a lot of nerve. Yes, I fucked you, but I'm not happy. Me and you still have issues that we need to resolve. We are not good. Do you understand *me*?"

"What the hell does that mean?"

"It means your dick, no matter how good it is didn't solve a thing. You're still a liar and did a lot of out of order shit that I'm still pissed about."

"So what are you going to Chauncey's for?"

"Fortunately for you, like I said earlier I'm going to tell Chauncey to fall back. Let him know I can't keep him as a client, and not to contact me anymore."

"That's right." He smirked.

"There's that cockiness. Again, don't mistake this as saying I agree with your actions. As Chauncey said, I'm tired of all your surprises and orders. Nothing's final."

"Yasmin," he warned.

"Braxton, don't push me farther away."

19

Bedda At Home

That fool had my neck all marked up. To a stranger, it looked like he laid hands on me. I ring Chauncey's door dressed in jeans and a top with a scarf.

"Hey, Miss Lady. Are you okay?" He opens the door and I walk into the vestibule.

"Yes, I'm good."

"So that punk ass husband of yours still showin' his ass?"

I follow him to the family room. I get straight to the point because I know Braxton would knock on this door. "Chauncey, stop, I can't do this anymore."

"Why?"

"For the last few months I have been very vulnerable. I admit I've leaned on you more than I should have. You've been a friend. I genuinely appreciate all that you've done but I'm going to have to end our relationship, business and personal."

"That insecure punk got to you."

"Chauncey our relationship is wrong in so many ways, for so many reasons. I know you have feelings for me. Me keeping you as a client and friend is wrong."

"We've been working together for some months without a problem."

"The other day I came too close to having sex with you."

"You came close because you have feelings for me. You realize you need more. You're not getting the love you need or deserve."

"Chauncey, Braxton does love me. He's not the calmest person. His temper can be challenging, but he does love me."

"So that's what you telling yourself? That it makes sense because he has a temper? It makes it alright to act like an ass? Yasmin it doesn't, does it?"

"No."

"So why you acceptin' that? How is he loving you right when he's telling you what to do, how to feel?"

"It's complicated," I grab my face, "He doesn't handle things the best way, but overall he does have good qualities."

"I want you here with me. I want you in my life. I love you."

"You don't mean that."

"Yas, I do. I am the better man." He grabbed my hand.

"You are the better man for someone else, not me. I am with who is best for me."

"Yas, he constantly lies to you. He doesn't respect you."

I remove my hand. "Chauncey nobody's perfect. Braxton has made a lot of stupid, stupid, stupid decisions, but I know his heart. He loves me. Braxton and I have our problems, communication is one. It definitely needs to be better, but he's committed. I'm committed."

"Yasmin, you don't deserve that. You deserve more. I don't mean to be cruel, but you need to face the facts. He had a kid with your sister, and he lied to you about Melania. Stop making excuses, justifying shit for him. I know you can't force a relationship."

"Chauncey, I appreciate what you trying to do or make me see, but I'm not forcing anything. Braxton does make me happy and he loves his kids. He is a good husband and an even better father."

"I'll take care of you and your girls. You can stay with me. I got you."

"Chauncey, you do realize his ass is crazy. But it doesn't matter, I'm staying with my husband."

"So you scared? That's why you staying."

"No, I'm not scared of him. You should be."

"Ain't nobody scared of him."

"Chauncey I'm so sorry for sending you mixed signals, for leading you on. I'm going to work on my marriage. It's not over. As crazy as it sounds we balance each other. We love each other. I'm not ending my marriage."

"He gonna hurt you again."

My scarf slips off when I shake my head no.

"What the fuck, that mutherfucker put his hands on you?"

"Hunh?"

"Your neck," he took his hand and moved my head side-to-side.

"Oh, no that was from earlier," I said, embarrassed.

He gives me a crazy look, "You into that S&M stuff now?"

I couldn't hold my laughter, "No S&M. It was just intense."

"So you stayin' 'cause you like to fuck?"

"It's more than fucking. I told you Braxton knows me. He helped me love me. He supported me when I found out about my paternity. He was there holding me, telling me it would be okay. The ordeal with Landon, losing my mother, so many other occasions, he was there. He's not perfect, but when I need him, he's there. He's there holding me, assuring me it will be okay, showing me he loves me."

"I've done that, *can* do that, and more."

"He knows what I need without me saying. We have a connection. The extremes he went to in planning our wedding, proves his commitment."

"How we get so close? If he is all that, our relationship would have never gotten this far. Those things you said are in the past. What has he done lately besides bark orders?"

"I won't deny that lately things haven't been the greatest, but that doesn't mean give up. All relationships go through something. You have to decide if the relationship is worth saving, mine is."

"It's not. Yasmin you're in an emotionally abusive relationship."

"I'm not. You and I wouldn't work. The other day I stopped you because when you touched me it didn't feel right. Your touch…you weren't Braxton. Chauncey every time we were together I thought of him. That's how I got through."

"You're making a mistake."

I walk closer to the door. "Please Chauncey, even if I was leaving Braxton, I wouldn't jump from a marriage into a relationship with you. That's why it didn't work before and can't work. You never were or could be him. I kept comparing him to you. Even now, Braxton has my heart. He always has. The good outweighs the bad. I know it's crazy, but he is my one, bi-polar and all. He is who I want, love, need."

"Yas, you can't force it with him like I couldn't force it with Toya."

"I'm sorry things didn't work out with you and Toya. I understand what you're saying. People do grow apart. That hasn't happened with me. We still have a connection. I feel at peace when he holds me. I see love when he looks at me. My marriage is not over."

"Alright Yas, since you like being lied to, go home," he said, frustrated.

"I'm sorry. I'm sorry." I felt terrible. I really should have done this months ago.

"Are you?"

"Yes."

"You say all that, it *sounds* good. But deep down I know you questioning if he will stay loyal. You wondering if one day he gonna get in one of his moods and tell you he's done. Isn't that why we started dating before?"

"Goodbye, Chauncey."

I left very sad. What I said was true. I was committed to my dysfunctional marriage, but this was yet another loss. Chauncey was more than a client he ***was*** a friend. Just like his relationship with Toya, our relationship had come to an end.

However, Chauncey struck a nerve. Would Braxton….

20

In Ain't Hard To Tell

I look over at my ringing phone and dread the incoming call. It seems like I've lived three lifetimes since I last spoke with him.

"Hey, Eric."

"Yas, first my condolences on your mother's passing. Normally, I would be more tactful, but have you found anything that can help me?"

"I'm so sorry, Eric. I haven't. It's so much going on right now. Lawrence and Jackie are not very…. cooperative or ready to listen to reason. They are only seeing what they want. I don't know what I can do."

"Yas, I believe you tryin', but are you sure you can't get in Landon's house or office?

"I'm sure."

"What about Kevin?" He asked, hopeful.

"He's following behind Jackie and Lawrence."

He hung up sounding defeated and my heart broke again for him. Eric's trial was set to begin. Things were going horribly for him. There was no doubt he was going to be convicted. I knew he didn't do it, but Lawrence and Kevin was set in their ignorant ways. I'd try again.

Braxton and the kids were sleep. I left him a note saying I'd be back shortly. When I get to the law office, I see the title was now Taylor, Taylor and Powell. I shook my head. It was good Kevin was promoted, but his ego. I would use restraint, but my patience for all of them was thin.

I walk into Lawrence's office to see Kevin sitting in one of the chairs. Good, I was relieved to see Jackie wasn't there. I didn't have the energy to argue with her.

"Hello Lawrence. Kevin."

They both stand to hug me. I hold my hands up letting them know that was not a good move."

"Yasmin, I know you're upset. I'm sorry. I'm glad you're here, we need to talk. I just wanted to give you some space," said Lawrence.

"Yeah, I know distancing yourself from me seems to work for you."

"That's not true, darling."

I roll my eyes, "Another day, another time."

Kevin tries, "Yas, it's been so chaotic around here. I apologize. I know you have a lot to deal with. I'm sorry I haven't been there for you."

"Yes, I do Kevin. My husband's mess as you said before, right? Anyway, I did not come here to talk to any of you pathetic men about your treatment towards me. I came to discuss Eric's case."

"Yasmin, I told you before, I have everything under control. Eric is a done deal," Kevin declared.

"Yes, he will pay for what he did to your sister. The prosecution has a solid case. He will die in his confined cell," Lawrence added with conviction.

"Lawrence, Kevin. I know you don't want to hear this, but I know Eric didn't do it. I've seen him."

"Yasmin, what is wrong with you? I told you to stay away from him. Braxton did too," reprimanded Lawrence.

"Hold it, when did you talk to Braxton?"

"Months ago. He mentioned Chauncey stopping past his office. He told me he resolved the issue, I now know he didn't."

"I will tell you now, and I will reiterate to Braxton, I am capable of making my own decisions. Unlike you, Braxton, and Kevin, I went and heard all the facts before convicting him. Isn't innocent until proven guilty part of your oath?"

He ignored me. "You're not a good judge of character. I know criminals. They're desperate, they lie. They will have you second guessing yourself. He told you that for sympathy. There is more than enough evidence to support that he is guilty," argued Kevin.

"Don't insult me. Do you know all the activities Landon was involved in? The people she was in cohorts with?"

"It doesn't matter, Eric had motive. Witnesses place him at the scene, his sporadic behavior, and he's left threatening messages," continued Lawrence.

"Your testimony alone is enough to throw out the reasonable doubt theory."

Inwardly, I cringe at the thought of having to contribute to Eric being falsely imprisoned. "I'm not saying she and Eric didn't get into a physical altercation, but he's had opportunity before. I do believe he crossed the line and there was abuse, but he didn't shoot her."

"Yasmin, stay out of this? The right person is being charged. How are Braxton and my granddaughters?" said Lawrence, closing the subject.

"Braxton is still pissed about you and Jackie's stunt. The girls are fine."

"You know Jackie is struggling. This is very difficult for her."

"Didn't realize she was the only one struggling. Her little stunt was the cause of papers being filed which made this situation messier than it had to be."

"Yes, but Braxton played his part in his past."

"Like Landon played her part."

"You're saying she deserved this?" he said, appalled.

"Not at all. She didn't deserve that. I never would say that. I loved Landon like a sister before I knew she was. We were each other's only friend for a long time. Truthfully, it still was that way. I knew her, she knew me. For instance, Landon had a very strong personality that a lot of people didn't care for. There are many more Tonya's. Remember her? She is the wife of Eric's former teammate, Thomas. She claims Landon gave her husband an STD and he, in turn, gave it to her. I'm saying all this for a reason. Just like Braxton's past came out, Landon's skeletons are even more scandalous."

They both look at me.

"Is there something you need to tell us?" asked Kevin.

"No. I just know this is going to get ugly. This will be public record and I hate for little Eric to see his mother in a negative light." I couldn't tell them about Eric's assumption because they would dismiss it, so I tried a different tactic since they were being stubborn.

"Lathan. Please start referring to him by his name," persisted Lawrence.

Another battle I was not going to take right now. Braxton wasn't cosigning on that bullshit and I definitely agreed. Poor thing is going to be confused and twisted like my sister.

"Can you take me to Landon's? I need to feel close to her again. Has Jackie gotten rid of her things?"

"No." He puts his head down.

"Can you give me the keys? I want to go get some closure, get some pictures for... Lathan,"

"No, it's too much for you to handle."

"Lawrence, you don't know me well enough to tell me what I can handle."

"Yasmin, trust me. I've been there myself. It's hard, you don't need to go there by yourself," cosigned Kevin.

Kevin's brown-nosin' ass was getting on my nerves. "I don't want to trust you two. Just give me the keys. I can handle it. To deal with the crap I've dealt with in my life, I am strong. Neither of you could handle half the stuff I do and continue to."

"Yasmin, once the trial is over, we'll go together. I'm doing this for you. I don't want to isolate you anymore. And despite what you think, I do love you, my daughter."

I shake my head, "So you're not going to give me the keys?"

"No."

"Let me go on record saying, Eric didn't do it. The person or persons who did it is still out there. You're not serving Landon any justice."

21

Only Wanna Give It To You

It had been a long winter and today the sky was clear, the sun bright, and the temperature 78 degrees. Braxton drove a moderate 45 MPH down Interstate 295, in his new silver Maserati GranTurismo Convertible, an early birthday present, to himself. I took in the landscape of trees, and enjoyed the brisk wind on my face. I was using the time to clear my head.

"Hey, beautiful."

I roll my eyes, even though he couldn't see them behind my dark Ray-Ban sunglasses.

"I don't like the way things are with us. I miss you." He grabbed my hand, placing it on his thigh.

"I'm still mad at you for trying to collaborate with Lawrence and keep me from seeing Eric."

"That was months ago. I told you I was looking out for your safety. I can't have anything happen to you, beautiful." He squeezed my hand.

"Eric didn't do it. He wouldn't hurt me."

"That's what you think?"

"Braxton, I know. Maybe you should talk to him. You hung around the same people."

"Hell, no!"

"Asshole."

"Yasmin, I don't want to argue anymore. You have your opinion, I have mine. Can we leave it at that?"

"What about Javon? You know he suspect."

"Stay the hell away from him! Yasmin, enough."

I bite my lip.

"I love you. You love me?"

"Yeah."

"Yasmin you know my temper gets the best of me a lot…ok, the majority of the time."

"This is another. 'Accept this is the way it is' conversations."

"Your mouth." He shakes his head no.

"Your attitude. How long are you going to be tolerable? You drain me."

"Yasmin, come on. Why can't you talk to me?"

"I am talking to you."

"You're holding back. You're physically here. I'm not connecting with you mentally though. I want all of you."

Don't you get it? I'm scared to be vulnerable. I want to scream.

"Where do you want to go?"

"It doesn't matter."

We end up at the National Harbor in D.C. and I'm pleasantly surprised when we run into Horace and Monica. I hadn't really talked to Monica since our lunch a few months back. Her groupie behavior put me on notice. For my favorite brother-in-law's sake, I would be alert and very observant. No more Ty's.

I give Monica a hug and my, 'I'm not sure about you' side-eye smile.

"Hey."

"Yasmin, I'm glad to see you out. How are you? I wanted to give you some space."

"Thanks, I'm fine. Thanks for asking. What have you been up to?" I said, still apprehensive.

"Nothing much, working. I like the hair."

My curly hair was swept up in a long ponytail, hanging over my shoulders. The style looked good with my long diagonal print dress.

"Thanks. I love your do."

Her newly styled hair was dyed a honey blond with a soft wave, and stopped below her chin.

"I wanted a change."

"Well, nice change. What were you and Horace about to get into?"

"We were going to get on the Ferris wheel, then get something to eat. Do y'all want to come?"

I shrug, "We can."

The ride on the Ferris wheel, I admit, was fun. It had me being affectionate with Braxton. Braxton took advantage of my nice mood by hugging and kissing on me. I didn't mind, we needed this. It was beginning to feel like before my miscarriage, before the drama.

No one knew what they had a taste for, so we choose Panache restaurant. Panache offered an assortment of Mediterranean, French and Spanish style tapas, so everyone's palate was satisfied.

I order a glass of Sauvignon and Braxton didn't say a word. Even by the second, he was quiet. I was impressed. Tonight, he just might get some love. Horace and Monica were on the dance floor enjoying the electronic mix. Braxton had gone to the restroom. I was alone and content when Lisa Stevens approaches. As always, her Spongebob-shaped self has on too much makeup. Purple and fuchsia eye shadow, red lips, and one-inch eyelashes. She'd gone from bad to clown. Her dress was too long for her 5'6 frame, dragging the ground like a wedding gown train. I had no patience for her at this time.

"Yasmin."

"What do you want?"

"Are you happy now?"

I look at this chick, "Yes, I am."

"I see you out spending money, enjoying yourself."

"Lisa, now is not the time or place. Don't do nothin' stupid."

"Now is the time and place. Your asshole husband got me fired."

"You got yourself fired. Funny how he's an asshole now, but you've been trying for five years to be with that asshole." I yawn, and do a dramatic stretch moving my feet in position in case I have to drop kick this chick.

She laughs, "I did get some laughs though. Gotta love the news. Your husband's dick has been in every available crotch."

"Not yours, and you still want him."

"No, I don't. He was really taking a gamble messing with prostitutes. Those prostitutes will ultimately cause him to lose his job. It's just a matter of time before he gets the boot. You should be saving money."

"You are the one who took a stupid gamble. You lusted after a man who never wanted you, made yourself look desperate, and just ruined your chances of getting another reputable job because you've shown you are stupid. Again, you want my life. You will never get it. You are damaged goods in more ways than one. And don't worry about my finances, they're well taken care of."

"You're stupid."

"No you're stupid. Don't think I forgot about that incident at my shower. Next time you try to call me out, make sure you clean up your mess. Your ex-husband is now one of my clients. He's a contributor to my household. We both know his money is very good."

After dropping Chauncey, I had to pick up another client to compensate for the loss of income. It just so happens her ex, Michael, who's a software engineer, was referred to me.

"He hired you?"

"He did. I know all about you JB. Or would you prefer me just to call you Jawbones. Heard those jaws were strong. Also heard about that nasty infection of yours. Medical minute: your vijayjay should not disperse skittles or smell like death."

Michael was bitter about Lisa's indiscretions, gossiped more than the queen of media herself, Wendy Williams.

"Wh..wh..what?" She stuttered.

"You heard me."

Lisa storms off, my shoe still on her train causes her to fall. On her way down, her face hits a chair and I see some things fly from her mouth. I swiftly remove my foot.

"Oh my god! Are you okay?!" I fake concern.

The staff rushes over to get her up. Her dress is caught on something and rips right up the middle of the back, exposing her too small G string. Lisa gathers her dress in the back, trying to hold it close. Blood is dripping from her mouth and nose, landing on her yellow dress. Unable to walk properly, Lisa, clearly embarrassed, scoots her way out of the restaurant refusing help.

I push my food away, she had definitely killed my appetite.

"I saw that." Braxton takes a seat next to me placing his arm around me.

"I know. She shouldn't have wore that long dress. She tripped over her own feet."

Braxton snickers and kisses me on my cheek.

I lean in, resting my head on his shoulder. I enjoy listening to his heart beat in sync with mine. I missed this feeling. The wine had me feeling some kind of way, if Braxton just keeps his mouth shut, it'll be an awesome night.

"I know I'm not the easiest person to deal with or be with. Thank you." He said sincerely.

I smile.

With his free hand, he moves my chin towards him before kissing me deep.

There's a loud noise that interrupts us. We look to see a commotion just as Horace and Monica return.

"What's going on?" asked Braxton.

"Groupies were acting like girls gone wild because some basketball players were coming in. I see what you mean now, Yasmin." Monica says matter-of-factly.

Just like that, the affection was gone. Braxton removes his arm.

"Yeah, one girl took her shirt off. Crazy," added Horace.

Horace bro, if you saw Ms. Thing a few months you wouldn't be laughing, I thought.

"Yeah Yasmin, Chauncey was one of them. A couple of the girls ran after him. I should have told him you were here. I know he would have come to see you."

No this chick didn't. Granted, she doesn't know all about what we've been through, but she saw how Chauncey interacts with me. We did not need to run into him. If I had clearance that Chauncey was gone from the premises, we'd be out the door on our way home.

"I'll be back," said Braxton, as he attempted to get up, but I throw my leg over his and grab his arm.

Oh no, Braxton would not be fighting Chauncey again on my watch. I knew Braxton. "No, stay with me."

"Yasmin."

"Are you two okay?" asked Monica.

I don't even hide my displeasure. Monica looks at Horace, who looks just as puzzled.

I hold on to Braxton's arm tighter, get the waitress's attention and order him a shot of Hennessey, and me a vodka and pineapple.

I stood outside with Monica for 30 minutes waiting on Braxton and Horace to come out of the restaurant. Thanks to the alcohol, we'd both mellowed out. I couldn't wait to get home.

"Monica, never mention Chauncey around Braxton."

"I'm sorry, is that where all the tension came from? What happened?" she said, appearing sincere.

"Yes."

I see Monica's eyes get big.

"You…" is the only word I get out before I feel my hair being brushed to the side. Next, I feel moist lips on my collarbone.

I reach back, stroking Braxton's face.

"For you." He hands me a single lavender rose.

Feeling erotic, I turn around, grab his face, and give him a deep kiss. I give him a look, taking in all of his sexy caramel, fresh goatee, sexy grey eyes, with dark colored button shirt, black jeans and Giuseppe Zanotti sneakers. He knew what I wanted. It's a good thing he wore a long shirt because he was about to get wet.

We said our goodbyes and found a secluded spot. He took a seat on a bench. I look at him, he knows what's up and unbuttons his pants. Sugar Daddy is up, ready for attention, ready to be put to sleep. I kiss him while his hands make their way up my dress. Our kiss deepens, becoming more sensual. Within seconds, my panties are being eased down. The kiss is broken long enough for me to step out of my panties. My back to his chest, I hike my dress up, and slide on my candy. His legs wide open, with mine in between, I glide on and off my candy. It's so sweet, instantly I feel sugar rush.

His arms wrapped tightly around me, I lie back, slowly rotating my hips round and round. One hand is fondling my breasts, the other up my dress, rubbing my clit, teasing me, begging me to cum. Somehow, I resist the urge, all the while responding to his pleasure, back arched, hips moving vigorously. Hot breath on my neck, has my clit pulsating, threatening to send me over.

Aching for more, I stand, cutting him off, he reaches for me. As I look over my shoulder, Sugar Daddy is glistening, calling my attention, telling me to stop teasing. Turning around, I place my hands on his shoulders. He pushes my dress up while I straddle him. Chest to chest, lips intertwined, candy to my mouth, candy becoming a tongue, filling all of me, exploring all within.

He scoots down some, the simple movement has Sugar Daddy sticking, hitting that GOOD spot, paralyzing me, and causing my legs to shiver. My honey so thick and abundant, it's pushing that candy out. Braxton won't allow it, he takes my hips, gently rotate them while he gives me subtle pumps creating more sensations, stirring up more honey. He then pulls back my ponytail, and sucks on my neck before he gives me five solid pumps. I hold on to his neck pulling him with me, my clit touching the base of his dick. Each thrust casing friction. I'm about to cum. I'm about to cum. I'm cumming. I moan, my body elated, overcome with involuntary spasms. Tears rapidly roll down my face.

The wind is steady, feels so good against my skin, my tears. The stars are bright, the perfect contrast for the violet sky, hypnotizing, heightening my love trance.

Braxton places sensual kisses down my neck adding to my arousal. Braxton still hard and strong begins a deep grind in me that takes my breath. Sugar touches places not meant to be touched causing a tingle of pain and pleasure. My honey is hot, running over. My feet flat on the bench, I rock back and forth relishing the feel of his candy. It's flickering inside, hitting all sides like a ping pong ball, up, down, side to side, G spot 1000 points, G spot, G spot, G spot, G spot. My muscles contract, holding, sucking all that candy in, being stingy, not wanting it to leave.

I look up and gasp. Braxton never stops. Continuously he moves in and out never losing his rhythm. I'm relieved that Braxton never notices my unease. Only a few feet away a tall body stands still, watching our every move, never making a sound. Eyes transfixed on me, I don't know what to do. I didn't mean to roll my eyes back, I didn't mean to let out a moan, but the candy in me warranted attention. And that candy had me squeezing, pumping, rocking, and bouncing all over it. Honey falls hard, fast as if in a thunderous rain. That candy creating a puddle of honey so rich it makes a rhythmic beat, music, harmonizing with our moans.

Chauncey's cold menacing stare was the last thing I saw before my eyes closed and I let ecstasy blossom.

22

Diary

All this loss, I know I was depressed, rightfully so, but I had to get it together. Chauncey had respected my request. It didn't make it easy. I felt alone again. I missed his jokes, the conversation, and yes, his presence. Seeing him that night only made me miss him more. I feel bad for hurting him yet again. I contemplated calling him, but what was I going to say, *'Sorry you had to witness me coming so hard on my husband's dick?'* Besides I meant what I said, I was committed to making my marriage work.

Braxton had been calm. I knew it was because Chauncey was gone; he felt vindicated, but it angered me. I know it had to be done, but he should not get to have his way, yet again.

Braxton had taken the kids to Jeff Jr. house. I opted to stay home, busying myself with neglected housework. I was cleaning behind the étagère in the hallway when I came across a stack of mail. I rummaged through a lot of junk mail before I saw a bulky letter. It rattled me, it was a letter addressed to me from Landon. I take a seat at the nearby couch. My heart beats fast and I struggle to open it. I take a deep breath and begin reading:

Hey Yassy,

I wish I didn't have to write this letter or communicate to you this way. If only I could talk to you, call you, hangout, have one of our girls' day ventures. Maybe it would make it easy to say what I'm about to say. So much has happened since we stopped talking. I never realized how much I depended on you. I royally fucked up in too many ways. I take full responsibility, but it doesn't make it easier. I hate to tell you things this way but I have to.

I'm writing you this letter because I don't think I'll be here much longer. For the first time in my life, I am scared. I fear for my life and I've prayed every day that if he did take me that you and I could make peace. So if you're reading this, I am gone. Wow, so surreal. I know I had a lot of nerve and I guess God agreed.

I know you will, but please let my baby know I love him so much. Let him know he is the best thing to happen to me. Tell him I honestly thought I was doing what was best. Tell him I'm sorry I couldn't be here to raise him. Don't let him grow up hating me for the things I did and the monster I know they will portray me to be. Make sure he knows that even though our time was brief, I cherished each moment. He is the love of my life and I will be with him watching over him.

Yassy things have been strained between us, as they should have been. I've missed you so much this year. It's true you never miss anything until it's gone. This has been the hardest year of my life. I never appreciated your positive influence over my life. You always had my best interest in mind and really looked out for me. You are who kept me grounded. I wish I would have taken heed. Maybe I would have been wiser. Now, I'm caught in a world I can't escape.

I know I said it before, but please believe me. I am so, so, so, so sorry. I know there's no excuse for the way I betrayed you. I swear to you, I never intended to have sex with Braxton. I admit I didn't like him. I was jealous. I thought he was taking you away from me, but having sex with him was never my intention. I wanted to break you up. I tried, but not by having sex with him. That was being dumb and getting drunk. I know cliché, but it was. I honestly wanted Eric to be his father, thought, hoped, and prayed he was.

Eric was such a good man. I didn't appreciate what I had. I can admit now I did love him, but I was scared. I wish I would have allowed myself to love and experience Eric's love. But it's too late for woulda, shoulda coulda, my destiny was created by me. Although he may not want to hear this, tell him I'm deeply sorry and I did love him. I'm really sorry for ruining things for him and mostly taking his son. He is the better father (sorry Yassy, he is.) and I know he would have raised little Eric to be extraordinary like him. Also, can you tell Eric don't let the hell I put him through shut off his heart. He is a genuine, kind soul. He deserves a woman who will appreciate him and give him the family he deserves.

I am so sorry for the hurt I caused you and Eric.

Now that I know death is inevitable for me, I see my selfish misguided ways. Jackie instilled in me I was gorgeous, the best, a jewel, and should be treated accordingly. There's nothing wrong with knowing your worth, however, I see now she also taught me to resent men and miss out on love. She never wanted me to feel any of the hurt she experienced. She did what she thought was best and I would never ask for another mother. Ultimately, I know she loves me and all she did was for me.

Lawrence was in my life, but we never had a real relationship. I held so much resentment towards him for his womanizing ways. I learned to use him and other men. The rule was never to allow any man close enough to hurt me. I saw first-hand how, despite how strong my mother appeared to be, he made her weak. She was vulnerable. Vulnerability scared me. In college, I fell in love with Chris and you remember how that turned out. I saw how you got with Braxton, sorry Yassy, but you lost your mind. Even though I was the cause of your relationship's demise, which I repeat again, I swear I did not plan, it broke you. I could never allow myself to get vulnerable like that for any man. When Eric came along, he scared me. He had me feel emotions I never felt before. I tried to fight it, be with other men to get my feelings in check. He was my first love and I destroyed him. I was toxic for him. He didn't care. He proved he loved me over and over and I pushed him away over and over. I was never good for him. Our marriage was based on a lie and deep down I knew it would all come to an end. Although brief, it was good having someone there who had my back and dealt with my trying ways. It felt good letting go and feeling love. I also couldn't continue to be naïve. The truth would come out, I had to prepare myself.

I did some things I'm not proud of. I got involved in things I shouldn't have. I don't recognize who I've become. Let me just admit I entered a partnership with Javon and a guy by the name of Rocco. I know, I know, what was I thinking? No excuses Yassy, I wasn't. This is why I'm not here. I lost my mind and when I got it back, it was too late. The damage was done and my world was spiraling so fast, I was dizzy and it was too late.

In my office, you will find tapes and surveillance. Also, there is another letter that describes my involvement in this fiasco. Mama didn't raise no fool (smile). That letter will go into detail about my business partners. I have three copies, one at my house, one at my office and the final in a safe deposit box. Please make sure you are careful. I know daddy and Kevin are stubborn and will be in denial, so make sure it's given to the authorities. I'm not concerned about my image. So many wrongs, I can't correct them all, but I can correct some.

I know again I'm asking you too much, but you know me. I don't let anyone threaten me or back me against a wall. This chick right here is not leaving peacefully.

I hate to leave you and my baby. PLEASE don't let him forget me. Please let him know I love him.

I miss you Yassy and love you even more. My best friend forever.

One last thing, you know I have to say what's on mind. STOP BEING STUBBORN! I know stubbornness is a part of that Taylor DNA. Nonetheless, the asshole (he is and you know it), as much as I can't stand him (really I can't) he is who you belong with. I know no one can and will replace me (tears), but he got your back and he will protect you. But most of all, HE LOVES ONLY YOU and is COMMITTED. He's literally CRAZY for you. You two have some crazy telepathy connection and make each other better. So basically, you need him and he needs you. Told you I got wiser, lol. You have a friendship with Braxton and genuine love. I've seen the way he looks at you, seen the way you look at him. It's real. Your foundation is strong. Yassy I know you're scared. I know you're vulnerable, but let go, fall. He will catch you. You hear me, HE WILL CATCH YOU. He isn't going anywhere. You have done the impossible, tamed the beast. Let go and receive his love. If he gets out of order, show him the other aspect of the Taylor DNA, we don't take no shit. Seriously, he makes you happy and he has finally got you to recognize how beautiful you are and have always been. I am so happy for you. The twins are beautiful. I wish I could be there to see them and my baby grow. Let me also say this, your outfits, as of late, have been marvelous. It's about time. You definitely get my stamp of approval.

I wish our time could have been extended, however I'm at peace because I did know you. I'm glad I did at least get to see the woman you've become. Don't cry Yassy, I made my bed. Don't dwell and feel bad for what you cannot change. My spirit will always be with you. Raise your three kids together. Break the cycle, show them love the correct way.

Thank you for always being there for me, even when I didn't deserve it.

Until we meet again,

Landon

P. S. The green key is too my house. Security code is little Eric's birthday, 0716

The blue key is to my office. The code is your birthday, 0108

And the red key is a safe deposit box located at Wells Fargo Bank. The code is 11/18/09

I take a few minutes to get my thoughts together. Landon told me not to cry, but how could I not. As crazy as it is, I never fully accepted her being gone. In the back of my mind, she was on hiatus and would be back. But her letter is a sign for me to let go.

I wipe my tears, go to the bathroom to wash my face, and lock Landon's letter in a safe place. I knew I could not go to her place, I was sure to break down. The bank had too much traffic and I knew this revelation would be explosive. I needed to sit and process this. I think I'll go to Landon's office because it will be the safest being located in a busy traffic area, with plenty of security.

23

Testify

I pull up to Landon's office. It looked like a different world. It had been almost a year, so much had changed. Businesses had moved a few blocks over to the newly constructed office space nearby. The area was almost abandoned. I take a few minutes trying to calm my nerves before I go to the office door.

I step in the office, everything is sterile, vacant. Far from the usually lively, yet productive office Landon ran. She never believed in moping or quiet. As with this office, my life had the same void without her.

Her personal office is the same, plenty of pictures of little Eric, pictures of her parents, and us. Her desk also held copies of Vogue where she had tabs of fashion styles she would emulate, I'm sure. I rummage through the magazine, nervous of what I would find. After procrastinating, I finally open the drawer. In the drawer, under a forged metal divider laid a safe deposit box.

I punch in the code in the box. It opens and I see CDs, tapes, and a letter like Landon said. I take a deep breath before unfolding the letter:

I, Landon Taylor am writing this letter because I am in fear of my safety. The cause of my concern is based on two individuals' actions. Over the last few months, they have harassed, threatened, and abused me. I believe these individuals will inflict bodily harm, or even worse, kill me. Their names are Javon Davis and Rocco Esposito.

In September 2010, I was approached by Javon Davis about a business proposition. Mr. Davis, who I will hereafter refer to as Javon, expressed interest in becoming a real estate investor. He appeared to be very eager and anxious in learning the business. At that time, I suggested Javon enroll in a real estate program. Javon was very persistent, insisting that I taught him the basic laws. Javon was not interested in obtaining a real estate license or acting in the duties of an agent. His sole purpose was to build his financial portfolio with real estate investments. Javon and I discussed the time and effort involved in this task. At that time, we were able to negotiate a fee for my services. Javon signed a contract agreeing to this and gladly paid the fee. With my assistance, Javon was able to purchase several properties.

Javon, impressed with my services, thanked me and suggested that I offer my services to other athletes. He went on to explain that there is a huge market for athletes as injuries and salary caps plague the league, leaving a vast majority of athletes in financial strain. This would be the perfect forum for them to learn how to invest their money. He readily offered me money to invest in the business. Weeks later he would introduce me to another interested investor, Rocco Esposito. After several meetings and negotiations, I finally agreed to enter into a partnership with the gentleman.

The business was run accordingly. I offered several classes that included, foreclosures, short sales, tax liens, rent to own, etc. Each class was offered for a set fee. Enrollees could take one class or choose from several packages. To give a more a relaxed feel, our classes were held at different rented homes. The classes ranged from two weeks for the daytime schedule of 10 AM - 5 PM. Six-week classes were held from 6 PM - 9 PM, to accommodate the athletes training schedules during the day. Enrollees could take the class as often as needed as long as they paid the fee. Several athletes would later go on to become investors, as detailed in the attachment.

The money would then be split and distributed into three separate accounts. The agreement was that I would receive the largest portion of 66 1/3% since it was my business. Javon and Rocco would split the remaining 33 2/3 %.

Unfortunately, I learned later that Rocco and Javon used the rented houses to host parties of a sexual nature. I also found that I was being drugged. Javon and Rocco drugged me to the point of sedation. In turn, I was repeatedly raped. After a breakdown, I voluntarily entered Mountain Springs located in Colorado. There, I tested positive for multiple STDs: gonorrhea, syphilis, and chlamydia, as well as drugs: cocaine, mollies, ecstasy and others that I have never had any affiliation with, but were found in my system. This is also documented.

Upon my return, I immediately tried to dissolve the partnership, but neither Javon nor Rocco allowed it. I was forced to continue. Also, I was threatened for money and forced to give both Javon and Rocco 90% of my business. I adamantly tried to cease all operations, even threatened legal action, however, the threats were frightening.

An acquaintance, Melania Vaquez, who assisted with operations, would turn up dead. While I do not have any proof, the deceased and I had several conversations where she expressed concern and indicated that she had tried to get away. Attached you will see text messages Javon sent to me; one being the link indicating Melania's death.

Again, I am in fear for my life. If anything were to happen to me, I know it will be because of Javon and Rocco.

Also, as painful as this is to admit, I acted inappropriately. Javon took video of me with missing 16-year old, Janay Watkins. I do not recall the encounter, but you will see that we were engaged in very lewd sexual acts. I'm sure Javon and Rocco had me, as well as Miss Watkins, heavily drugged. I do pray that Miss Watkins is found safe and did not meet her demise like Ms. Vaquez and myself.

Please note attached to my letter you will find multiple documents to support my testimony, cancelled checks, along with audio, video, and discs.

Thank you, I pray the evidence collected will be sufficient in putting Javon and Rocco behind bars. My dying hope would be that they are stopped and unable to hurt innocent people anymore.

Landon Alise Taylor.

Wow. Landon, wow. Oh my God, Oh My god. I re-read the letter again and reviewed the attached documents. The first showed where Javon signed a contract with a cancelled check attached. Many more documents backed her claim showing, just as she said, athletes buying property, the threatening text from Javon, and the email indicating Melania's death. But I couldn't view the tapes. I didn't want to see the drug induced, shell of my sister being raped and abused. I stood up placing the contents into my huge purse, preparing to leave. It was still early and the sun was out. I had to get out of this office and handle this.

I open the door, feeling on edge. I look around and don't see anything out of the ordinary. I step out to close the door to lock it when I'm pushed back in.

Panic fills my body, quickly I get in attack mode. I turn around quickly to get away from my attacker. I am shook when I see Javon.

"Javon, what are you doing?" I ask in a shaky voice that I unsuccessfully try to settle.

"Why you so nervous?"

"Because you scared me. You just came behind me and forced me back in here."

"It's just me. You can relax."

"I'm good now, but I was on my way home."

"You can't talk to me for a few minutes," he said coolly.

"Not now. I have an appointment. That's why I was leaving out." I lied.

"Oh, is that so."

"Yes," I manage to say calmly.

"What made you come here?"

"Why are you here?" I counter.

"Just still in shock about Landon. It's a shame what happened to her. We got close when y'all stop talking. I miss my buddy. I ride pass here from time to time. I keep on expecting to see my buddy walk out of here."

"We were here for the same reason," I say uneasily. "It's honestly too much though. I need to get out of here."

"This is my first time in here since you know," he continued.

"Well, I gotta go. Lock up for me when you leave." I try to walk pass him, but he blocks me.

"Javon, let me go to my car."

"No."

I scrunched my face, "Javon."

"I wasn't done talking to you."

"Oh," I look to the ground too nervous to look at him.

"So how's my friend, Braxton?"

"He's good."

"Yo, why you tell him I tried to fuck you? That was supposed to be our little secret."

"I don't know."

He looks me over, focusing on my breast, making me even more nervous. "You know."

I swallow, "I was mad at the time."

"I'm mad now."

I don't respond.

"What do you have?"

"What are you talking about?" I play naïve.

"Listen, I ain't got time for the games. I know your ass got something. What you got in the bag?"

"Javon, really, I don't know what your problem is, but I'm leaving."

"Give me your bag."

"No."

"We can get rough."

"Now you sounding stupid. You want to attack me over a bag. I need to go home to my husband, Braxton. Remember him?"

"I thought you had an appointment?"

"I do."

"Bitch, stop lying." He slapped me across the face.

I hold my stinging face.

I look for an escape. "Here, take the purse, now move."

He snatched the purse. "Good girl. You owe me something though."

"Javon, I gave you the purse, we even."

"No, we not. I need to sample this." He grabbed my crotch.

I smack his hand away, "What the hell is your problem?"

He grabs my neck, grabbing my crotch again.

"Ummm feels nice and plump even through them jeans. I know it will feel even better fucking the shit out of you," he laughed.

I was so glad I wore jeans; he would not be getting my pussy easy. I would fight it to the end.

He released my neck and private area.

I back away, "Javon, get the hell away from me."

"Nope."

"You doin' all this for some pussy?"

"Yes and no. You know something."

"I don't know anything."

He dumps my purse. Everything comes falling out, wallet, phone, lip gloss, gum, lotion, keys, papers, cd's. Javon looks at me. "Pick up the paper and give it to me."

"No."

He strikes me across the face, even harder than before. I smack him back this time. He grabs my hair, yanking it hard. The strength of his muscular 250-pound body forces me down.

"Hand me the got damn papers."

I do as he says, handing them to him.

He scans the document.

"Um um, damn. Your girl done fucked up now. Just like you, she couldn't keep her mouth shut. What am I going to do with you?"

I start hyperventilating.

"Calm down, I didn't do anything.....yet."

I cry, breathing still strained, "I will keep my mouth shut."

"Like I would trust you."

"You have all the evidence now. Everyone thinks Eric shot Landon. I won't say anything. I won't tell."

"Tell what?"

"You sh,sh, sho-t her." I stutter.

"Who said I shot her?"

Tears rush down my face. "Please, please, please. I won't tell. I won't tell. I don't know anything. It's too much traffic around here. Someone would notice. Don't hurt me," I attempt to rationalize.

"Fuck me good and I won't. Then again, I might."

"Please. Please." I begged.

"You just had to fight me. This was going to be our little secret. Now, I'm going to have to hurt you."

"You think nobody will put two and two together?"

"If they do, it'll be too late."

I screamed like a mad woman, my pants halfway on my butt.

He wraps both hands tightly around my neck. "You're going to take these pants off and spread these legs. I don't care if I got to fuck you with my fist, I will fuck you! Do you understand?"

I don't respond, restricted air, I feel dizzy. I nod.

Just as I was about to pass out, he releases my neck. His breathing is still labored, but he's still and for a minute, I think I have time. "Bitch, do you hear me talking to you? I want these pants off. And you better not try any shit."

Two police officers come rushing through the door immediately grabbing Javon off of me. My kicks from earlier still had him struggling to gain his composure, making it easier for the officer to handle him. They cuff Javon, drag him over to the corner, and call for backup. What Javon didn't know was that Landon had a panic button on the side of the drawer. Lawrence insisted that it was installed when Landon first started this business, for stalker or other crazy clients she came in contact with. Fortunately, for me, she did or else… I wipe away tears.

One of the tall male officers walk back over to help me up, "Are you okay ma'am?" he asked.

I wince from pain, the pain causing me to hold my breath, unable to speak.

"Ma'am.

I nod while I pull my pants completely up, fastening the top button.

"Where are you in pain?"

"My hip. He pulled me down," I said with tears rolling down my face.

"Do you want me to call an ambulance?"

"No."

"Were you assaulted in any other way?" The officer looks at my ripped shirt and unbuttoned pants. Quickly, I try to close my shirt, completely fasten my pants, buttoning the second button. I fold my arms across my chest to keep my shirt closed.

"No, he tried."

I turn my back to the officer and scan the desk for anything. I pick up a stapler and staple my shirt close with 10 staples. The shirt is jacked up and the staples only unravel the delicate material.

"Ma'am, you sure you don't want an ambulance."

"Yes," I said trembling, trying to calm my frazzled nerves.

By now, the other officer is reading Javon his Miranda rights. He is bent over suffering from the kick from my heel.

I limp up to him and spit in his face. "Rot in hell, mutherfucker."

Javon lunges forward catching the officer off guard making him fall forward. He almost head butts me, but the officer who was talking to me prevents it by stepping in and blocking it. He then pushes Javon back hard causing him to fall on his ass.

"Fall back!" the other fallen officer warned.

The tall officer touches my shoulder, "Are you okay?"

I nod.

"Ma'am, we need you to give a statement."

"Can I please call my husband first?" I look over at my shattered phone. I know Braxton was 1000 ways of crazy by now.

"Yes."

"Actually, can you call him?" I take a seat in a chair in the opposite corner.

He does. I hear the officer telling Braxton that I was involved in an altercation, but couldn't give any details over the phone. The officer then requested he come.

"She's fine, sir... I can't answer that… Please come to 55 Millers Road."

"What do you mean you can't answer that? How you going to tell me my wife was involved in an altercation and not give me any details?!" I hear Braxton yelling.

I shake my head, *this fool.*

"Sir, you have the address." The officer hung up.

"Sorry about that. He's very protective," I explained.

"It's okay. I'd be the same way. I do suggest you go to the hospital. Are you sure you don't want any ambulance?"

"I will go."

"I need an ambulance," Javon whined. "I'm suing y'all asses. Excessive force, police brutality."

"Shut the hell up!" the fallen officer yelled.

Javon laid on the floor playing the victim role, screaming as if he is in agony, about to die. While the officers collected evidence, it allowed him a few minutes on the floor. When the additional officers arrive, they begin pulling him up. They sit him in the chair to catch their breath because he is uncooperative and 250 pounds of dead weight.

Braxton arrives in record time. I see him through the open door and window. He jumps out of the truck, engine running. He runs through the door to see my ripped shirt, my cheek, which I'm sure is red, and pauses. In a manner of seconds, I see relief, to panic, to fear of what transpired cross his face. He looks around and spots Javon in handcuffs. His eyes of fear rapidly become a blackout, and that's just what he did. I swear, in a blink he was punching Javon. I saw Javon go down and Braxton go down with him as he continued to punch him. Two cops are trying to restrain Braxton, but it's useless. He continued to assault a lifeless Javon. A third and fourth officer come and struggle to restrain Braxton.

"What the hell did you do? You touched my wife?! What the hell did you do?" he roared. He kicks at Javon landing multiple blows to his sides.

I try to stand, but the pain in my hip sits me back down, "Braxton! Braxton! Stop! Braxton, come here!"

Braxton is still in need of restraint. Three officers restrain him while two officers put him in handcuffs. They escort him outside cuffing him to a metal fence. Braxton delusional thinking he could break free, tries. I push through the pain and walk up to him. I wrap my arms around him and lay my head on his chest. "I'm okay. I'm okay. Please calm down."

He bends down and kisses me on top of my head. His free arm wraps tightly around me. "Look at me, Yasmin."

I ignore his request, not ready for him to see my stinging cheek.

"Look at me," he demanded.

I didn't want him going off again, but fortunately he was handcuffed. With hesitancy, I look up, "Calm down."

Of course he tries to break free from the fence. I step back, wincing like he really was going somewhere. My obvious pain puts him on alarm.

"That motherfucker didn't, that mutherfucker didn't," he paused, unable to get the words out becoming more enraged by the millisecond.

I grab his face, "No! He didn't. No! I'm okay, I just fell."

Relief washed over his face and he pulls me close and I shudder from the pain in my hip.

Shortly thereafter, Javon is escorted to the police car. Braxton again unsuccessfully tries to go after him. The cops leave Braxton cuffed, which was a good thing. I had to give my statement again. As I recanted the story, Braxton's demeanor unraveled. I know his fists were bruised from the many times they hit the fence. The police advised me to go to the ER to check my hip out and document the injury. Reluctantly, Braxton was freed after multiple reassurances on his end that he would not cause more of a scene. When he was freed he swooped me up and carried me to the car.

24

Emotional

I was examined at the hospital. Mommy, Mr. Jeff, and Horace were called. Willingly they came, tending to me. It was overwhelming, but appreciated. I had a nasty bruise on my side that set my protector off, but nothing was broken. I asked the doctor to give him something to calm his ass down. Of course, they didn't. Mr. Jeff fortunately was able to settle him down. Patrice and J.R. kept the twins for us since I wasn't discharged until after eleven.

Braxton helped me upstairs since it was so painful to walk. He ran me a hot bath filled with Epsom salt, coconut oil, and some aloe vera.

Braxton sat on the chaise inside of our massive bathroom watching me, "You're not getting in?"

He shook his head no. I knew he was pissed.

"Baby, come get in with me."

He's quiet, meaning he was about to blow, 5, 4, 3, 2, and 1.

"What the hell were you thinking? Do you think sometimes? What are you trying to prove?

"Braxton, please get in the tub with me. I will answer all of your questions."

"No, answer my questions now."

"Braxton, get in," I said sternly.

He disrobes and slides in the huge Jacuzzi tub sitting across from me so he could stare me directly in the eyes. "Speak."

I look him in the eyes. "Landon wrote me a letter before she was shot. In the letter, she touched on some of the things she got into. She wanted me to go to her house, her office, or a safe deposit box to get evidence. She knew something would happen to her." I paused. "She said she was being blackmailed by Javon and Rocco."

I watch Braxton's body tense.

"Who is Rocco? How do you know Rocco? And to what capacity do you know him?"

"Rocco is someone you don't need to deal with."

"Braxton, tell me."

"Rocco is involved in a lot of illegal activity. I don't know all the details. I do know he is ruthless."

"How do you know so much?"

"I've seen him at parties, so I have been in his company. Heard stories, but I never dealt with him on any level."

"If he was so ruthless, why were you in his company?"

"Yasmin, I come across shady characters all the time in the entertainment industry. I wasn't dealing directly with him. I went to the parties to be entertained, not business, so our paths never crossed.

I study his face, body, for any sign of untruth. There was none.

"Landon said she, Rocco, and Javon would have exclusive parties. I assume you attended some of these parties. Especially since you admitted to having sex with 45 women when we broke up."

"That's not important. What's important is you not using any sense and going to places you should have had the common sense not to go to ALONE in the first place," he snapped.

"Who was I going to go with? I didn't know what I was going to find or that I would run into Javon?"

"Yasmin, that letter told you Landon was into shit way over your damn head. Javon almost… damn!" He knocked over the soap dish.

"Braxton, please calm down."

"You too damn calm. You don't realize what almost happened and what else could have happened. That sheisty mutherfucker!" He stood up.

"I do know what almost happened! I lived it. Shut the hell up! I know!" My body began to tremble and tears fell freely.

Braxton takes a deep breath. He comes behind me, easing his body into the tub behind me. "Beautiful, I don't mean to yell. I just love you so much. I'm mad I use to call him a friend and I think of what he would have done to you. I just keep thinking you could have ended like Landon."

"I know, I know. Just hold me, please. And be quiet."

He does.

After several minutes, I speak. I let go. "You have a tendency to isolate me when you get upset. You do. It's a double standard. You expect me to be able to deal with everything. You forget I have feelings. I'm supposed to deal with your moods and accept whatever you say or do."

I'm sorry."

"Sshh. I need you to listen. I am tired. Every time I turn around there was something. I tried to be strong, but I couldn't catch my breath. When I stayed over at Chauncey's it was a bad decision. But, it was never intentional. I should have called you, but I admit I was very angry and part of me wanted to get back at you."

He takes a deep breath.

"I lost a lot. I'm dealing with a lot. I confided in Chauncey because he was there. He didn't put any expectations on me. Hanging out with Chauncey was relief. It was an escape from the chaos. We did crazy things like pillow fight, play Uno, karaoke. It was never serious stuff, we just had fun."

His body tenses.

"I did feel terrible that you caught me at Chauncey's like that. But you wouldn't talk or listen to me. All you were concerned about was I didn't do what you always expect me to do. I embarrassed you. You forgot everything I did to show you I love you, that I was committed to you. Instead you flipped on me. I couldn't be trusted and you pushed me away. The pelvic exam, really? You didn't talk to me, you ignored me. I made a lot of sacrifices, put up with your shit and your moods."

"You're right."

"Which is why it was so easy for me to go to Chauncey. You have to talk to me. Tell me the truth, no matter how hard it is. You haven't done that. Lately, I haven't. When we don't talk to each other it allows disruption. Ty telling me how you and Melania were so good together, were supposed to end up together."

"That's a damn lie. I was never gonna marry Melania. You know her ass ain't too bright," he said adamantly.

"I told her that too, dismissed her claims of you giving Melania money as her trying to start shit. However, I find out the dumb chick was accurate and I'm looking dumb instead. No, not a good thing at all especially since I asked you. She planted that seed. Your lie watered it, made it grow."

"I'm sorry."

"You should be. You pushed me to Chauncey. He was there being honest, gentle, sincere. He was willing to give me everything I needed." I pause to let it sink in, "But, I didn't want it from Chauncey, I wanted it from you. Although I may have said no, emotionally, I was screaming yes to him. I played his emotions, allowed his feelings for me to manifest. I'm not saying he never would have crossed the line, but it didn't help. So any issue you have with Chauncey drop it. It's not his fault, it's mine." I turn my neck to look at him.

He gives a look that said he wasn't cosigning with the bullshit. "Okay."

"By me turning to him it gave him opportunity. You have to understand and accept Chauncey was there for me each time YOU fucked up. He didn't yell, he didn't turn off his feelings. I'm not saying all this to hurt you. I'm just trying to get you to understand where I was. I was at a loss, too much was happening."

"What are you trying to tell me, Yasmin?"

I take hold of his arm, "I want you to know although I grew closer to Chauncey, you are the only one I've been with since 'I do.' I have ended my business and friendship with Chauncey. I have not talked to Chauncey at all since the day I told you I was going over there. And I apologize for bringing Chauncey into our marriage."

"Thank you."

"I love you, Braxton. You are who I want, who I need."

"I love you, beautiful."

"We're in this together. You are supposed to come to me. Physically we've always been good, but I need you more than just physically. I need you emotionally."

"I'm here."

"I need to be able to be weak sometimes. I need to be vulnerable. I'm scared to be weak. Scared that if I do, you will push me away and won't be there." I hold my breath.

"Yasmin I'm not going anywhere. I love you don't worry about that. You can be weak. I got you, beautiful. I'll always be here holding you," he pulled me closer, whispering in my ear, "I love you. You can be vulnerable. You and me. You are the only woman I ever wanted. The only woman that had me. You are my queen, my life."

I exhale. I don't fight it or hold it in any longer. I hold on to his arm and do something I needed to do for a long time, grieve. I cried for being attacked earlier, cried for Landon, cried because he did love me and I knew he would be that strong man I needed. But finally, I cried for the loss of a mother and the mother's love I never would receive.

When I finally stopped, the water was frigid and my skin was wrinkled. Ironically though, I was comfortable, at peace because Braxton remained holding me, kissing me softly, and rocking me slow.

Even after he carried me from the tub, he covered my shivering body before his. He robed himself, returning with massage oil and lotions. Lathering my body gently, he was everything I needed and more. When my aching body was soothed he climbed in bed with me, wrapping his strong arms around me, whispering in my ear, he again told me he loved me, assured me he wasn't going anywhere. Told me I was his life.

25

No More Tears

I lived the past year without Landon in my life, I always felt loss but now the finality left another void in my fragile heart. I was so tired of heartache. Discovering her letter, seeing all she went through, and understanding how her unfortunate choices caused a chain of events that caused her demise, didn't make it easier. How was I going to move on without having my girl, my best friend, my sister in my life?

I slowly walked hand-in-hand down the corridor with Braxton. My body was still sore from Javon's attack two days prior. While the swelling on my hip had gone down, my limp was still prevalent. We had made the two-and-a-half hour dreaded trip to Pennsylvania. This visit was necessary, yet painful. When I reached the door, I paused trying to get my nerves together. I opened the door, the sight as horrific as I remember. Landon's lifeless body lay comatose in a hospital bed, her body and head swollen from excess fluid. A complete contrast of her former self. The sight not easier than before, I lean on Braxton for support. He holds me up, I close my eyes praying for strength.

Yes, Landon was physically here, but her spirit was not. Stuck between two worlds I suppose. The doctors resuscitated Landon that day. Although her body said it was tired, Jackie said otherwise. Jackie determined, made them bring her baby back. She didn't care that blood flow was lost to the brain for an undisclosed period of time, that she was brain dead, legally dead, only surviving due to the aid of life support. Her baby was only sleeping, resting, gaining strength, would eventually fight and become the survivor she was.

I ease slowly in, taking a seat next to the bed, and grab Landon's hand.

I begin, "Hey Land. I miss you so much. I have so much to tell you. First, your baby is beginning to look just like his Mama. He was already adorable so you know now, he is gorgeous. He is also full of personality like his mama; he don't take no ish. He is very inquisitive too, loves to talk and has to be entertained. Yes, just like his mama. He is your child. I tell him all the time that you love him most."

I look at her, looking for any movement or sign that she could hear me. I received none.

"My daughters are almost one. Eric is very protective of his sisters. The twins are beautiful. Everything I prayed for and more. Personalities are the same yet different. Reagan is the calmest, really subtle and sweet. Khouri she's sweet, but she runs the show. They're both too spoiled. I know you would spoil them too. I can only imagine what their wardrobe would look like."

I take a few moments. Braxton squeezes my shoulders.

"I finally read your letter. I never knew you got so caught up. I'm so sorry you had to go through all of that. I still don't know who did this to you. Only you can answer that question. Javon is getting some of what his ass deserves. Four women have come fourth saying he drugged, raped and abused them. Sadly, I know they're many more. Rocco whoever he is, is still walking the streets. The girl Janay, unfortunately, she didn't make it."

I wipe away tears.

"Unfortunately, Eric is locked up. Our father and a lot of others believed Eric did this to you. I did too for a while. Nonetheless, I talked to Eric and I knew he wasn't guilty. Your written confessions I'm sure will exonerate him."

Braxton rubs my shoulder.

"I'm glad that we were able to talk and make amends that day. I wish we had more moments together. We have so many memories, so much we should be doing. What's important though is, we made up."

Still nothing but a lifeless Landon, machines forcing her chest to rise and fall.

"Land, even though I made amends with you, I never got a chance to with my mother."

I pause, "Land my mother is dead. She died and we never got it right. She died with so much resentment towards me. I'd never thought it would be like this. It still hurts. I wish I could hear your voice. I need a word from Landon on how to deal with this,"

I inhale deeply. I didn't want this mute Landon. I need her voice. Landon got me through the toughest times.

"Kevin is marrying Nicole. I'm sure you'd have a lot to say about her. Something is definitely off, but hey, Kevin loves her so, oh well. I support him. Can't pick our friend's spouses, as you learned from me," I laughed.

"I know you regret how things went down. Land, I know it was not intentional and I know how sorry you are. It still hurts, but if I could have you here fussing about my hair and uptightness..." I paused. "Every day is a struggle. Life just isn't the same without you. We've gone through so much together. I never thought you'd leave so suddenly. It's hard, but I know you're near so I'm going to somehow get through. I love you, Land."

Jackie walks in startling us. She speaks, I nod. Braxton ignores her ass. It will be a long, long, long time before he spoke to her ass. Who could blame him?

I back away to give her access to her daughter, she encourages me to stay, but I've said all I had to for this visit. Besides, the energy had been shifted. She takes my seat. I stand by the door observing her.

She loved Landon, believed she was making her strong. And in many aspects she did, however she also robbed her of experiencing love. Landon had plenty of self-love, but she never got the chance to fully experience being in love, having someone love you back. For a brief time, she did with Eric. Ill-advised by Jackie telling her that love equaled weakness and was never an option, ultimately lead her to make horrible choices.

Looking at both mother and daughter was heartbreaking. I glance at Braxton, seeing compassion and sympathy as well. Jackie was suffering. Jackie never in a powerless position, didn't know what to do, how to handle this. I could never tell a parent to let a child go. Medically the answer is easy. The doctors make a point telling you the quality of life she would have is horrendous. How she would never function or be viable. Medical term after term, but the key is she would have life. All our life, we're told to have a piece of the pie, you can't have it all. Something's got to give. As with that analogy, Jackie would rather have a piece of her daughter, than not have her at all. Like in many relationships, some women would rather have a part of a man, than no man at all. For her, Landon was her world, her only. She has little Eric, he helps fill some of the void, but she wants her daughter. She would not let go. She held out hope. Her heart was still beating which meant her baby was alive, not dead. God had the final say.

I say a prayer before turning to leave.

*

"Are you sure?" Braxton grabbed my hand.

"Yes, I can do this. I need to do this alone."

"Alright, I'll be in the car."

I walk slowly over the rocky, patchy grass in search of Michelle's grave. I stand over her elaborate headstone with an engraved picture of my mother. I study the inscription:

In Loving Memory of

Michelle Sinclair

Devoted Wife Dedicated Mother

One loving heart stopped beating.

Your Heart so genuine and pure

You gave so much

How will we survive?

We hold onto the many precious memories

Use your love as a guide

One day we will meet again.

Until then ....

Love you always, you will forever be in our hearts

Ashley's honor no doubt. To her, Michelle was all of those things and more. For me, this woman was a stranger. The flowers on her grave are fresh, the area neatly maintained; obviously, she'd been missed. Where do I begin? How do I talk to a woman who I've never *talked* to before?

"Hello Ma,

I'll never forget the looks you would give me when I was younger. At first, I thought it was your way of saying you didn't hate my existence. Quickly, I learned it was because you couldn't stand the sight of me. You always pointed out everything I did wrong, never acknowledging anything that was right. I worked hard in school, made sure my chores were done, stayed out of your way, tried not to ask you for anything, all to appease you.

I remember the first time I brought Landon to the house, the look on your face when you met her. The look of disgust, the only time I recall you taking any interest in anything concerning me. Later, I would find out why. Every birthday there was always something more important. No need for you to go to my graduations. You never came to my defense when John's mother would comment about my eyes. She would say they were green, evil, and monstrous. Tell me no one would ever love me. You remained silent. Help me create a complex. See an image I hated and live in a body I was not comfortable with.

Despite it all, I never hated you. I just wanted you to be proud of me, acknowledge me. Even at your funeral. Do you realize how it hurt me to hear so many people say, I never knew Michelle had another daughter? It was a slap in the face, another blow from the grave. So many times I asked myself why you hated me so much. You never even made an attempt to see your granddaughters. You couldn't accept my kids. I can't remember one time of you hugging me, or saying I love you. All my life, I only wanted your acceptance and love.

I don't know all the details of your relationship with Lawrence, maybe you made me pay because of your hate for him. Even now all I can do is speculate. I do love you. After all, you gave me life. I pray now that you are resting in peace. I pray that in the afterlife you are happy and don't hate me.

If you do, you do. Still, you will receive no hate from me. It takes too much time and energy to hate anyone. Regardless of what you said, I am not stupid. My struggles have been hard, but they made me stronger, made me the woman I am. Now I have love, acceptance, devotion and dedication in my life. I have a purpose. My children will know I love them and support them. I am happy. I love me. I'm done with focusing on what I didn't have or get from you. Instead I'm focusing on what I do have.

So goodbye, Michelle.

For the first time there were no sad tears. I let go of all of the negative energy concerning Michelle. This chapter was closing, the weight had been lifted.

26

We Can Be New

"From the beginning of this tough situation for all involved, we believed in and supported Eric Ayres. We also believe in the court system and the due process that found Eric to be innocent of the very serious charges. He can now get on with his life, including his work with the Wizards."

Eric is a good young man. Even during these difficult past months, he has made the effort to help his family, his teammates, and others who rely on his good will and generosity.

"It will be great to see Eric back in our faciities and on the field soon."

I mute the TV. Jerry Kaiser, owner of the Wizards had just released a statement in regards to Eric's trial.

Eric Ayres was acquitted, found not guilty on all charges, even assault. I knew he was at least guilty of that, but with all the pain and suffering he endured he served his time. The Wizards offered him a one-year contract which was wonderful. I was so glad that things were looking up for him. He called to thank me and I wished him well. I also read him the letter Landon wrote. It would never erase the damage, but I hoped he did not know she never intended to hurt him. Maybe ease some of his pain knowing that she did love him.

Braxton was officially back at work. The twins were crawling. Daddy, Nana and Pop Pop finally let them get on the floor long enough to learn. The twins both learned Dada. You talk about a Kodak moment when Braxton heard them both say it. They had him. They could have had whatever they wanted. No doubt, he and I would battle with that theory.

I got an invitation for Ashley's wedding. John has been persistent, wanting us to bond, since we are sisters. I'm not mad at Ashley or have any resentment towards her. I'm just not feeling it. Right now, it's being forced and not natural. I've been uncomfortable too long. I was finally feeling free and wanted to bask in the feeling. If I attended the wedding, like the funeral, I would have to explain my existence in Ashley's world. It was not the right time to construct that bridge.

We were having the twin's one-year birthday celebration at his parents. They actually turned one a few weeks ago. However, with my assault and other things going on, we postponed the celebration. Over a hundred people were in attendance for their birthday. Oh and Braxton's birthday too, he'd been overshadowed. He didn't care though, it was all about Reagan and Khouri. He bragged that he had the most beautiful girls in the world on his birthday and how they looked just like him.

Lawrence had dropped off little Eric, who was running around a while ago. An invitation was extended for him to stay, and he opted to stay. Jackie had wisely stayed away. Braxton had reluctantly agreed to allow Eric whose name had been officially changed back to Eric, to stay over. As it stands now, Braxton has full custody. He, off the record, agreed to allow Lawrence and Jackie every other weekend. He also made them aware that at any time they tried to pull any underhanded trickery, the agreement would be rescinded permanently. Things were settling.

Braxton also had invited Kevin to the twins' birthday party. Our relationship was still strained. I counted the balloons on the package, ignoring my present company, as Kevin approached with Nicole.

"How are you, Yasmin?" asked Kevin.

Braxton walks over to stand beside me.

"I'm well, especially since an innocent man isn't being sent to jail by some ruthless, arrogant attorneys."

"Ok, I deserve that."

Nicole grabs Kevin hand and I roll my eyes.

"Yes, fortunately Landon had the foresight to see how stubborn you would be. Seriously though, I hope you both learned not to allow your emotions to control your judgment."

"Says the woman who ended our friendship because you got caught up in your emotions."

Braxton laughs.

I give him an evil stare.

"He right, beautiful," he leaned over, kissing me on my check.

"Whatever, not the same," I pouted.

"Nicole, you want something to drink?" Braxton asked, trying to give Kevin and me space to talk.

"No, thank you."

Braxton narrows his eyebrows.

"Nicole, can you get me something, please?" asked Kevin.

She walks off with Braxton looking back at Kevin. "She can't get enough. A little clingy now," I commented.

"You think so? Weren't you the same way with Braxton?"

"No, I was not."

"You wasn't?"

"No, I never clung. Braxton got to talk to his friends and hangout alone."

Kev seemed a little apprehensive.

"Are you okay?"

"I'm nervous. I can't believe I'm getting married. And you are exaggerating, Nicole isn't that bad…is she?"

I'm mute.

"Why you so quiet?"

"No reason."

"You think I shouldn't marry Nicole? Lately, I've noticed she has been a little clingy, dependent."

I felt bad because I am the one who helped him propose, but I agree as of late that chick been off. Landon would have broken it down.

"That's your call, Kev. You have to live with her. Do you love her? Do you think she's in love with you? Committed?"

"I do."

"I support you in whatever decision you make."

"You're giving me the diplomatic answer. Landon would give me the raw, uncut."

I laughed, "She would. It's just not my place to tell you who to marry. You told me at first not to mess with Braxton. I didn't listen. Then, when I was trying to leave Mr. Bipolar you were on the Braxton choir, singing, give him one more chance."

"You're right about that."

We both laughed.

"How are things with you?" asked Kevin, with concern.

"Better. It's been tough. Since you were being an ass I had to lean on Chauncey and let's say all ties have been severed."

"What the hell happened?"

"I'll never tell. Your punishment for being an ass."

"You didn't."

"Braxton is still free walking the streets isn't he?"

"Yeah. How far did it go, Yasmin?"

"I'm not telling you. I'll just say it was close, and there was an altercation involved. Enough said. It's too much to attempt to summarize."

"You gotta tell me what the hell happened."

"I don't and I won't."

"You're wrong for teasing me like that."

"So were you for being a jerk," I laughed.

"Altercation? Really?"

"Yes, fortunately Vince was there."

"You do got a crazy one."

"Yours don't seem so sane. Seems like she got a case of obsession and fatal attraction."

"Not at all. Nicole is shy. This is a large gathering, she's not use to this. Both of our families are small."

"If that's what you have to tell yourself."

"I recall years ago you hiding your face and staying in the shadows."

"True."

"I really regret not listening to you. Javon could have hurt you. I feel real bad. Just thinking what he did to Landon, the other women. It could have been a lot worse and that would have been on my conscience. I'm real sorry. I should have listened to you, heard you out. I'm at a loss of words, just thinking about what happened." He gave me a hug.

"Thank you, but I still don't like you," I teased.

"You love me."

"You are really annoying."

"Yas, can you do me a huge favor?"

"What's that?"

"Sing for me at my wedding. I want my sister to be a part of my wedding. Can you do that for me?"

"No."

"What? You not going to do that for me?"

"You know I don't like singing for an audience."

"Yas."

"No," I said sternly.

"Yas, are you really going to make me beg?"

"Since you have a problem disassociating our friendship with the courthouse, plead your case."

"Yasmin Simms, I stand before you today requesting to hear the sweet melody of your voice. As you know, weddings are joyous occasions meant to be shared with friends and family. You, Yasmin, are my family. We've been through a lot. We argue, but at the end of the day, we're here for one another. It would be an honor and a pleasure for my sister to show me the words I speak are the truth. Make a contribution of love by singing to me and my bride."

I stop him, woo he is so long winded, "Alright Kevin,"

He gives me another hug as Nicole comes out with his drink. She approaches going right for Kevin's arm.

I contemplate pulling Nicole to the side, see why she's so uneasy around me. I see Braxton returning and decide against it. This is a happy day, I wasn't focusing on her neurotic energy. This was my husband and my daughters' day.

"Hey, baby." I give Braxton a kiss on the lips.

"Hey, you." He kisses me back.

Kevin and Nicole walk off into the yard to mingle with the other guests.

We both look out in the yard as mommy and Mr. Jeff play with the twins. I have love, acceptance, devotion and dedication. Nana,

Grandpop, and daddy had the event catered with choices of grilled deli meats, stuffed shrimp and salmon, pasta bar, fresh fruit, too much food. Of course it was a princess themed party. The backyard had tents designed as castles, horses, and a jumbo castle moon bounce. The kids wore tiaras and crowns. My daughters sat on a throne made with pink and purple plush pillows, per their daddy's request. It was over the top. The gifts were abundant. We were specific, telling guest two gifts for two different girls. Too much for a one-year birthday.

Braxton and I went into the kitchen to escape the madness.

"You are so smart," he said.

"What I do now?"

"Suggest we have the party here."

We laugh. While our house was large enough to accommodate the guests, Braxton and I were not entertainers. We didn't like so many people in and out of our house. Some family was okay, however, after a few hours, Braxton was ready to do his Martin impersonation and tell them, "*You don't have to go home, but you got to get the hell out of here.*"

"Yes, it's too many people."

"My daughters are one. Wow, it's been a year. A little over a year ago, you was cussin' me out, putting me out of hospital rooms." He tickled me.

"Ha ha. You deserved it. I was in pain. That was a labor of love. I need to go on the books for that. You got twins for your birthday. "

"It was. The best presents in the world."

I kiss him, "Happy Birthday. I know I told you, you weren't getting any more gifts from me, however I made an exception."

He smiled, "Hmm. What you get me?"

"I'll give you a hint. Let's say you'll have me every day of the year."

He looks puzzled.

"I need more than that."

"You can get it.... Later." I wrap my arms around his neck, pulling him close into a passionate kiss.

"Aww, aren't y'all so cute. Look at the punk and his smart mouth wife."

"Look at Don Juan and his hoe," I snapped back.

"Yasmin, be nice," Braxton chuckled.

"He started it."

"Y'all ready to make some more? It makes sense, since they think that's *their* babies." He nodded to the window.

"You ready to have some more," asked Braxton.

"No, we're done."

"What you mean, we're done?"

"What I said. No more babies. We're not having anymore. Labor is a bitch. I'm done and so are you."

Is this fool serious?

"Not even one more. I thought you were game."

"We can practice as much as you want, but there will be no game."

"Fight, fight, Fight!" chanted Vince.

Mommy walks in, "Please I can't take y'all fighting and breaking up. Get along and stop the craziness. Y'all workin' my nerves. Braxton you stop doing stupid. Yasmin you stop running. These girls can't keep going on this emotional rollercoaster."

All of us laugh, even Ty.

"Mommy, we're good. We were arguing about kids. Braxton trying to get me to have more kids in nine months. I told him we're done."

"Ma, you know you want some more."

"Braxton you have lost your mind. You and Yasmin and pregnancy don't mix. My little angels need to enjoy being babies and having the spotlight. You can't handle two kids now. You have Eric and you want another?"

"Thank you."

"I think they should. They only have one really because you and Pops think the twins are yours."

"Shut up, Vincent!" said Mommy irritated.

Braxton and I share a laugh.

"Why you mad at me. I'm feeling neglected. You don't have any time for me anymore. When was the last time you said my favorite, absolute best son, how was your day? I hate to see how you act when you get some more grandkids."

"What do you mean, some more?" She looks at Vince, then Ty. "You not pregnant are you? Please, tell me you're not pregnant?"

Ty looks taken aback.

Uncle Charles and Stella walk in, noticing the tension right away.

"Bev, everything alright," asked Uncle Charles cautiously.

"Vincent," said Mommy nervously.

"No ma, Ty isn't pregnant."

"Hallelujah. Vincent you don't need any kids. Over 30 acting like you're 10. Ty don't get pregnant. No kids. You hear me?" lectured Mommy.

"Ain't that the truth. You two need not procreate. Here take these." Uncle Charles throws some condoms across the counter. "Use them."

Braxton and I bust out laughing.

"That's not my style, Unc. Ty and I use other precautions."

"Take more. Use the damn condoms," ordered Mommy.

"Ma, why you getting on me? You never get on Horace. You ain't never get on Braxton either."

"They are more responsible."

"Braxton, more responsible?" Vince laughed.

"Vincent don't make me go there. I will say some things that aren't nice." Mommy looks at Ty.

"Come on Ty, let's go see the babies."

"Take the condoms, Vincent," ordered Mommy.

"I'm allergic to latex," Ty said condescendingly.

"Well take an allergy pill," blurted Uncle Charles.

A very hurt looking Ty follows behind Vince.

"My patience is running thin with her," declared Mommy.

"Yeah, I don't like her. I don't trust her," agreed Stella.

"I can't understand why that son of mine still got that tramp glued to his side."

"Superhead revamped." I whispered in Braxton's ear.

He puts his head down laughing, trying not to be so obvious.

"Braxton, what's so funny?"

"Nothing." He grabs me and kiss me on the cheek.

"Now, that's what I like to see," said Uncle Charles.

Mommy smiles.

"Ma, what you get your son for his birthday?"

"I know my baby boy." Mommy walks over and grabs his face. "What my baby want?" She kisses all over him.

"Alright ma, I was playing. The twins missing you."

"Oh, my babies." She runs off.

We follow behind her. The twins reach for us when they see us. I grab Reagan and Braxton grabs Khouri. They both were dressed in yellow sundresses. Khouri had pink barrettes while Reagan had lavender. We take some pictures, even managed to get Eric to pose for some. The twins had fun mashing their hands in their custom birthday cakes. Just like the shower, the twins received a lot of gifts and love. Uncle Vince put together a video chronicling their first year. There were clips of Braxton and me at different locations holding and kissing them. He added subtitles letting them know how much they were wanted, how much they were loved, adored, a blessing and as their daddy says, the most beautiful girls in the world. He had everyone saying *aww*, even some tears, Mommy and me mainly. Mommy even apologized to Vince, not Ty though. She would embarrass him though, making a fuss over him by kissing all over him like she did Braxton earlier. Vince was speechless. That in itself was priceless.

The twins' party was a huge success. Braxton would have a private party later.

27

Bittersweet Symphony

Nicole and Kevin's wedding was held at a local winery, very intimate and romantic. Nicole's colors were champagne and a pale pink which served well with the many fruit trees and fields of green. All together, they had roughly 75 guests in total. Lawrence served as Kevin's best man. Kevin's brother, Nathan, whom I only met once, served as a groomsman. Nicole's, I assume friends, served as maid and matron of honor. Their pale pink dresses were frilly with too many ruffles. They made them look like they didn't have necks, in my opinion, with the dresses stopping below the knees. Nicole's dress was very pretty, a sweetheart gown with crystal embellishments. The train was long, making her small, size two frame appear statuesque. She was a pretty bride, but I think she should have worn a padded bra or cutlets to enhance her nonexistent cleavage. She wore her hair in a chic ponytail, a style I wouldn't have done.

I tried to be uniform, sticking with the champagne color. My dress was a coral, champagne, and white semi-sheer maxi dress with an intricate pattern. My hair was worn straight, parted down the middle, hanging long, stopping at the middle of my back.

Before the nuptials began, I was called to the podium. I try not to look at anyone. I do see a smile when Kevin grabs Nicole's hand and stares her in the eyes. I focus all of my attention on Braxton as the pianist begins to play the melody. Braxton smiles at me. I close my eyes and sing to my husband.

Time after time, when I'm feelin low
Something inside of me, lets me know
It's alright, love's on my side
When the world, seems a lonely place
I've got a dream that won't leave a trace, of the blues
I just think of you, baby, I know

I've got a real thing, here by my side
Someone who needs me, holding me tight
And these special feelings, won't ever fade
'Cause I knew, I knew from the start
You put a move on my heart

I was startled by the applause. I opened my eyes to a standing ovation. Braxton comes up grabbing me from the podium, kissing me. Embarrassed, I let the fool lead me to our seats. Braxton has me hugged up in the seat. I meekly look at Kevin, who is laughing, shaking his head. Lawrence encourages Braxton giving him a thumbs up. Nicole's expression is blank.

"Love is definitely in the air," the reverend begins. "You got the real thing." He pointed at Braxton.

"Yes sir," bellowed Braxton.

The audience laughs.

"Marriage is not to be entered into lightly. It takes love, understanding, honesty, patience, and kindness among other things. Kevin and Nicole, as you pledge your love here today before God, family, and friends I want you to remember to put each other first. Depend on God and each other, in that order. Let us begin.

Dearly Beloved, we are gathered here today in the presence of these witnesses, to join Kevin Powell and Nicole Johnson in matrimony, which is commended to be honorable among all men; and therefore is not by any to be entered into unadvisedly or lightly, but reverently.

Despite Nicole being aloof, the wedding was beautiful. The ceremony was quick and to the point. The reception began shortly thereafter. Nicole and Kevin are by the entryway greeting the guests. Braxton and I stand in line, hand-in-hand to wish the newlywed couple well.

"Congratulations, Kev and Nicole." I give them both a hug.

Braxton follows. "Congratulations, marriage is a beautiful thing."

Braxton kisses my hand, then me.

"No, you two still getting along, no drama, *that's* a beautiful thing."

We both laugh.

"It's because our love goes deep. We're very emotional about each other. Our expression like our love is aggressive," I justified.

"Yeah okay, that's what you call it. I call it crazy." Kevin laughs.

Nicole laughs with him.

"I must say thank you. You sang that song. Everybody was feeling that song. I didn't know you had all that in you." antagonized Kevin.

"Great job, Yasmin," complimented Nicole.

"Yes, that's my daughter. Beautiful." Lawrence comes over kissing my cheek.

"My wife is talented."

"Thank you, your dress is pretty Nicole," I said modestly, ready to change the subject.

"Thanks, Yasmin."

More people stop over to congratulate the newlyweds and give me acclamation. I gladly ease away from the newlyweds and head to the table we were assigned. Kevin's mother and brother, Nathan, were also at the table. I'd met his mother quite a few times. She was one who didn't bite her tongue.

"Hello, Ms. Powell, you look nice."

Braxton and I take a seat.

"Thank you, Yasmin. You look nice as well."

"Have you met my husband, Braxton?"

She looks Braxton up and down, "No."

I sip on my water.

"Hello, nice to meet you." He offered his hand, but she ignored him. He does shake Nathan's hand.

"So you the one who took Yasmin from my Kevin."

I choke on my water.

"I'm guilty as charged. But the decision was mutual."

"Ms. Powell, you know Kevin and I were never together like that," I shook my head.

"I know. You never were into him."

"Exactly."

"You're a lucky man, Braxton. I see you two genuinely love each other. I'm warning you though. You better treat my girl right," grilled Ms. Powell.

"Yes ma'am. I am and I will," said Braxton politely.

"Well, glad to see real love. I don't know what kind of mess my son just married."

Braxton and I look at each other.

"Ms. Powell, why don't you like Nicole?"

"'Cause that chick crazy," said Nathan.

"She's off, I wouldn't call her crazy yet." I voice my concern.

Braxton squeezes my leg.

"That thing crazy. I know what I'm talking about. Something in her eyes just ain't right. Kevin just don't have common sense," said Ms. Powell matter-of-factly.

"Kevin has sense," I reasoned.

"That crazy chick look like you, Yasmin," said Nathan.

"No she doesn't," I said repulsed. She's not ugly but just the idea of being compared to her.

"I have to disagree with that one. My wife is beautiful, she's plain."

"That she is," flirted Nathan.

"And she mine." Braxton puts him on notice.

"I hear you. If you can't fulfill your duties. I'll be waiting to fill the position," antagonized Nathan.

"You Powell brothers like what you can't have."

"Nathan, when he knocks your ass out remember you deserved it," said Ms. Powell matter-of-factly.

He laughs.

Ms. Powell still wasn't feeling her daughter-in-law's parents. Nicole's parents were staring from across the room. I was ready to leave and I had a feeling in my gut to run. Nicole's parents approach. Braxton and I give each other a knowing look.

"Barbara, everything was just lovely wasn't it?" Nicole's mother gleams.

Ms. Powell just nods her head.

"Your son better do right by my daughter," Nicole's father said half-jokingly.

"Your daughter better do right by my son," Ms. Powell said seriously.

"Well, your son is lucky to have my daughter as a wife."

"I'm not convinced. I pray I'm proven wrong, but your daughter is touched."

"Ma," warned Nate.

"Our daughter is fine," they both said appalled.

"I enjoyed the ceremony," said Braxton, trying to alleviate some of the tension.

"I know you did. How long have you two been married?" asked Nicole's father.

"Almost three years."

Nicole's mother still pissed about Ms. Powell's comments offers a half smile.

"Do you have any kids yet?"

"Yes, we have three. A four-year-old and a set of one-year old twins." Braxton pulls out his phone and shows them pictures.

Nicole's mother gives a genuine smile. "Aww, they're all so cute. The girls look just like you. I know you spoil them," she tells Braxton.

"He does," I confirm.

We all make small talk for a few minutes with the exception of Ms. Powell.

All we could do was laugh. Mrs. Powell wasn't feeling this union at all. Nicole will need a backbone to deal with this woman.

Being polite, I suffer through the reception, but I was bored, getting sleepy from the wine and lack of excitement. Nate and Braxton talked sports while Ms. Powell was engaged in a conversation with another guest about the casino at Charlestown. The DJ was decent. A few people were on the dance floor. Soon the DJ stops the music, opening the floor to people who wanted to say words of wisdom to the bride and groom. I abruptly turn when I hear Braxton's voice.

"Kevin and Nicole, I want to first congratulate you on your nuptials. Like I said earlier, marriage is a beautiful thing. If you do it right. Kevin you're a good man. I'm glad you found love in Nicole. I definitely wish you the best. Words of advice I have is to be honest and communicate."

Kevin and I both look at each other shocked.

"Kevin with your permission, I'd like to say something to my wife."

Kevin gives him thumbs up. I cover my face.

"Y'all met my beautiful wife earlier. Yasmin stand up."

I look at this fool and shake my head no.

"Yasmin, if you don't, I will sing." The audience laughs.

I do.

He walks over to me, "Hey, beautiful."

"She's beautiful, isn't she?"

The audience claps.

"Yasmin, we've been through a lot. It takes a special person to deal with me and that's you. Thank you for the love, my beautiful kids, and making me a better person. You make me better and know everything I do, I do for you. All for love. Earlier Kevin and Nicole she was singing for you, but she was singin' to me."

More laughs.

"So with that being said, I'd like to dedicate this oldie but goodie to you. Thank you for loving me and all that you do. I do act like a fool but it's all for love."

I touch his face.

"This song is for you beautiful. Oh and Kevin and Nicole, I wish you years of happiness, prosperity, and love. May you experience the love I do every morning I see my wife's face, and at night when I get to hold her tight."

The Dj begins playing Stevie Wonder, *Always.*

I touch his face, trying not to cry.

Did you know that true love asks for nothing
Her acceptance is the way we pay
Did you know that life has given love a guarantee
To last through forever and another day
Just as time knew to move on since the beginning
And the seasons know exactly when to change
Just as kindness knows no shame
Know through all your joy and pain
That I'll be loving you always

I bury my head in his chest, but he takes his hand lifts my head, and makes me stare in his eyes. His eyes singing to me every word letting me know he would love me always.

He sings horribly, but still the sincerity is genuine.

We all know sometimes life's hates and troubles
Can make you wish you were born in another time and space
But you can bet your life times that and twice its double
That God knew exactly where he wanted you to be placed
so make sure when you say you're in it but not of it
You're not helping to make this earth a place sometimes called Hell
Change your words into truths and then change that truth into love
And maybe our children's grandchildren
And their great-great grandchildren will tell
I'll be loving you

Braxton gets a standing ovation for his effort. And of course a big kiss from me. My face a mess from the tears, I excuse myself to the restroom.

I return from the restroom only to be stopped by Nicole. She pulls me into a corner.

I look at her like the nut I now know she is. "Nicole, what's going on? Is everything okay?"

Mobbing closer to me, "No, it's not."

"Okay, what's the problem?"

"You. You're the problem."

I exhale, "Why am I the problem?"

"You know why?"

I was really tired of going back and forth with her. I wished she'd just say what her issue was.

"Nicole, I don't know what the problem is. I'm not a mind reader. Can you tell me what the issue is?"

She grills me with her eyes. This chick was about to blow. A guest walks by and just like a switch, the chick's mood changes. She smiles and laughs like I told her the funniest joke. The guest smiles until she sees my face which screams this chick crazy.

"Yasmin, thank you so much for the gift. Can't wait to use it on Kevin tonight, I know he will love it."

On that note, I turn to leave.

"Alright enjoy. See you later, Nicole."

Her cold hand grabs my arm, "Wait, I didn't give you your gift. It's in the dressing area."

She attempts to yank my arm, but I pull it away. By now the guest had disappeared into the reception area.

"What the hell is your problem? First, don't you ever yank my arm like that or put your hands on me again. Do you understand?" I snapped.

"Do *you* understand?" she retorted.

"My tolerance for you is over. You got two seconds to tell me your issue," I said annoyed.

"My tolerance for you has been up. This is my wedding. You and your husband's show was inappropriate. This is not your show. It's mine. I am the Mrs. Let us get a few things straight now. First rule, your annoying phone calls to my husband any time of night ends. You have a husband. If you have a problem, talk to him. Second, you are only to come to my house by invite, which will be rare. This co-dependency you have ends today. You got that?"

I laugh.

"Nothing I said was funny," she said curtly.

In the calmest voice I can muster, "I can get why you're feeling so annoyed in regards to my husband and my display of affection. I do apologize for that. However, you will not dictate orders to me, especially when they hold no truth."

"I can and I am."

"Nicole, why are you really so threatened by me? I don't want your husband. Never have for that matter. I have my own who I love, who I **am** committed to."

"Yeah, a husband that cheats and lies."

Do I break this chick down on her wedding day? I will try being nice one more time just because she's Kevin wife. "There was no need for you to go there. It wasn't even that serious. Yeah it happened, he did it. What's your point? Fortunately for you, I won't embarrass you on your day. But don't you ever insult me or throw shade my way again."

"I will do whatever I choose."

"This entire conversation is frivolous, Nicole. I'm not trying to go there with you," I warned.

"You've already gone there by disrespecting me. I am the queen of the Powell house now. I don't trust you. You're manipulative."

"Manipulative?" My mouth opens with surprise.

"I was not done speaking. Yes, manipulative. Obviously, you're unclear on the definition. Therefore, I will give you the definition. Manipulative meaning… "

I cut this bitch right off. "Instead of insulting me you need to be thanking me. I am the one who convinced Kevin to marry your desperate ass. After many years of Kevin persuing me and me telling him *NO, I don't like you in that way*, he finally got it. He finally realized I didn't want him or would ever be with him. So yes, I was offered the ring before, during, and after you were in the picture. Luckily for you, I never wanted it. I am the one who helped plan the proposal. So, if it weren't for me, you'd be still… hmm…waiting. In regards to my husband, who you just insulted, that issue occurred prior to my nuptials. He on the other hand, didn't need persuasion with saying I do. I know you heard the fabulous story on how he showed, well, really proved, his commitment. By the way, he offers me so much more. I don't have to fake moans for show."

She looked hurt, but I didn't care. One of my pet peeves is trying to make me look dumb and she insulted me. I really tried. It was her fault I unleashed the beast.

I storm off to the table to see Braxton sharing a laugh with Ms. Powell and Nate. I don't try to hide my disdain. "Braxton let's go, now."

"What's wrong?"

"I'll tell you in the car." I don't wait for a response instead I walk straight to the car.

I hear Lawrence, Ms. Powell, and Nate call after me. I was hot, fuming, had to go, so all were ignored.

Braxton is right behind me. He clicks the button to open the car door. I slide in, my anger has me in tears.

He comes to the passenger side of the car and opens the door "Yasmin, talk to me. What's going on?"

"Drive off."

"Not with you like this." He tries to pull me from the car.

"I will tell you. Just get me away from here now. Pull around the corner. Just get me away from here."

Reluctantly, he gets in on the driver side. Just what I don't want to happen, Lawrence and Kevin come out to the parking lot to see the reason for my abrupt departure. Quickly, I fix my face, wiping away the angry tears.

"Yas, what happened?" Kevin asked bewildered.

I shake my head like nothing's wrong.

"Kevin!" one of Nicole's bridesmaid calls out, startling all of us.

"Aisha?"

"Kevin, Nicole is very upset. She says she needs you."

Kevin races off to check on Nicole.

The beast in me couldn't be tamed. "That phony bitch," I blurted.

Lawrence and Braxton look at me. I tell them everything that transpired word for word.

They're both stunned, convinced I made this crap up.

"I hope Mr. Know-it-All Kevin signed that crazy chick to a prenup. I got $1,000 saying they won't make it six months."

"Does my daughter need anything?" Lawrence asked apprehensively.

"Yes. I need Braxton to take me home."

Braxton gets in the car to drive us home. He's silent the first fifteen minutes of the ride.

"I knew Nicole was off, but damn." Braxton shakes his head.

My mood was beginning to mellow out.

"She ain't off. She just crazy. I know one thing, Kevin don't ever have to worry about me going to his house or her coming to mine."

"Yeah."

"That damn crazy, delusional heifer trying to talk about my baby," I winked, "I had to let her know don't fuck with me about my man." I lean over and give him a kiss.

"That's my girl."

Braxton is opening the garage door to our home when my cell phone rings.

"It's Kevin," I announced.

Braxton raises his eyebrows.

I put the phone on speaker.

"Hello, Kevin."

"What the hell is your problem? What kind of shit did you try to start? I asked you to my wedding because I thought you were a friend and would respect the sanctity of my marriage."

"Whoa, Whoa, Kev. Nicole has a problem that requires psychiatric admission."

"Yasmin!" Nicole cried. "How could you say that? I thought we were friends. I really tried to be nice to you. Kevin all I was doing was thanking her for the song. She started saying I should be thanking her for getting you to marry me."

"Yasmin!" yelled Kevin.

I look at Braxton, "Kevin contact Spring Grove. Your wife is a got damn liar, and she got you acting like a got damn fool."

"You insulted my wife earlier and just now. You will give her an apology. Stop the ignorance. " He practically growled into the phone.

"Hold your damn breath. I'm not apologizing to that conniving, manipulative bitch."

"What the hell is your problem insulting my wife!?" yelled Braxton.

"Braxton this is about Yasmin and that smart ass mouth of hers. Her mouth, like her, was out of line."

"I don't give a fuck if she cussed her ass out or what the hell she said. You're not going to talk to my wife any kind of way."

"Kevin, I don't want to see her again. She's just evil. Yasmin, for Kevin's sake I tried, but you're just so mean. Why did you have to talk to me that way? You embarrassed me," cried Nicole.

"Yasmin, I'm very disappointed in you! You have lost your damn mind acting like you don't have any sense! You need to grow the hell up!"

"Didn't I just tell you watch your tone and how you talk to my wife?"

"Obviously, you two irrational, drama-loving folks deserve one another. This imprudent behavior is second nature to you both. Somewhere in your vows there must have been a clause to be disrespectful and ignorant; you both are ridiculous. I'm not dealing with you. Don't contact me anymore. When you visit your father at our law firm, don't speak." He slams down the phone.

"That mutherfucker," we both said in unison.

28

Human Nature

As crazy Nicole said and Kevin blatantly affirmed, he had no words for me, and was done. I even stopped past the office a few times, not to apologize, but the dummy ignored me like I was a stranger on the street. Lawrence made several unsuccessful attempts to get us to reconcile. Neither of us would budge. I couldn't believe that dummy was so sprung. It's been months, I lost another friend but this time I was okay with it. I missed Kevin, but I couldn't tolerate Nicole, and if that's who he was with her, then the best thing was for him to stay away. Pushing that negativity from my mind, I slip in bed with Braxton handing him a nicely wrapped package.

"A gift for me."

"Yes, your birthday present."

"I thought you were making this gift up."

"Ha ha, there were a few technical issues."

"Good answer."

"Since you love me so much, I wanted to give you something to admire me every day of the year."

He kisses me before ripping the package. Inside was a calendar of me in a lot of risqué attire. Braxton's favorite color being blue, the premise was *Shades of Blue.* Bustier, garter belts, lace lingerie all blue with accents, tastefully done. I know the picture Chauncey sent was a stab in the gut, I had to top that. This calendar featured a few alter ago shots. Shots such as bad girl, good girl, church girl, call girl, there were a few underwater, holiday props, definitely variety and satisfying.

"Damn," he flips through the calendar, month-by-month drooling.

"You like?"

"I love. Damn." He blows out a breath.

I laugh, Sugar Daddy was on a rise.

"All that ass. Damn!"

"It's yours."

"It is."

I roll over giving him a perfect view of my assets, he slaps it.

I purr, "Meow."

"Um, um, um, you did your thing."

"I even signed it."

He reads my message:

Every day my love grows for you more and more.

You are the only man to have my heart

Not only do you call me beautiful, you make me feel beautiful

I'm yours every day day of the year

Looking forward to my years with you

Thank you for loving me,

Your wife

"Aww, beautiful. Give me kiss."

"Just a kiss?" I lick my lips.

"You know I'm always open for more."

"How you want it?"

"Hmm, I want you on your back with your legs spread, ass up in the air."

Quickly, I untie my robe, I lay flat on my back, my legs spread, and hips up high, per his request.

Braxton grabs my legs and forks his tongue in me so forcefully, I instantaneously climax.

"That's a record. Less than 30 seconds," he said cockily, hovering over me.

"You're not done." I wrap my arms around his neck, pulling him to a kiss.

He uses his fingers to play me like an instrument. His thumb flicks my clit like a guitar while his two fingers inside me move in my like he's playing a violin. With my hands I stroke him. I stop, touch my self, taking my honey, using it as a lubricant on him. I alternate, we both go back and forth teasing each other. Minutes later, my hand is filled with his cream. He wants another taste. He places my legs on his shoulder. Taking three long licks and one long suck on my clit, my knees lock. My pussy wanted more. As much as I wanted to wet his tongue, I wanted to wet his dick more. I wanted him to put all got damn hard 9 ½ inches in me, push it hard until he can't go anymore, until my cervix couldn't take no more and my pussy is gushing over him.

Lick, lick, lick, lick, suck, suck, lick, finger flick, lick.

My ass in the air, legs shaky. I try to push his tongue from my clit. He holds me still, continuing his torture.

Lick, suck, suck, suck, liiiiick, suck.

"Put it in me! Put it in me! Put it in me!" I squealed.

He ignores my request. He licks, licks, licks. Licks. My shoulders the only thing on the bed, I'm so high.

Braxton begins to strategically place pillows under me.

"Fuck me hard! Put it in me. I need it. Baby. Braxton. Put it in me!"

My ass high on five stacked pillows. He grabs my legs and pulls me close. The time on the clock, 11:02 was the last thing I remember before his dick made it's way up my pussy, sending me screaming orgasmic pleasure.

Exhausted, I collapse on the bed after my seventh orgasm, ready for a power nap. The phone begins to ring unceasingly, just as I close my eyes.

Braxton has me in a bear hug, making it impossible to move.

"It might be your mother calling. Remember we told her we'd be there by one."

Which we had. She came over at ten that morning to get the kids for an annual Simms cookout. I look at the clock, which read 1:32. Scanning the caller ID, I see the display reads Suburban Hospital.

I answer in a panic, praying everything is okay. Braxton looks over sees the display and is up dressing.

"Hello."

"Yasmin." I hear Vince on the other end of the line.

"Vince, what's wrong?" Braxton takes a seat on the bed. I place the phone on speaker.

"Ty and I was in an accident and I need you to pick us up. Can you tell Braxton to bring me some clothes?"

"Yeah big bro, what happened? You gonna be okay? You call Ma and Pops?" asked Braxton.

"No, it ain't that serious. Actually, don't tell them. Just bring me some clothes and come pick us up."

"Alright, we on our way."

Braxton hangs up.

*

Since it wasn't life threatening, Braxton and I shower, getting in a quickie before taking the drive.

We're escorted to the back. When we get there, Vince is on a gurney draped in a hospital gown. Ty is by his side, splint on her finger, looking unfazed. Makeup flawless, outfit consisting of short cutoff denim shorts and a white off the shoulder top.

"Are you okay bro-in-law?" I stand on the other side of Vince.

"I am your favorite brother-in-law."

"No, Horace is." I stick out my tongue. His comment let me know he was okay.

Ty leaves the room to make a call.

"Was Ty hurt, Vince?" I asked genuinely concerned.

"Ty hit her head."

"Did you knock some sense in it?" I asked. I couldn't resist.

"Yasmin, seriously, stop talking about Ty. She the one." He grinned.

"She the one, what?" I give him a look that lets him know that he is being STUPID!

Braxton shakes his head no. "Bro, Ty is not the one."

"Braxton, she is?" he said seriously.

"Call the doctor 'cause this fool obviously is suffering head trauma. I'm convinced you hit your head too."

"Yasmin, smart mouth, chill. I know you and Ty started out rough, but get use to her. She ain't going nowhere. I like her. Yeah, she cool."

Braxton starts laughing.

In my sincerest voice. "Vince, did they test you for syphilis or any STD's because some do affect the brain. You're not making any sense."

Braxton laughs harder.

"Y'all got jokes. I'm telling y'all Ty the one."

"Bro, she got your ass whipped. You ain't in no damn love."

"Exactly, you ain't say you love the chick once." I cosigned.

"So y'all gonna be in my wedding or what?"

"Is this some candid camera joke or some other foolishness? I know you are not committed to one woman."

Vince looks around, "I am, in a sense. She the wife, but we will have an open marriage."

"What's the purpose of getting married?"

"We a good team. You seen my videos lately. Ty sees the vision. She gets me. We have our fun together and separately. I don't have to worry about any stalker chicks. They will know I'm married I just wanna fuck."

"You are stupid." I throw my hands up.

"So Vince what happened?" asked Braxton.

"Long story short, Ty and I were having our morning run. From time to time we do a little detour and handle business. So we in this wooded area. We were kind of high up, we like getting it on high up while other people walk past. You know we see them, they can't see us. So I'm in my zone, holding on to the branch and going in. I went to grab the other limb and lost my balance. I fell down in a bush, Ty fell on me. A branch fell on my leg, and because of my position, I couldn't move it. Ty went to get help. Another jogger came by before Ty made it back and called 911."

"So y'all thought y'all was monkeys and could swing from trees? Monkey see, monkey do."

Braxton howls in laughter.

"You know the crazy part, I'm laying their naked and something bit my ass, literally."

I can't hold in anymore, I laugh at this fool. Braxton and I are laughing so hard the staff came back to make sure we're alright.

"Y'all done? I don't care, it was worth it. I ain't embarrassed."

"You been around Ty too long, you need help," I said seriously.

"Anyway, so I'm here getting a tetanus shot, make sure I didn't hurt anything. They said I was good. So y'all can take me and Ty home."

"Where is your car, Vince?" asked Braxton.

"At Ty's, but I need you to take me home first to get my other set of keys."

"Where are your keys?" asked Braxton.

"I don't know. Lost them when I fell."

"I thought Ty fell too. She don't look like she fell in the bushes," I said.

"Ty went home to change her clothes."

"Why didn't she bring you clothes?"

"Because, I don't know. I guess I didn't have anything there. I still needed y'all to pick us up."

"No, it's cool. I was just wondering why she didn't drive." Braxton hands Vince the bag of clothes.

"Ty was going to drive me, but she can't find her keys. She think they're at my place."

"So let me get this straight. Your car and Ty's car are at her place. You lost your keys and she thinks hers are at your house." Braxton scratches his head.

"I'll tell Mommy you sick." I shake my head.

"We'll be over there. I just need to get my keys and take a quick shower."

"You sure your ass aiight?" cracked Braxton.

"My ass, like the rest of me, is fine." Vince smirked.

Ty walks in and gives Vince a kiss.

Me and Braxton look at each other and just shake our heads.

"You didn't speak to Ty earlier Yasmin?"

"I know."

Braxton gives me a look. I give him one back.

"We all are family."

"No, we're not. My last name is Simms. Ty's isn't. I don't know what hers is. I have a guess, but I'll be nice."

"Yasmin, really this is getting old. We might as well be nice, we're practically sisters." She holds up her left hand revealing an enormous Asscher cut diamond ring.

I blink, shocked.

"Aren't y'all going to congratulate us?"

Braxton nor I respond.

Vince is smiling.

"I hope we can't let bygones be bygones. I'm happy to be gaining you all as a family. I can't wait to teach my nieces fashion sense and take them shopping," she said jubilantly.

Braxton grabs my hand, squeezing it. I squeeze his back, we're both in agreement that shit wasn't happening.

The nurse comes in handing Vince his discharge papers. We leave the room so Vince can get dressed and we can leave. Those two are Stupid and Senseless.

"That's your brother."

"I ain't claiming him." Braxton shakes his head.

"Yeah, I agree."

Braxton and I walk to the cafeteria for a drink. On the way, I see a man bent over with bloody clothes. I didn't want to stare, but there was a familiarity about him. I nudge Braxton. He, in turn, gives me a look that says stop being nosy.

I ignore him, continuing to stare. On instinct, the man looks up, my heart drops, and fear fills me.

He looks surprised and relieved to see me.

I rush over to him, Braxton right behind. "Kevin! What happened to you? Why are you bleeding? Why aren't you in the back being examined? What happened?"

He closes his eyes and bangs his fist on the wall.

"Kevin!"

I'm scared to touch him. I look around for a nurse, doctor, anybody.

"Kevin, what's going on, man?" asked Braxton.

"Nicole. Nicole. Nicole." He babbled.

"Nicole what?"

"Nicole… She tried to kill herself. She slit her wrist." Kevin falls back into the chair.

Kevin's Story is next ………………… And its craaaaazzzy.

Pieces of Me

Something to ponder on….

Throughout my life's journey, I've been constantly challenged. From learning how to love myself, to learning how to forgive, I've struggled. Each obstacle however, I have overcome. Now I'm faced with death and loss, the hardest yet endured. I don't know where my journey will lead next, only time will tell. I won't ask why or how. I will stand strong, ride the tide. I will appreciate the lesson.

Landon's prognosis is hard. I won't say she's dead, but she's gone. I'm at peace because we did make amends. With my mother, I never got that chance. Although I said goodbye, it's a struggle. I pray daily to God for peace and his guidance to accept things as they are.

My relationship with Kevin has been challenged. We hurt each other a lot this year. My mouth I admit is often reckless, uncensored. It's a defense mechanism, it's not right. Hey, I'm a work in progress, but I'm learning. I do wish the best for him. Kevin was a real friend to me. Just as he was there for me at my lowest, I will be there for him.

Now Chauncey,

I can understand Braxton's reasons for not telling me he gave Melania money, he was wrong for doing so. But he was also right, if he told me while our marriage was hanging on a thread, I probably would have ended it. He should have told me when Ty brought it up. Not right then and there, but later in privacy. As I said before, that seed was planted, the lies watered it. That seed pushed us farther apart, allowing discord.

Something as simple as that almost caused a domino effect to our marriage. Looking back, it seems stupid, however, life happens without cause, warning, or reason. I didn't know Eric would have press coverage, that I'd end up at Chauncey's, that Chauncey would become my confidant, or that my mother would die. Life's travesties had me lean on another because I couldn't, wouldn't, talk to my husband. I looked at what was wrong in my marriage rather than everything that was right. I turned to Chauncey and came so, so, close to doing the thing I condemned Braxton and Landon for. Fortunately, common sense prevailed and I did not completely break my vows, but I did break my vows. I confided to him things I should have confided to my husband.

Chauncey, in turn, opened his heart for me, became vulnerable. He laid it all out for me. He was willing to sacrifice, be a provider, a lover and confidant. Continuing to go around him only gave him hope. I made him believe that we had a chance. For a while, I thought we did too, but I was acting out of anger and frustration. Regrettably, I hurt someone who was a friend. More importantly, I turned my back on my husband who I vowed before God to love through the good and bad times.

I do accept responsibility for my part in my marital problems, but Braxton was also at fault. We both did things to hurt each other. Marriage is something you work on 24/7 it doesn't just work because you said, I do. In actuality, once you say I do, the real work begins. It's then that you put forth effort daily to not only communicate, but listen. You cannot become complacent or ignore each other's feelings and concerns. You will not see eye-to-eye or always agree. What you must do is respect each other. We didn't do that. We started doing "I", instead of "we". "We" almost destroyed our marriage.

It takes more than sexual chemistry to make a relationship work. Braxton and I never had problems in the bedroom, our struggles came outside the bedroom. Those struggles being communication and being there for one another emotionally. While my part in this was running and keeping things bottled up, Braxton had a tendency to shut down, avoiding the problem, catching an attitude instead. Pushing me away, ultimately pushed me to Chauncey.

It's not justification. He was wrong, so was I supposed to be wrong too? If I had that attitude it wouldn't have accomplished anything. Instead I would have hurt him, myself, ruined a great love, destroyed a friendship, a bond. In the end, I would have cheated myself like Landon cheated herself of love with Eric.

It's inevitable we all get hurt, play the fool sometimes, and do crazy things. All for love. But the question is, is it worth it? Is it the right kind of love? Is that person we're fighting for worth it? Do they deserve our love?

For Braxton, I say, YES, YES, YES, YES!

◇◇

Please connect with me on FB @ https://www.facebook.com/nakia.robinson.35 Or IG/Nykia8, Twitter @AuthorNakiaR

www.RightAboutItPublication.com

Check out the trailer for You Call That Love:
Production and lyrics by Bmore Ben. Vocal performance by Ashley.
https://www.youtube.com/watch?v=6W9cC8VHooo&feature=youtu.be

"You create your destiny."